A Place to Belong

# Also by Cynthia Kadohata

# A Place to Belong

CYNTHIA KADOHATA

Illustrated by JULIA KUO

atheneum

A CAITLYN DLOUHY BOOK

NEW YORK LONDON TORONTO SYDNEY NEW DELHI

$\mathcal{A}$ atheneum ATHENEUM BOOKS FOR YOUNG READERS | An imprint of Simon & Schuster Children's Publishing Division | 1230 Avenue of the Americas, New York, New York 10020 | This book is a work of fiction. Any references to historical events, real people, or real places are used fictitiously. Other names, characters, places, and events are products of the author's imagination, and any resemblance to actual events or places or persons, living or dead, is entirely coincidental. | Text copyright © 2019 by Cynthia Kadohata | Illustrations copyright © 2019 by Julia Kuo | All rights reserved, including the right of reproduction in whole or in part in any form. | ATHENEUM BOOKS FOR YOUNG READERS is a registered trademark of Simon & Schuster, Inc. Atheneum logo is a trademark of Simon & Schuster, Inc. | For information about special discounts for bulk purchases, please contact Simon & Schuster Special Sales at 1-866-506-1949 or business@simonandschuster.com. | The Simon & Schuster Speakers Bureau can bring authors to your live event. For more information or to book an event, contact the Simon & Schuster Speakers Bureau at 1-866-248-3049 or visit our website at www.simonspeakers.com. | Also available in an Atheneum Books for Young Readers hardcover edition | Interior design by Mike Rosamilia | Cover design by Russell Gordon | The text for this book was set in Adobe Caslon Pro. | The illustrations for this book were digitally rendered. | Manufactured in the United States of America | 0420 MTN | First Atheneum Books for Young Readers paperback edition May 2020 | 10 9 8 7 6 5 4 3 2 1 | The Library of Congress has cataloged the hardcover edition as follows: | Library of Congress Cataloging-in-Publication Data | Names: Kadohata, Cynthia, author. | Kuo, Julia, illustrator. | Title: A place to belong / Cynthia Kadohata ; illustrated by Julia Kuo. | Description: First edition. | New York : Atheneum, [2019] | "A Caitlyn Dlouhy book." | Summary: Twelve-year-old Hanako and her family, reeling from their confinement in an incarceration camp, renounce their American citizenship to move to Hiroshima, a city devastated by the atomic bomb dropped by Americans. | Identifiers: LCCN 2018043629 | ISBN 9781481446648 (hardback) | ISBN 9781481446655 (paperback) | ISBN 9781481446662 (eBook) | Subjects: LCSH: Hiroshima-shi (Japan)—History—Bombardment, 1945—Juvenile fiction. | CYAC: Hiroshima-shi (Japan)—History—Bombardment, 1945—Fiction. | Emigration and immigration—Fiction. | Immigrants—Fiction. | Belonging (Social psychology)—Fiction. | Identity—Fiction. | Japanese Americans—Fiction. | Japan—History—1945-1989—Fiction. | BISAC: JUVENILE FICTION / Historical / Asia. | JUVENILE FICTION / Social Issues / Emotions & Feelings. | JUVENILE FICTION / Social Issues / Emigration & Immigration. | Classification: LCC PZ7. K1166 Pl 2019 | DDC [Fic]—dc23 | LC record available at https://lccn.loc.gov/2018043629

To the memory of Wayne Collins

CHAPTER

ONE

This was the secret thing Hanako felt about old people: she really didn't understand them. It seemed like they just sat there and didn't do much. Sometimes they were rude to you, and yet you had to be extremely, extremely polite to them. And then when they were nice to you, they asked you lots and lots of questions. Lots!

Her mother's parents were both dead—Grandpa from being run over by a tractor while he was drunk, and Grandma from drowning in a giant wave off the coast of Hawaii. They had already passed away when Japan bombed Pearl Harbor. But when Hanako had worked in her family's restaurant, she'd encountered many old people with their families for dinner. Mostly, as said, they just sat there.

And now her family was on this gigantic ship, going across the ocean to live with her father's elderly parents in Japan.

This was the thing about Japan: she had never been there. Her parents had told her for her entire life that it was important to be American. It was important to talk just a little more loudly than some of the girls who were being raised to be more Japanese. It was important to make eye contact and not cover your mouth when you laughed, like some of the more Japanese girls did. Basically, the way to be Japanese in America was to be more American than the Americans. And now she was being told she would need to learn to be more Japanese.

Her family had been imprisoned for almost four years—since she was eight—and now that she was kind of free, she did not know what was out there in the world for her, in the future. She had no idea. All she could hope was that from now on, and maybe forever, she would never be in jail and nobody would ever point a gun at her again.

"Hanako, do you have any candy left?" Hanako turned to look at her brother, who was standing in his underwear, his pajamas in his hands. He had pale eyebrows and a ton of black hair, with a big wine stain covering the skin around his right eye and beyond, like a pirate's patch. She kissed his stain the way she liked to do, because it was so beautiful. It was shaped like Australia, except sideways.

Reaching into her pocket, she pretended to be searching, though her fingers were already clutching a candy. "Hmm, I don't . . . oh, wait, I do!" She pulled the candy out and held it up triumphantly. Akira grinned and took it from her. She liked to make him happy—some days it was all she lived for, really. The candy was a butterscotch, his favorite. They had bought a bag of it a few weeks ago at one of the co-op stores in Tule Lake, where they'd last been imprisoned. Located in Northern California, Tule Lake was a high-security segregation center with almost nineteen thousand inmates. Each of the three camps where they'd been imprisoned had been different, all awful, but not in exactly the same ways. Plus, there was a different prison where her father had been held for almost a year. That was the most serious prison of all. In the freezing cold of Bismarck, North Dakota, he'd been housed with German prisoners of war. Hanako had never been freezing, but in Tule Lake she had been very cold for several days at a time, and she did not like it at all. Papa said that when you were freezing, your feet started to hurt a lot.

"Mmm, butterscotch!" Akira said now, holding it up like he was looking at a marble.

Akira had a teensy, squeaky voice—sometimes Hanako thought he sounded like he would fit in your hand. She had to admit he was a strange little creature, with his squeaky voice and with Australia on his eye and with the way he was several inches shorter than other five-year-old boys. When Akira was only a baby, Mama had said, "He was born sad." She had rarely spoken of it again, but Hanako had not forgotten it. She was always looking for signs of sadness in his face, and she often found such signs. Sometimes, even when nothing bad had happened, he looked like he wanted to cry from something—maybe loneliness?

After Akira put the candy in his mouth, she put his pajamas on him because he looked so helpless.

"What if we sink?" he asked suddenly.

Hanako tried to think of something comforting to say. It was hard, because she didn't know how something as big as this ship *could* stop itself from sinking. "It's impossible for us to sink," was what she came up with. "It's a US Navy vessel. It's probably one of the best ships in the world." The ship they were on was called the USS *Gordon*, and it was about two football fields long. She didn't understand how airplanes flew, and she didn't understand how ships floated. She'd been quite scared about that. But at this point, who even cared? They were on the ship, and they weren't getting off.

Akira grabbed her hand and started digging into it with his nails. Hanako always cut his nails into sharp spikes, because he liked them like that. He called them his "sharpies." He said he needed to protect himself from . . . he could never say what. Hanako tried to wriggle her hand free. In response, he dug in harder.

She concentrated on keeping her voice calm like she (almost) always did with him. "Akira, can you hold on to my sleeve instead, *please*?"

"All right," he said, grabbing her purple coat and pulling at it. She didn't like him to pull on her purple coat—it was her favorite thing, and it was from a store instead of sewn by her mother. But she didn't scold him, though that took a heap of self-control. She didn't want him to say what he'd said to her twice in the past: "You like your coat more than you like me!"

She looked around but didn't see where their

mother had gone off to. Mama always liked to know what was going on. At the Tule Lake camp she used to go out every morning after breakfast and talk and talk to people. That's what Hanako had heard, anyway; she was at school. Mama was obsessed with *what was going on*. It was like she was desperate to know more. Always *more*. Mama used to be a calm person—serene, even. She never used to care that much about what was happening in the outside world. But in camp her eyes became filled with a hunger to know things.

Hanako wondered if anybody here actually knew anything about what was going on. But how would they? It was very crowded here in the sleeping quarters, and you couldn't see much because the aisles—the space between each set of bunks—was maybe two feet.

She scrambled up to the top bunk, looking around and seeing more bunks. But not that many. Sixty? In stacks of four, so 240 people sleeping here. Supposedly, there were thousands of Nikkei being sent to Japan on this very ship. Nikkei were people of Japanese descent, whether they were citizens of America, Japan, or any other country. Only women and children were in this room—all the men and older boys were on another part of the ship. It was strange how quiet the whole crowd was. Probably scared and depressed. Then Akira whimpered, "Hanako, I'm afraid. Why do we have to go on this ship?"

Trying to get down quickly, she tumbled to the floor and then immediately dusted off her coat. "Because we don't belong in America anymore," she said as she dusted.

Akira closed his right eye and tilted his head. That's what he did when he was trying to decide something. "I think I *do*. I do belong in America."

Hanako thought this over. That was a hard one, because she wasn't sure about it. "Belonging" was a difficult concept at the moment. Really, for the people on this ship, they "belonged" with their families, if they had them. Where else was there to belong at this point? They had no country.

It was a complicated and confusing story, why they had to be on this ship. There was no way to think about it and have it make sense. First, Japan had bombed Pearl Harbor, Hawaii, in early December 1941, a little more than four years ago. Second, that caused America to enter World War II. And third, more than 110,000 Nikkei—mostly American citizens—living on the West Coast had been imprisoned in ten different places, for no good reason. And then about six thousand more had been born in the camps! What had Hanako's family done wrong that they had to be held captive for almost *four* entire years? They ran a restaurant in Little Tokyo in Los Angeles!

They were sent to a temporary camp nearby, then a permanent one in Jerome, Arkansas. Jerome was a bad camp, because the director was really tough and made some inmates cut down trees for the whole camp for heat in the winter. Logging was one of the most deadly professions in America, Papa said. At Jerome it was grueling work with old equipment. The men—like Papa—who were forced to work as loggers there had no prior experience, so Hanako was always worried that her father would get killed. The other camps were provided with coal, but Jerome's director, Mr. Taylor, wouldn't stand for that. He was only thirty-four, and Papa said he did not have the least idea of what the difference was between right and wrong. But, still, he insisted Hanako and Akira call him "Mr." She'd called him "Taylor" once, and Papa had reprimanded her for being rude. "But he didn't hear me, he's not even here," she had replied. Her father hadn't answered, just frowned at her.

One time she had complained to Akira, "I don't know why we have to call him 'Mr.'" And Akira had

said patiently to her, "Because he's the *boss man*, Hana."
And he was only three years old when he said that!
Actually, Hanako had realized she agreed with him,
because that's the way she was raised: She could not
stand the idea of not showing a grown-up respect.
Even if it made her angry and sometimes made her cry,
she could not stand it. Even if it ripped her whole heart
out, she could not have stood it. So she always called
him Mr. Taylor after that. Even though she hated him.

But now Akira was staring at her. "Why do you
look mad?"

"I don't! You need to get in bed," she said in her most
official voice, the one her brother usually listened to.

They had decided he would sleep right above her.
The "beds" were hung by chains. Each one was only a
sheet of canvas, maybe two feet above the one below.
On every bed lay a muddy-green blanket, with no linen
and no pillow. This is where the American soldiers had
once slept when they were helping to save the world
during the war, Hanako thought. And then she remembered the American soldiers who'd occasionally pointed
guns at her in camp. Papa said the good and the bad
thing about people like soldiers—and for that matter, *all*
people—was that they usually did what they were told.

That sometimes made them act bravely, and it could also make them act right sometimes, but wrong sometimes, too. So you needed to have the right people telling them what to do. Papa said that was the hard part. Maybe, he said, it was the impossible part. Hanako thought about how she sometimes did the wrong thing when she didn't think her parents would find out. Like when she and some other kids found several empty glass bottles once and threw them against the barracks in camp. For no reason. Then they ran away. She wasn't sure if it was easier or harder to always do the right thing when you were a grown-up. She actually had no idea.

Akira's eyes were closed already. He could fall asleep anywhere, anytime, in about ten seconds. Sometimes you had to scream to wake him up.

She took off her precious coat and thought about hanging it on the hook where her duffel bag was. But what if the hook tore the fabric? She laid it on the bed instead. But what if she wrinkled it when she slept? Suddenly she felt like crying. She did not want her coat to get wrinkled! She did not want to spend two weeks inside this ship! She did not want to go to Japan! There was so much that she didn't want, but at the same time she didn't even know what she *did* want.

"Are you all right?" a woman asked.

She realized her eyes were tightly closed, tears squeezing out. She opened them quickly. In front of her was a tired-looking lady holding a baby. "Because we're all here to take care of you," the woman continued. "Nothing will hurt you now."

"Thank you," Hanako said, embarrassed. "I'm fine. I'm sorry . . . I shouldn't cry." Crying wasn't very brave.

But the woman was now gazing down at her baby, who was suddenly whimpering. Beyond her, Hanako spotted her mother looking wild-eyed as she walked toward someone new. Mama laid her hand on the new woman's arm, leaned toward her, and began talking. Mama had a habit of getting too close to people when she wanted to know *what was going on*. Hanako began to undress, having decided to lay her coat over her blanket while she slept.

Women and children all around were also changing into their bedclothes. Nobody was shy, because in the camps there had been showers and latrines with no partitions between them. So none of them had had privacy for years. When you'd been forced to be naked in front of strangers every day for years, you didn't have much shame left.

She got into her bottom bunk and thought about a magazine photograph she had seen in camp, of American soldiers sleeping in a room much like this one. They were wearing their uniforms, though they were in bed. She thought about how some of those men might be dead now. Maybe a soldier who had slept in this very bunk had been killed in the war. For a moment she felt as if she could sense him. Maybe he had been scared, or maybe he had been brave. Probably both.

Her bunk was about two inches from the ground, but there was no sag, so she couldn't feel the floor. There was so little sag, she could hardly tell Akira lay above her.

She touched a seam in her pajamas. The US government had allowed each family to bring only sixty dollars on board this ship. Mama was holding that money. This was because even though the war was over, the government wanted to control every last thing they did, until the last possible moment. But Hanako was carrying another twenty dollars that her mother had hidden in a seam in her pajamas. Akira's pajamas held twenty as well, so altogether they had a hundred dollars. Maybe Papa had managed to hide some money too.

She felt her thick braid on her back. Briefly, she considered undoing her hair, but she didn't want to lose her rubber band. It was her last one. She was quite concerned about it. She'd tried ribbons and string, but they always slipped out of her hair. Her rubber band was dear to her. When you hardly had anything, even a lowly rubber band could fill you with *feelings*.

But she needed to think of something happy. So she thought, *Japan will be fine. It will be beautiful. Everyone will love me.* She closed her eyes and pictured the three most beautiful places in Japan. She'd never been there, but in class at Tule Lake the children had painted watercolors of the three beautiful places: Matsushima, Miyajima, and Amanohashidate.

Matsushima was a group of more than 250 small islands in blue, blue water. Miyajima was the island of the gods. Amanohashidate was a sandbar covered in pine trees. So all three of the most beautiful places in Japan had to do with water. Miyajima was near Hiroshima, where they were headed. She hoped it would be beautiful too.

# CHAPTER
## TWO

When Hanako opened her eyes, Papa was by the bed, and there were men everywhere visiting the women. The ship was swaying gently. "Papa!" she cried out. Other than for the few hours while they were waiting to board the ship yesterday, they had not seen each other for almost a year.

Papa lifted her up and said, "You've lost a pound since yesterday!"

It was crazy, but somehow Papa could tell whenever she or Akira had lost or gained even a single pound. Mama said it was because he used to buy flour from a man who Papa suspected was cheating him. He used to lift the bags of flour one by one and contemplate them, to see if they all truly weighed the amount the man said they did. He thought the man had "fixed" his scale. Mama and Papa were funny in that they trusted everyone, and at the same time they didn't trust anyone at all. It made no sense, but that's the way they were.

"I haven't eaten since yesterday morning," Hanako said now to her father. Before Papa could answer, the PA system was announcing that men's visiting hours were over! So soon! "Why didn't you wake me up when you got here?" she asked accusingly, wriggling down.

"You looked so peaceful," he said. He nodded toward where Akira still slept. "Him too." He kissed the top of her head. "My sleepy, sleepy children."

She leaned against his chest as he wrapped his arms around her. She was almost as tall as him, because she took after her maternal grandparents who had been tall for Japanese. Papa's hug was tight—he was much stronger than he had once been, because he and some of his fellow prisoners in North Dakota had spent a lot of time exercising. Papa said that once they took everything away from you and all you had left was your body, it made you want to make yourself as strong as you could. He exercised for three hours a day, six days a week, sometimes out in the freezing cold.

Besides getting stronger, Papa had changed in another way. He looked older now, and kind of feral. Before, he had always seemed civilized, even sophisticated. Most days at their restaurant, he had worn a simple shirt and slacks with an apron and spent all day in the kitchen. But every Friday he would put on a beautiful suit and greet every person who came through the fancy wooden door. He remembered all their names. Just before he left the house on Fridays, he would admire himself in the mirror and say, "Your mother married a handsome man." Hanako had heard him say that probably a hundred times. He owned just the one suit, and one beautiful blue tie, and he liked them as much as she liked her purple coat. He had brought his suit to camp, but then after they got there and he saw how they would be living, he threw it away. Just like that. "That part of my life is over," he said. You did not need a suit when you were surrounded by barbed wire. He accepted this immediately as reality.

Mama walked with Papa toward the doorway—is that what it was called on a ship? Once her parents were out of sight, Hanako turned her attention to her brother.

"Akira!!" she shouted. People around her looked

over in alarm, but that was the way to wake him up.

He opened his eyes and squinted at her in that defi-
ant way he did when he thought she might be mad at
him but he had no idea why. "What?"

"It's morning."

"So? Hey! It feels like the ship is moving."

"It is. You have to get up."

"Why?"

Hanako hesitated. "Because . . ." But there was
really no reason. So she added, "Well, never mind."

He closed his eyes again. Once, Mama had taken
him to the doctor to see why he slept so much. But
the doctor had just said that some children slept more
than others. After he seemed asleep, Hanako spotted a
group of kids by the door. She rushed over and immediately cried out, "I'm Hanako!"

They glanced at her, then a girl said, "We're not
supposed to go anywhere, but we're going anyway!
Come on!"

They sped through the doorway all at once. Hanako
hesitated for just a second, then ran after them. It was
suddenly just like in camp, where the kids went wild
and the parents couldn't control them. They stormed up
some very steep stairs, hardly looking where they were

going. Hanako's face felt hot with excitement, just like that time they threw the bottles. Energy! She had so much energy!

She and another girl glanced at each other excitedly as they reached a different deck and sprinted down a long, long, narrow hallway. All that mattered was running! She didn't even know these kids, but at the moment they were all one single entity. They reached a door and stopped—altogether. A boy flung it open, and one by one, they stood in the doorway and stared.

A bunch of soldiers were sitting around a table playing poker, and there was real money in the center of the table. More money than Hanako had seen in a long time. She thought soldiers didn't get paid that much. They were big and looked strong. They gazed curiously at Hanako and the other children, and Hanako gaped at them. She tried to put her finger on why they were so . . . surprising. It was just that they were so different from her. You only needed to look at them to see they had lived totally different lives from hers. And not that long ago, maybe they could have been guards in her camp.

Then the boy who'd opened the door called out "*Hakujin!*" and slammed it shut, and they all ran away laughing hysterically. *Hakujin* meant "white person." They would not have dared to call out such a thing in camp. But they were no longer in camp.

Hours later, lying down again, she thought about seeing those soldiers and remembered something Papa had said about Mr. Taylor when he was very angry. She didn't remember his exact words, but it was something like, "Mr. Taylor has a life. He was a baby once. Maybe he has children, maybe not; maybe he will someday. He has hard days and easy days. He has emotions. These are the things that keep me from killing him."

That was pretty shocking coming from a restaurant owner who had never hurt a fly. But that was Papa in camp.

And so. Those soldiers had a life. Maybe they had children, maybe not; maybe they would someday. They had emotions; they had been babies once. Just like her, really. Just like her.

CHAPTER

# THREE

The next morning Hanako woke up smelling vomit and immediately retched. She realized that the ship was going up and down. It seemed to be swinging wayyyyy up and then wayyyyy down. Hanako knew exactly what was happening: the ship had left the harbor and was now in the ocean, and she was seasick. She leaned over the bed to retch more, trying to cough something up, but nothing came out. Then she couldn't stop gagging, over and over, like she wasn't in control of her body. It felt like a demon had taken her over!

"Mama!" she shouted. "Akira!"

Nobody answered, but she thought she saw the outline of her brother's body above her. "Akira!"

"Shut up!"

So he was sick too. She had a sudden, desperate desire to get up and check on him, but there was nothing she could do, because she felt like she was on the verge of vomiting again.

"Hanako!" Mama was kneeling down, literally holding her own eyes open with her fingertips. She looked like she was insane!

"It's going to be rough seas all the way!" Mama blurted out. "I must lie down! There are people who can help you!" Then Mama leaned over and went "HAHCH!" Then she gagged. Then she fell into her bunk, which was also on the bottom, directly across from Hanako's.

The smell of throw-up was overpowering. Hours passed, or maybe it was minutes. Hanako closed her eyes, but all she saw in her mind were chaotic lights. She badly wanted to sleep—there was nowhere else besides sleep where she could go to feel better. She wished she knew what time it was, but on the other hand, what difference did it make?

She lived in a daze that wouldn't end. Sometimes she slept. Sometimes she cried. Sometimes someone who wasn't sick brought her food and water.

Sometimes, through the spinning, she thought of her brother and tried to will herself to feel better so that she could help him. But it was so hard to concentrate on feeling better. It was so hard to think. So she tried to concentrate on something that focused her mind and woke her up in camp: an anger that she always felt in her fists. She would squeeze them so long that her forearms hurt. But here, now, she could barely even close her fingers. She was too weak. She was trapped. She would rather die than live like this forever, but she kept murmuring to herself, "This will pass, this will pass."

And yet it didn't pass.

# FOUR

And then it did. One day Hanako opened her eyes and felt . . . nothing special. And she knew exactly what had happened—the ship was no longer in the ocean. She had lived all her life in America, and then she had spent the last two weeks in a dizzying half-world between America and Japan. And now she was in Japan! She had to be!

Women and children were milling about. Mama was standing up chatting with another woman, and Akira was laughing as Mama held him. None of it seemed real. Hanako tentatively stood up and still felt fine.

"Good morning, Hanako," Mama called out, exactly as she might have on any other day.

"Hello?" Hanako replied like a question. Mama held Akira as if he were an infant, his hands around her neck the way he liked to do when Mama felt like babying him.

Mama nodded at the floor. "I brought you a tray of food from the mess hall. I didn't want to wake you."

Hanako stared at the food for a moment, then fell upon it and didn't bother with the fork, just picked up the eggs in her hand and shoved them into her mouth. They didn't taste good or bad; she was beyond caring either way. It took her about three minutes to eat the entire tray of food and drink the orange juice beside it.

Then the PA announced that they were in Uraga Harbor. They *were* in Japan! She'd been seasick the entire trip! She'd hardly eaten. She held out her arms in front of her—the bones in her wrists protruded. Mama said it was Saturday, January 12, 1946. They had left Tule Lake on December 26 and boarded the ship on December 28. All those days. Five thousand miles— America was five thousand miles away now. *Americans* were five thousand miles away . . . although she was American. President Truman was five thousand miles away. President Roosevelt, who had imprisoned her family, had died last year—his final words were sup-

posedly "I have a terrific headache." Nobody she knew
in camp had cried when he passed. Her father hated
him, so she did as well. But Papa never called him
"Roosevelt," always "President Roosevelt." Hanako did
not know if it was legal in America to even think about
hating him. She thought for certain it would have been
illegal to say out loud. Even in private, her father would
only whisper it. This was the thing about President
Roosevelt: he had personally made every decision that
had destroyed their lives. She tried to think about how
he was a baby once, how he had kids . . .

Now that her stomach was full, Hanako suddenly
felt . . . stuff. Like she wanted to cling to her mother
the way Akira was clinging. Like she wished Papa
were here right now. Like she wondered if all the terrible things she'd heard about Japan right before camp
were true, but she also hoped all the wonderful things
she'd heard about Japan inside of Tule Lake were true.
Like she still felt like throwing up, but not in the same
way she did during the trip. Everybody was talking to
everybody else: *Where will you live? With whom? What
will you do?*

She changed her clothes and underwear, right there
in front of everyone, and rebraided her hair. Akira

changed himself, standing naked for about a minute as he decided what underwear to use. She tried not to pull too hard on her rubber band so it wouldn't break. She concentrated on feeling calm, but instead she kept feeling overcome with the seriousness of their life now. It was an absolute fact that America had won the war, yet some people in camp did not believe it. Could they possibly be correct?

Her family was headed to her grandparents' farm outside the city of Hiroshima, and she'd been hearing for months that a single big bomb had been dropped there and destroyed the city. But in camp rumors were constantly spreading, dying, and spreading again in different form. There were rumors about where the government was sending them next, rumors about the food supply, rumors about the war, and at one time even rumors about the government possibly killing them all. That was a rumor that had spread very early on, on the train to Jerome, Arkansas, a few years ago. But a giant bomb? How could a plane even carry such a thing? And what exactly would be the point? Was it more efficient than using a lot of smaller bombs?

These were the kinds of thoughts and worries and fears that had plagued her for years—thoughts and worries and fears about every rumor and every real thing that could fit into her brain.

Many times, to let her mind escape the worries that filled her head until it hurt, she had gone outside with an older girl who liked rocks *a lot*. Yes. Rocks. Ugly ones, too, not shiny or sparkly or colorful. The rocks in Tule Lake were volcanic and old—supposedly formed two and a half million years ago. They looked plain instead of pretty. But as Hanako had picked up and held those rocks that had formed so many years ago, she'd felt comforted, steady. Calm. She kept one of them by her bed. It was a dark gray basalt, and she used to hold it to her forehead, and it would immediately make her feel better: two and a half million years, right there against her skin. A few hours before they left camp for the last time, however, she had walked to an open area and flung her basalt among all the others over the fence. Then they had left for their train. She did not ever want to see that stupid rock again.

# FIVE

The PA was already making announcements about disembarking! They were starting with names from *A* through *C*. Hanako's last name was Tachibana, so they would not be called for a while. "Tachibana" meant "tangerine," and "Hanako" meant "flower child." So her name was Flower Child Tangerine. That was why she liked bright colors, or anyway, that was her *theory* about why she liked bright colors: because flowers and tangerines were bright.

Mama had set down Akira, and his face was screwed into a grimace.

"What is it, Aki-chan?" Hanako asked. "We're here now." She paused. "And just think, we'll positively never be sick like that again." She didn't know why she lied to him like that. That is, she lied to him to make him feel better, but sometimes she thought about how ridiculous some of her lies were, and she wondered if she should stop.

But now he looked very hopeful. "Really?"

He looked so hopeful, she heard herself saying, "Yes, never again!"

He hugged her hard, as if she personally had made it so that he would never be that sick again.

She spotted a soldier walking through the room, and her heart sped up. The soldiers always made her nervous. As he passed, he stopped for a moment when he saw Akira. Akira *always* caught people's eyes. The soldier reached into his pocket and said, "Here ya go," handing Akira a package of Juicy Fruit gum! Akira's mouth dropped open; so did Hanako's. The man walked on.

Juicy Fruit had been taken off the civilian market during the war, so Hanako had not seen any for years. Only soldiers got Juicy Fruit, although probably rich people could get it somewhere if they wanted. Papa said rich people could get whatever they wanted, except happiness and living forever. But Juicy Fruit would probably not be a problem.

Mama said to Akira, "You must share."

"I will," he squeaked. With a serious look on his face, he tore open the package and handed Hanako three of the five pieces of gum.

And that was why Hanako lied: to give him something, even if it was only a lie, just like he would give her anything. She really didn't have anything else to give him but her lies. She put a single piece in her mouth, pocketed the other two, and said, "Mmmm, thank you, Aki!" It tasted like heaven. She let the juice flow through her mouth and found herself smiling. Akira smiled back as he chewed.

The taste was like something powerful, like the time her father was drinking some home brew that one of the inmates had made, and he let her have a couple of sips. She had felt it coursing through her body, through her blood, into her brain. It was the same with this gum.

Then suddenly came the announcement: "Japanese repatriates will begin disembarking beginning with $R$ through $V$." They were calling out of order! It was an American who didn't know anything about Japanese making the announcement, because there was no $V$ in Japanese.

Also, she knew, because her teacher had told her, that the proper word for her family was "expatriate," not "repatriate." A "repatriate" was someone returning to his native country, while an "expatriate" was someone withdrawing himself from his native country. Like her, many of the people on this ship had probably never been to Japan.

Suddenly, someone was scooping her up. Papa! He set her down quickly, though, and the whole family huddled in a circle, their heads leaning forward, touching. They had done this only once before: right after the announcement that they were going to be imprisoned. Then, Hanako had leaned against her family, thinking not about them or where they were going but about her cat, Sadie, whom they would be leaving with a neighbor. Hanako had paid the neighbor her entire savings of twenty-seven dollars, earned through working at the restaurant when she was six and seven years old. Sadie was an orange cat with eyes as green as a blade of grass. Papa had told her that cats were not like dogs in that they did not get their hearts broken when their owners left. Hanako hoped this was true. She would rather have her own heart broken than Sadie's.

"In America you learn about having things," Papa

was telling them now. "You have a house, a restaurant, a car, and you work hard for the future. It won't be like that in Japan. In Japan we'll need to learn about something else. I don't know what yet."

"Do we have a future, Papa?" Hanako asked. She lifted her head to gaze at his face. His eyes were out of focus.

Then he said, "I'm looking . . ." And he did seem to be looking at something in the air. Finally, he said honestly, "I don't see one. I'll keep looking, though."

"Why can't we work hard in Japan and start a restaurant?" she pressed him. "That would be a good future!" The whole time in camp, she had dreamed of when they would be let out to work hard and start all over with nothing. Having nothing was not as bad as not having the chance to work for more.

"We can work hard," Papa said. "We will. But it won't be for the future. It will be to survive."

Hanako wasn't sure what that meant. To her, "survive" meant like if you were out in the desert or jungle or maybe the Alaskan wilderness. In school they had learned to speak simple Japanese and paint pictures of the three beautiful places. Things like that. Nobody had said "survive" and "Japan" in the same sentence.

Then they began following other people out—the
PA had told them to head to where they'd boarded the
ship two weeks ago. For some reason, Hanako kissed
Akira's cheek. "Thank you," he said, which Hanako
thought was a funny thing to say. So she kissed him
again to see how he would respond this time. "Thank
you," he said again. Then suddenly she felt a little dizzy,
like somebody had just whacked her on the side of the
head: nervousness hitting her with a *thud*.

"Are you all right?" Mama asked. She squinted into
Hanako's face—Mama did that when she wanted to
read her or her brother's mind.

"Yes," Hanako said, trying to open her eyes wide,
like she wasn't dizzy at all. "Yes, I'm fine!"

Mama kept squinting into her face—Hanako
sometimes felt like her mother was physically trying to
get into her brain. Then Mama relaxed, petted her nose,
and turned away.

Everybody was crowded so closely together that all
Hanako could see around her was people. They climbed
down a ladder to a boat. It was overcast, and the sky
looked exactly the same as it had in camp. For some
reason, she had thought it would be different. Everyone stood crowded together without their belongings,

which were being brought to shore separately.

Hanako buttoned her coat. Most of the small children on the barge wore knit caps, probably made by their mothers. Kids Hanako's age didn't wear hats so much, though some had scarves around their necks. The older boys—the ones who'd stayed with the men—had styled their hair into puffy ducktails, and they wore expressions like they were not afraid of anything in the world, and never would be. Like they had seen everything there was to see. Those were probably Los Angeles boys—they had picked up their hairstyles from the Pachucos, who were some of the young Mexican American boys and men in Texas and Los Angeles. There used to be some young Nikkei men who liked to dress like Pachucos. She remembered how she couldn't help but stare at them, because they were so stylish.

Everyone wore neat, plain coats except for Hanako, who of course wore her purple one. She had always been a little desperate to fit in with the other kids, except for her coat. The moment she had seen the coat in the Sears catalog in camp, she knew she had to have it. Even after Mama had ordered it for her, she had longed for it with a passion that surprised her. She had never really wanted anything that badly before. And when it came, it was just as perfect as it had looked in the catalog! She'd had it for just five months.

Now she looked to her father, in his plain, old black coat that he'd come to camp in. His eyebrows were scrunched up. He almost looked like he was in pain. She tried to think of what she could do to make him feel better, and pulled at his arm. "When we get to Hiroshima, do you want to go see Miyajima, one of the three beautiful places?"

"Someday we will definitely see the three beautiful places." He paused, then gave a slight smile. "I look forward to it. Let's have something to look forward to. Why not?" He seemed like he paused a lot now. He must have become that way while he was locked up with the other prisoners of war. That's what they all had actually been. President Roosevelt had decided to take Americans as prisoners of war as well as Germans, Italians, and Japanese.

The wind was hitting her face hard. This was the thing about Japan: the water was gray, not blue or pretty. The sky was gray, not blue or pretty. She didn't see the sun; it was as if there *were* no sun. Nearby a woman was weeping. Nobody wanted to be here—Hanako was sure of that. Because most of them had been born and raised in America. And yet they were not really Americans anymore.

She could just make out the blob of land in the distance, beneath the plain sky. It was so depressing that she wondered if Matsushima, Miyajima, and Amanohashidate were famous because they were the only beautiful places in Japan. The way the boat moved across the water made it seem as if they were driving over a road, something solid. It wasn't floating peacefully the way she would have thought.

When they reached shore, they were herded into trucks. "Don't worry," Papa assured her. But she was worried.

This truck wasn't covered like the ones that had taken them to the first camp—called an "assembly center"—in America. An "assembly center" sounded like somewhere in a school where everybody went to sing songs or listen to the principal speak. Papa said naming things was a government specialty. He said government employees probably sat around a table and talked for an hour about what to call the camps.

Hanako gazed around at her new country.

Truthfully, Japan looked a little dismal. The road was rocky, and the buildings were made of cracked wood.

Everything looked like it was a hundred years old and hardly ever repaired. She had a feeling that practically everyone in Japan was depressed. They were let off at some barracks that Mama said had been a center for Japanese soldiers who were being shipped out during the war. She had heard this somehow, like she heard so much. A Japanese man in uniform was telling them, in Japanese, to go inside the barrack for their *ken*. *Ken* were like states in America. Another man asked him a question, and after he answered, the two men bowed to each other. The one in the uniform seemed polite, yet Hanako wondered if he had killed people during the war. So many had—killed people, that is.

"There's a sign," Mama said.

There was a miserable-looking, old barrack with a sign reading "Hiroshima-*ken*." The barracks here looked different from the ones she'd lived in for years in America. These seemed to be two stories. But they were plain, unpainted wood like the ones she'd resided in. She paused before going inside. She could not fathom it: living here before going off to war. On the wrong side of history. Then she went inside. She waited for her eyes to get used to the darkness. *I'm in Japan*, she thought. *I'm here.*

As her eyes adjusted, Hanako could see that the barrack was long and plain and empty. A soldier was already moving through the room throwing out bags of what he called *katapan* to eat, and everybody scrambled madly. Hanako pounced on some bags, grabbing them up greedily. She wasn't even sure what *katapan* was! She felt like an animal! Then she calmly handed all the bags to Akira, except for one each that she gave to Papa and Mama. Then Akira handed her a bag. "Here," he said. "I'll trade you for a piece of gum." So she traded.

*Katapan* turned out to be crackers. The hardest crackers in history, maybe. Biting them was like a battle between her teeth and the crackers, but then Mama told her to suck on one until it softened.

The crackers didn't have much taste, but they settled nicely in Hanako's stomach, taking away her hunger. After they finished eating, Mama told them to go to sleep since there was nothing else to do. There were hard platforms to sleep on. She and Akira lay down in their coats like their mother told them to, and they tried to sleep. Hanako was chilly and knew her brother would be too, so she wrapped her arms around him.

She was wide awake. In the dark barrack she could vividly picture their restaurant, the way she liked to do when she couldn't sleep. It was called the Weatherford Chinese & American Café. The restaurant had been their whole life, especially for Papa, but for Hanako as well once she got old enough to work, which was the day she turned six. During their last summer of freedom before the war, she would get up with Papa at four thirty a.m. to eat breakfast and go to work, even though she was only seven. In many Nikkei families, you began working as soon as you could, babysitting or cooking rice or cleaning floors. Or filling salt shakers. Wiping counters. When Hanako and her father arrived at the restaurant each morning, Hanako would heat up the grill and turn on the steam table in the kitchen while Papa made coffee. Then Papa would make the batter for the pancakes and waffles. Breakfast was purely American, though most of their customers were Nikkei. But first-generation Japanese Americans—called Nisei—had embraced America completely. They were more American than a lot of Americans. Hanako would take out ten flats of thirty eggs—one by one, so as not to break any—and place them near the grill. Then she would bring other foods—like hash brown potatoes, bacon, and sausage—out of the refrigerator and place it all near the grill as well, ready to be cooked when an order was placed. Throughout the breakfast rush, she would make sure whatever food was needed was in the kitchen for the cooks.

After breakfast ended, Papa would start getting the food ready for lunch. He always had a daily lunch special and a daily soup. Around ten a.m. he would make six pies for the day. Dessert choices were the pie of the day, ice cream, or Jell-O. The pies for the week were apple, lemon meringue, pear, pineapple, cherry, and egg custard—for Tuesdays through Sundays. They were closed on Mondays. While Papa made the pies,

Hanako would read a book in the office with Sadie.

Then during the lunch rush, Hanako again made sure the right foods were always in the kitchen for the cooks. They would yell out at her what was needed from the refrigerator. When lunch ended, she would blanch whole almonds by boiling them just until their skins puffed up. Then she drained the almonds onto a large, flat cookie sheet. After that she would squeeze the almonds from the fat ends, so that the nuts would pop out of the skins. The difficult part was to split the almonds in half. Hanako had to use a knife to split each almond on the seam. She would make seventy cookies with the almonds three times a week, plus one large cookie for herself and Akira to share. Toward the end she would be tired of making the cookies and didn't pay good attention to the baking. Sometimes the last batch was overcooked, and Papa would scold her. He used to say that being a perfectionist was one of life's most important secrets.

The restaurant closed at nine p.m., but Mama would come pick Hanako up at eight o'clock and take her home.

At night Papa would continue working until everything was clean and ready for tomorrow. Hanako wasn't sure what time he got home, because she would be asleep with Sadie next to her head on the pillow. Sometimes on top of her head, actually.

Mama worked too, when Akira was sleeping. She would save old grease and mix it with lye and water to make dishwashing soap. So nothing was wasted. Even the ugliest pan of grease was special.

It was all very hard work, but Hanako loved it because her father's ambition rubbed off on her. He was born ambitious to be a great cook, way back in another time, way back in America, which was now across the ocean. It was all in his mind now, though, wanting to cook.

Papa said all of that life—every single thing—was done and over with. Kaput. He especially blamed President Roosevelt for their whole situation, as well as the ACLU, who mostly didn't stick up for them. Papa had explained it all to Hanako. The ACLU was a bunch of lawyers who'd formed an organization to defend people's civil rights and stand up for the Constitution. Supposedly, they had a lot of integrity. But their leadership voted not to challenge Roosevelt's order allowing the government to "exclude" people—namely, Nikkei—from "military areas"—namely, the

West Coast, where most of the Nikkei lived. That had really surprised Papa, because he had always believed that there were special people—people born special, just like he was born to cook. He thought those people became president. He thought those people ran the ACLU. But in the end they weren't so special. "They're just like you and me," he had told Hanako. "Except they're lawyers."

And so here she was, in Japan, where her father could not see a future, but where he thought they could survive. If she were smarter, she would be able to understand time the way he did. There was a part of her that sometimes couldn't quite comprehend how things could just be gone. She had to tell herself over and over that her old life would not return. A part of her did not believe it the way her father did.

She felt a rush of love for Papa, and for her whole family, lying there near her, on these hard platforms in a new and strange land. She felt that anger that made her face hot and made her squeeze her hands into fists. She had no future! All she had was her trust in her parents. Then her anger started to subside. Even though Papa said he could not see the future yet, Hanako believed that he would see it again, and soon. Maybe more than wanting to cook, he was born wanting to see the future. He said that was why he and Mama got along. She took care of what was going on *now*, and he took care of the future. That way, Hanako and Akira were covered, in the present and hopefully forever.

# SEVEN

Papa had lived in Japan from when he was nine until he was eighteen, and he was thirty-five now. So, lying in the barrack that night, she felt secure in the knowledge that Papa would know his way around Japan.

In the morning Hanako woke to a huge commotion, people running out like there was a fire. She jumped up in a panic. Her whole family held hands and rushed for the doors. What now? Outside, people were excitedly saying that the Hiroshima baggage had arrived. "Hana! Aki! Stand back!" Mama shouted.

Hanako was happy to do this, because the grown-ups were frenzied as they tore through the baggage.

Hundreds of bags were strewn over the dirt ground! There were solid black trunks and flimsy tan suitcases bound with thin rope and more laundry bags than she could count. There were duffel bags and what looked like a yellow-and-blue-striped sheet wrapped and tied around some belongings. There were three suitcases that had the name SATO written on them that Hanako could spot just from where she was standing. She couldn't see Papa, but Mama was feverishly digging, flinging big bags around like she was a strongman. Hanako felt her face grow hot with excitement. She understood everyone's frenzy—those bags contained literally all they owned in the world. One by one, people found their belongings and left. But others kept searching, and some were crying. It took an hour to determine that somehow both Hanako's and Akira's small duffel bags were missing.

The air felt suddenly heavy, like she was breathing mud. "Maybe they're mixed up with baggage from other *ken*?" Hanako asked. "Shouldn't we go look?"

Nobody spoke. She didn't know why. Papa ran a hand through his hair and said, "We don't have time. We've all chartered a train to Hiroshima." He indicated with his hand. "Those trucks out there are ready to take us."

Hanako felt the depression in the air pressing in on her head, squeezing tears from her eyes. She fought an urge to grab somebody else's bag and run and run. "I'll make you new clothes, don't worry," Mama assured her.

"You didn't have anything valuable, did you?" Papa asked.

"Mama sewed twenty dollars into my pajama seam. Also in Akira's."

For the quickest second, Papa's eyes went wide.

"Well . . . I hope someone finds it," he said resignedly. "But it's not ours anymore."

"But it's still ours!" Hanako said.

"But you see . . . ," Papa said, gesturing at the remaining bags—bags someone else in another barrack was surely missing—then shrugging.

"Hanako!" Mama spoke sharply. Hanako looked at her, surprised. She looked tense and unhappy. "If the bags are not here, they are not ours anymore. We must leave."

Then Hanako understood: That was the way war was—things just became gone. Your house, your country, your duffel bag with skirts and underwear. Anyway, at least Mama and Papa were able to find their own luggage.

The family had been successful in that the restaurant had been busy and in that Papa had planned to have enough money to send Hanako and Akira to college one day. But they hadn't really owned *that* much.

They hadn't owned their house, and they hadn't owned the land the restaurant was on. Their most valuable possession had been the one thousand dollars in inventory and equipment at the restaurant. But they hadn't had time to sell it before the government swept them away like dust from their homes. After paying debts, they'd had three hundred dollars in savings, which they'd brought to camp. They had spent much of that while Papa was in Bismarck, and Mama was working only part-time for a low salary.

Three hundred dollars was a little more than the average person got paid in a month outside the camps in America. Inside the camps, however, workers had been paid less than twenty dollars a month, even if they were doctors!

Papa now said, "Hanako!"

She snapped to attention.

"Don't look so sad. Let me tell you: when I was in Bismarck, when I had nothing, not even a family, it taught me who I am. All right? You're still Hanako.

That twenty dollars in your seam doesn't make you Hanako. All right?"

"All right."

"Good. Now let's go see what Japan is like."

# CHAPTER
# EIGHT

People were already climbing into the trucks waiting to take them to the train. It was warmer than yesterday. The boys in their ducktails were mostly wearing plaid shirts underneath their open jackets, still looking like they weren't scared of anything in the world. The truck drivers gazed curiously at the teenagers. It was hard not to stare at them, the way they sauntered, the way they acted like nothing had bothered them—ever—even though they'd just been locked up for years. Heads high, backs straight. Hanako straightened her own back, lifted her head.

In the truck, on the way to the train station, she saw a few makeshift homes built out of what looked like scraps—even worse scraps than the barracks were made out of. Not homes, exactly—more like small shacks, such as those a couple of goats might be sheltered in. She watched Akira stare and stare. Nikkei migrant farmworkers had not lived in much better, but . . . these were worse. The farmworkers she'd met all thought their families had been on the way up in the world, but she somehow didn't think these people were on their way anywhere at all. She could not imagine a way that you could escape a goat house.

Their truck stopped at an old wooden platform at what must have been the train station. They got off. The truck driver, a thin man with a goatee and a cap, yelled out, *"Genki de ne!"* He was looking right at Akira. *"Genki de ne!"* he said again. *"Sayōnara!"* That meant "Be well! Good-bye!" Then he nodded and drove off.

"Everybody likes me," Akira said with satisfaction.

Mama leaned over, her face overcome with love. "Of course they do!" she said. "Of course they do!"

Nearby was what looked like a ticket office, but it was closed. When the train arrived, they found seats—wooden benches, really—facing each other and settled in. Mama sat with Akira, and Papa with Hanako.

A conductor came through collecting money. As

the train started to move, Hanako let herself feel a moment of joy: They were free! Weren't they? Could the government still control them? She didn't think so. She smiled at Akira, who sat by the big window across from her, but he just asked suspiciously, "Why are you smiling?"

"Because we've escaped," she said. "From camp."

But he screwed up his little face into a frown and leaned his head against Mama, closing his eyes extra tightly. He was so small and thin that there was room for Hanako to sit next to him right now, but she didn't want Papa to feel lonely.

So she just said, "Life will be perfect now, I promise."

The train was coal-operated, so according to Papa, they wouldn't be able to open the windows because the smoke got in if the wind was wrong. Hanako stared at the trucks driving away. They were not far from Tokyo, which she had heard had been totally destroyed by napalm. She had read somewhere that napalm was gooey stuff used in firebombs that burned everything. She imagined flames everywhere, reaching into the sky amid the zillions of buildings in Tokyo.

The train lurched along. It was the noisiest train she

had ever been on, and it shook like it was going over a track full of rocks.

Akira was still frowning, so Hanako reached out and smoothed his forehead. He got up and sat on her lap, leaning his head against her neck. "I don't like it in Japan."

"We've only just gotten here."

"I can tell."

Across the aisle a baby started screaming, and it didn't stop. And then it still didn't stop. It was rude, but Hanako turned around to look. Everybody nearby wore blank expressions except the baby and mother. Hanako tried playing peekaboo, but the child didn't want to play. The mother bowed her head to Hanako, calling out, *"Mōshiwake arimasen."* That was a formal and strong way of saying "I'm sorry." Hanako had actually never spoken those words outside of a classroom before. And she herself was only a child, too young to be spoken to so politely! Then the mother leaned forward, almost squishing the baby, and repeated more passionately, *"Mōshiwake arimasen."*

Mama had looked up and bowed her head and waved her hand, as if to say, "Oh, no, no, no. No!"

Akira stuck his fingers in his ears. The woman

looked exhausted, and she seemed to be alone. Had she crossed the entire ocean by herself with that crying baby?

"Oh, I'll take the baby!" Hanako exclaimed. "You sleep!" She gently pushed Akira off her lap.

The woman looked surprised, caught halfway between saying yes and saying no.

"I'm good with babies! I took care of my brother when he was little!" Hanako insisted. "I'm a genius with babies!"

At that the woman smiled and bowed her head, holding out the tiny child to Hanako. Hanako fingered some loose hair back behind her ears and eagerly reached out. The infant shrieked as Hanako took it, but the mother seemed relieved and immediately shut her eyes.

Hanako leaned in and said, "Hi. You're cute!" The baby let out a bloodcurdling scream. It seemed to hate Hanako! Its next shriek was louder still, like somebody was killing it! Hanako glanced over, but the mother still had her eyes closed. Then Mama was there, taking the baby. It grabbed desperately at Mama.

Hanako sat back and looked sheepishly out the window. They were going through a tunnel. Mama was making funny cooing noises, and finally, the baby quieted down. Hanako sneaked a peek. It was sucking peacefully on one of Mama's fingers.

Just through the tunnel, the train stopped at another station. Though this was supposed to be a chartered train that the deportees had paid for, a mass of Japanese soldiers in their khaki uniforms and caps pushed on board. One of them—he wasn't wearing pants!—dove for the empty area next to Akira, but Hanako stood up and shouted, *"Acchi e itte!"* Meaning "Go away!" Her heart was pounding. Akira sat rail-straight.

The soldier moved back into the aisle, and Hanako sat down again. Some soldiers wore coats, while some wore only their uniforms. Two had no shirts. They kept coming and coming, filling every space, small men with sunken cheeks, dirty faces, and black eyes that Hanako knew had seen worse things than she ever would, *ever*. She could tell that just from looking at them. Maybe they had done some of those worse things themselves. Horrible things. A year ago she would have been terrified of these men. And now here they were, small and dirty. She could see there was no need to be scared.

It was impossible for anyone to move through the crowded aisle to the bathroom, and as the train started going forward again, Hanako saw a man hold a small boy out the window so the boy could pee. From that point on, whenever the train stopped, a grown-up or two would hop out the window to pee and then quickly jump back in. Then one man didn't jump back in on time, and as the train started, he tried to catch it, his fingers clutching at the window. But the train gained speed, and he was left behind. Hanako stared back at him, astonished. He was . . . gone. He had come across an ocean to get left behind!

The train chugged along. Out the window were sleepy towns, assortments of dark wooden buildings that seemed untouched by war yet worn and cracked by age. Unpaved roads. Pretty slanted tile roofs. Old wooden signs with *kanji*, the most complicated of the three ways of writing Japanese. A *kanji* was basically a word. Each *kanji* was made up of separate lines, called "strokes," and a single *kanji* could have more than thirty strokes—sometimes many more. Someday Hanako would need to memorize thousands of *kanji*. Right now she knew a hundred. She did not know any with thirty strokes, but she knew the *kanji* for "military ship," which had twenty-one. Her teacher had taught the class that one because they would all be boarding a military ship soon. The other complicated *kanji* Hanako knew also had twenty-one strokes, and it meant "demon." This was a word that came in handy on the days when you hated white people like Mr. Best— the Tule Lake director—or Mr. Taylor, both of whom sometimes seemed like demons who smiled. But there were Japanese demons too; she knew that.

Sometimes, as they passed a village, there would be people standing by the tracks, just watching the train pass, as if they had nothing better to do. Beyond the old towns, beautiful mountains rose at the horizon. So far today, she'd seen different types of mountains: dark ones with snowy ridges, green-covered ones, and one unreal mountain with a blue-gray disk-shaped cloud right above it. Maybe that was one of the special, holy mountains of Japan. She tried to remember her school lessons. Japan was a country of mountains, many of them volcanoes. The people called their nation Nippon, which meant "land of the rising sun." As the train continued, they traveled through many more tunnels dug through the mountains. Hanako felt a little panicked in the longer tunnels. It seemed like they would never end; she had never been in the center of a mountain before. When they'd finally emerged from an especially long one, night had fallen, and there was not a light to be seen outside the train. In the camps there had been constant searchlights lighting the barracks through the cracks in the wood, day and night. So this kind of darkness was something she hadn't seen in a long time.

The baby had settled on one of Mama's shoulders as Mama sang to it. Akira rested against Mama's other shoulder, listening to the song with a faraway look in his eyes.

> *Nenneko, nenneko, nenneko ya!*
> *Netara o-kaka e tsurete ina!*
> *Okitara gagama ga totte kama!*
>
> Sleep, sleep, sleep, my child!
> If you sleep, I will go home to fetch your mother!
> If you stay awake, the goblin will catch and bite you!

The baby seemed quite satisfied with life! Hanako took out a bag of crackers and sucked on one. Then a feeling washed over her, and she looked around to see that every single soldier was watching her. She felt suddenly that she was in a bubble. She took out another cracker, reached through the bubble, and held the cracker out toward the man with no pants who was now sitting in the aisle. His mouth dropped open as he took the *katapan* and bowed solemnly. *"Arigatō, arigatō."*

*"Dōitashimashite,"* she replied.

"Oh, here," Papa said, noticing. He reached into his coat pocket, drawing out another bag of *katapan* and handed the crackers out to the men nearest them. The men reached out eagerly, their faces breaking out in smiles as they mumbled, *"Arigatō."* It was so odd to feel lucky—lucky to have food, lucky to have a seat. Hanako had not felt this lucky in a very long time.

Then Papa put an arm around her and kissed the top of her head. "How have your Japanese studies gone?" he asked. "You have a good accent."

Hanako felt a flicker of pride at that. "I've learned a lot, but I'm not nearly fluent, and I can't write well," she admitted. She paused. "It's been harder than I expected."

He nodded. "It'll come. Your grandparents will help you."

She studied the deep slashes, like his skin had hardened and cracked. They were not normal wrinkles—there was no better word for them than "slashes." Those were new; he hadn't had them when he left Tule Lake.

She asked tentatively, "Was it bad where you were in North Dakota?"

He seemed to think that over. "Well, as I've told you, it was very cold. The German POWs were amazed that we were Americans and yet in the same jail as them. They asked why I was there, and I said for trying to negotiate with the director of Tule Lake."

What had happened was that there had been a farm truck accident that injured five inmates and killed one. As a result, workers went on strike. They demanded improved safety and working conditions and compensation for anyone injured on the job. Mr. Best responded by firing everyone and bringing in strikebreakers from other camps. The strikebreakers' pay was fifteen times higher than the strikers' had been. One night Hanako had actually knelt with her father and dozens of other strikers while they prayed that their spirits would not be broken. She did not know whom they were praying to, and she didn't think they knew either. Or maybe they did. The man leading the prayer had spoken more advanced Japanese than she could then understand. But the prayer was mesmerizing; she had felt sure nobody's spirit could possibly be broken now.

So then the national director of all the camps in

the country, Mr. Myer, visited Tule Lake. It was kind of amazing that he was there; he personally knew President Roosevelt. In general, Papa said, the people running the camps were "low-level flunkies," so everybody was curious about Mr. Myer. A negotiating committee met with him and Mr. Best to discuss camp grievances. More than five thousand Tule Lake inmates gathered outside the administrative area to peacefully support the negotiating committee. She and her father were even there for about half an hour.

Later that night she woke to someone pounding on the door, crying out, "Come! Come! They're stealing our food!"

Papa jumped out of bed, and she ran after him—they were going to lose their food! A big crowd had formed. "That's our food!" men were shouting out. All of a sudden there was a half groan, half roar that moved through the crowd until it reached Hanako. She screamed, though she didn't know why. Suddenly, people started running. Papa pulled her away, but when they stopped, Hanako looked back to see several inmates being savagely beaten, one with a baseball bat, by guards.

Papa lifted her up, and she could hear his feet

pounding on the ground. He grunted as he ran, maybe from the weight of her. At some point he said breathlessly, "I have to put you down. Can you run?"

"Yes!" she cried out, and together they ran home— they lived halfway across camp. When they reached their little barrack, she fell into bed and curled up in a ball. Mama and Akira never even woke up.

The next morning, when Hanako tried to go to school, she saw inmates being teargassed as they walked through the barracks. The camp was filled with tanks, and jeeps mounted with guns. After that, when Hanako and the other kids walked to school each morning, the soldiers in jeeps would stare at them like they were criminals. Once, the military invaded her barrack without knocking, shouting and demanding to know if they were hiding "contraband." They took one of Mama's kitchen knives. Mama held on to Akira the whole time, his whole body pressing against hers, his face terrified and astonished. To be honest, on that particular day, Hanako hadn't felt astonished to see their "home" invaded. She had reached her limit previously, and now this was just more of the same.

The soldiers had begun running their hands over the floor as if searching for a trapdoor. They looked under the beds, saying, "Are they here?!" They turned on Papa, shouting the same thing. They screamed at Mama, which made Akira wail. Hanako suddenly felt calm but alert—she thought fiercely to herself, *Please, Papa, don't tell them anything.*

"I don't know who you mean," Papa said, but Hanako knew he did. They were trying to find the negotiating committee's main leaders, who were hidden somewhere in the camp. Since nineteen thousand people lived there, it would not be easy to find these men.

Soon, however, the leaders turned themselves in, so as not to cause harm and distress to the rest of the inmates.

And then one day they came for Papa as well, because they'd found out that he had met several times with the negotiating committee and had helped come up with the negotiation points. They knew this because there were Nikkei spies among the inmates.

Papa and more than two hundred other men were imprisoned in the stockade, some for as long as nine months, without a hearing or trial. Among the reasons the army was holding the men: "general troublemaker," "too well educated for his own good," and "definitely a leader of the wrong kind." "Too well educated for his own good" was what Hanako's father was accused of, and he spent seven months in the stockade. He was not well educated at all—he'd never even finished high school in Japan—but anyway, that was what he was accused of.

Now, on the train, Hanako noticed that Papa's head was still tilted over, his back slumped. His eyes were open, though completely dead. She thought about those teenage boys, with their straight spines and heads held high. With their swagger. They had not been broken, not the way Papa seemed like he was, with his slashed cheeks and empty eyes. Then a funny expression passed over his face. It was almost no expression at all. It was like all of a sudden he didn't even want to go on another moment. Too tired.

She wasn't sure what to say. She tried this: "Don't worry, Papa. We're going to have the best life in history!" Words such as those had always worked with Akira. But Papa didn't even seem to have heard her. Then the life came back to his eyes. "Yes, yes," he said almost desperately. "I hope you will, Hana, you and Aki. Let that be our goal."

Despite the jerking of the train, Hanako must have slept, because when she looked at her mother again, the baby was gone. She turned to see it sleeping now with its own mother, its face completely at peace. That gave Hanako a sudden feeling like all was right with the world! Then she turned to the window—and let out a gasp, then a soft cry. Hiroshima! The City of Seven Rivers. The red sun rising in the sky. Only, the city was almost all rubble! Everywhere she looked was chaos—piles and piles of wood and rock and metal. Quite a few single poles and blackened tree trunks stuck up from the ground, and here and there a skeleton of a building rose forlornly. Hanako gaped—

the destruction stretched on and on, only seeming to stop at the mountains rising on the horizon. Almost as if the spirits she knew lived in the mountains of Japan had stopped the chaos from spreading. Was that how it would work? She didn't know much about bombs, or spirits.

The destruction, though . . . there was so much of it. It was beyond comprehension—it couldn't possibly be real! She was starting to feel mindless. Like she wasn't exactly there. Like her brain was frozen. Papa and Akira were talking, but for some reason, their voices sounded so far away that Hanako couldn't make out what they were saying. She gave her head a shake. Then she woke

up. It seemed her mind adjusted to what she was seeing, and she could think again.

What she thought was how the city would have
been full of people going about their lives before they
were burned, flattened, ripped open. There were probably so many ways to die in destruction like this. It
was strange, she could almost see it, the moment it
happened. But then she had to turn away. Akira was
pressed as far away from the window as he could get.
He looked terrified, as if a bomb might fall at any time:
*now*, even. Mama still slept.

Planes and bombs. She knew these were a big part
of the war. She imagined Akira growing up, flying a
plane and dropping a bomb. *What have I done?* This is
what she imagined he would think in such a moment.
Maybe it was the question that many people had asked
themselves, Americans and Japanese and Germans and
everybody else in the war. Every soldier, every general,
every leader. They had done what they thought they
had to do, and then they had asked themselves, *What
have I done?*

She could suddenly grasp that over the past several
years, really big things had been happening—huge,
enormous things—with many millions of people

involved, even at the exact same time that she hid in their little barrack, even on the night she saw that man hit with a baseball bat. So much more had happened, to other people, not just her, her family, and the Nikkei imprisoned. She just felt amazed—smacked in the face, almost—that so much BIG stuff had happened while she sat in her barrack.

Papa glanced at her, his face pale. He dropped his eyes to the floor and said, "There was a rumor in Bismarck that the US dropped an atomic bomb on Hiroshima. Then, on the ship, people told me it was true," he was saying. "But I didn't believe it. I *couldn't* believe it. It didn't make sense."

"Just one bomb?" Akira asked, looking over.

"Just one. I don't really understand it. On the ship they said it had to do with an atom. That's why it's called an 'atomic bomb.'" Papa looked at Akira. "Do you know what an atom is?"

"No."

"It's a tiny, tiny, tiny, little thing. It's so tiny that you can't see it. That's what doesn't make sense."

Akira looked at him suspiciously. "Maybe other people can't see it, but I can see it. I have good eyes." This was true; his vision was better than 20/20.

Papa gave a small smile. "It's so tiny that even *you* can't see it."

Akira cocked his head, as though unsure if Papa was joking with him.

Then Papa said a little desperately, "Make me smile more, Aki, make me."

But Akira just kept looking at Papa with his head cocked. "Papa, I can see anything," he said stubbornly.

"I don't know how, but these tiny little things you can't see can destroy a city," Papa went on. "Maybe you can grow up, study science, and explain it to me."

"I don't want to grow up," Akira said flatly, crossing his arms over his chest. "Mama! Mama!"

Mama sat up abruptly, her eyes flaring open as she saw out the window.

"Mamaaaaa!"

Mama pulled Akira toward her, pressing her face into his hair.

Hanako stared back out the window and wondered what time the bomb had been dropped. She thought of all the people who might have been walking the streets when everything around them exploded. How would that feel? Would they have felt intense heat? Or just a force like a tornado? Both, she decided: *You would blow through the air with your hair on fire.* She imagined her family, hurtling into the sky with their hair in flames. *Stop.* She willed herself to stop imagining.

Hanako didn't think she would be able to walk out there. Were they going to have to do that?

"But, Papa?" she said.

"What is it, Hana?"

Tears started pouring out of her eyes. She shut them tightly. It felt good to cry, but awful, too. "What if it never ends?" she asked.

"If what never ends?"

"Everything. All of this. Everything bad."

He brushed the tears from her cheek. "It's over. The war is over. It looks bad out the window; that's war. But now it's over. I haven't really studied war. But I think when it's over, there's a time of rebuilding. I'm certain of it. Everything gets better. All right? It has already ended."

"But what if it *hasn't*?" What rises falls; what falls rises. That's what Papa told her once. But what if things hadn't stopped falling yet?

Papa took her face in his hands. "Hanako. Listen to me. The war is over. We're going to my parents' farm. Even during the war, it wasn't as bad on the farms." The way he shook her head so firmly almost hurt.

"How do you know? When did you last hear from your parents?" Mama asked now, her face almost burning with intensity. "How do you *know*?"

He paused and turned away grumpily.

"Papa?" Hanako pressed.

"I'm not sure," he said reluctantly. Then he added with annoyance, "I know what I know."

Mama was staring at Papa with disbelief. "You know what you know?"

Papa didn't get mad much, but Hanako could see tension building in his face, in his stiffening body. She braced herself, but then Mama didn't say more, and neither did Papa.

Somehow Hanako felt herself calming down instead of getting upset. This was just one more thing they would get through. If Papa said he knew something, then he did. Period.

"We aren't staying in the city, though, are we? We are going to the farmlands," she said. "We will change trains in Hiroshima and never even walk outside."

Papa kissed her head. "Yes," he said. "Yes. And I know my parents are there waiting for us. I wrote them in July, and in August, September, and October. I didn't hear back, but mail has been disrupted. But I *know* they must have gotten one of those letters." He paused, and Hanako again studied the cracks on the sides of his face. They went straight down from his eyes, splitting his cheeks into sections. But you could tell he wasn't old—that was what gave the cracks their peculiar quality. "I know—I *know*—that they're alive."

Hanako met eyes with Akira. She knew they were both thinking, *But* how *do you know?*

"I don't want to sit by the window," Akira announced. He and Mama changed places. "I don't like the window anymore."

"I hate windows!" Hanako exclaimed, and turned her back to hers.

"It shouldn't be bad where we're going," Papa tried to assure them. But Hanako did not feel assured, even when he added, "We're headed to where the small villages are. Why would they bomb those?" A look passed over Papa's face, like he had a sudden headache. "But it won't be easy. Everybody is very poor in Japan. While you were sleeping, your mother spoke with one of the soldiers. He said you can't imagine how poor."

But Hanako could imagine how poor. She could imagine it because of the faces of the Japanese soldiers, of the truck drivers, of the people watching the train roll by their villages. Papa had always told her, "Do everything you can do." For instance, she would say, "How long should I work for?" And he would answer, "Do everything you can do." That was one of his mottoes. The faces of the people she was seeing seemed to be saying, "There's nothing more I can do." What could a soldier do who had killed people for no good reason and then returned starving to his country?

# TEN

Nothing, that's what.

The PA announced Hiroshima Station, so Papa pulled down their bags from the rack. The whole train emptied out. Everybody else seemed eager to get off, but her own family waited and were the last out the door. Then, after having been so eager to get off, the passengers walked slowly, some gazing around with their brows furrowed. The teenage boys were frowning, looking worried—scared, even. No more swagger as they moved along with the crowd.

The station building was heavily damaged, but there were workers atop scaffolding at the ceiling. You could see the sky through the broken ceiling. Hanako held on to Papa's coat, and Akira held on to Mama's. But then he pulled his hand away and pointed, exclaiming, "Mama! Papa!" almost hysterically.

Akira was looking at a woman sitting on a blanket, with what appeared to be *mochigashi* sitting in front of her! Those were delicious, colorful cakes such as you could get in Little Tokyo, by downtown Los Angeles. It was like a mirage. Hanako was almost shaking with excitement. She hadn't seen these for four years, and they were her most favorite treat. Akira ran forward.

The woman was middle-aged, with her hair pulled back off her face, and she did not look like the people Hanako had seen from the train, the people who seemed to be feeling that there was nothing they could do. On the contrary, this woman looked quite motivated. She began immediately haggling with Mama and Papa about the price of the cakes, even though they hadn't said a word about even buying them. She was so motivated, she couldn't stop talking, making offers and taking them back and making new offers.

Finally, Papa said he would pay one American dollar for ten cakes, and she accepted.

Hanako could not believe their luck to find this woman in a starving country selling these beautiful cakes.

Pleasure flooded her chest. She and Akira picked out five apiece, pale greens and yellows and pinks. Akira gave her his to hold because he was afraid he would drop them. She wrapped five in her handkerchief and put them in one of her deep pockets. Papa gave her his handkerchief, and she wrapped the other five in that for her second pocket.

Mama said, "You must not eat them until we get to your grandparents' house. And you must share. They may not have had sweets for a long time."

"But, Mama! Can't we eat just one each?" Hanako turned to Papa, but he gestured toward Mama. She took Mama's hand. "Please?"

Mama seemed torn, but then she said, "We must respect your grandparents."

Hanako had never understood why she must respect people who weren't even there at that moment. For instance, Mama and Papa had never let her criticize kids at school when she was at home. Or her teachers. All this respect among the Japanese could get quite aggravating! She thought about begging further, and maybe even trying to work some tears out of her eyes so she could get at those precious cakes. But Akira had surprisingly not argued at all. "I respect my grandparents," he said, putting her to shame.

"I do too," she said. Her mouth was watering, though, so she said it reluctantly.

Mama smiled at Akira with pride, but she frowned at Hanako. Hanako felt embarrassed.

They all trailed Papa through the station, Hanako's mind on her heavy pockets. Then Mama called out in a panic, "Where is Akira?"

Hanako spun around. Where *was* he? And so quickly gone? Then she spotted him about twenty-five feet away, just standing and staring. "There he is!" she shouted, running over. She slowed down when she saw what he was looking at.

They were . . . people. Dozens of them. People lying down on single sheets of newspaper or sitting on the bare ground staring at nothing. Some with no shirts, a couple with no pants, like that soldier on the train. A man with only a shirt, and it was very dirty. Maybe ten or twelve children. Most of the children were sleeping, though it wasn't nighttime. A naked baby clung to a woman, both asleep. A dirty, shirtless boy lay with an arm resting over a toddler girl. A very dirty toddler girl.

It was so rude to be staring! But the people didn't seem to care; they just watched Hanako and Akira with dead eyes. The chest of the older of the shirtless boys was covered in scars. He didn't seem to have one of his ears. His face was pink, as if the skin had been scraped off and was still growing back. But at least he had a face; she saw one man who didn't. That is, two men didn't, although . . . actually, she wasn't sure if the second faceless person was a man or a woman. No face, baggy clothes, eyes peering out from a mass of scars.

She started to get that sense of mindlessness again. It was too much; it was hard to look at; her mind was freezing. She gazed down. When she lifted her eyes again, she focused on the pink-faced boy, because he did not look much older than her. She realized that although his eyes were closed and he wasn't moving, he might be awake. His lips were pursed, but then he relaxed them.

He didn't seem to have one single possession. Actually, not many did. Nobody had shoes or anything. She thought of the pile of baggage that the Nikkei from the ship had searched through so fervently. *Things.* Things they owned. Skirts and pencils and toothbrushes and underwear and probably sheets and pillowcases. Among these people, it seemed only the fortunate had even a sheet of newspaper to sit on. She did spot someone with a possession, though—a little girl clutching what looked like a piece of flowered cloth, not really big enough to be a blanket.

But the pink-faced boy . . . She went as if hypnotized to kneel beside him. She heard her family calling to her. *"Sumimasen,"* she said softly. Both the boy and the toddler opened their eyes tiredly. No hope in those eyes. Just fatigue and a little suspicion. She reached into her pockets, emptying out the handkerchiefs and placing the cakes next to them. The boy blinked a few times, then sat up abruptly and grunted like an animal, he and the little one suddenly yelling at each other as they gathered the cakes into their newspaper. Maybe the pink-faced kid was thirteen or fourteen, and the tot maybe three or four. Pink Face picked up the newspaper, and they both broke into a run, the smaller one struggling to keep up. Hanako watched until they disappeared into the crowds.

Now she noticed that *everybody* was staring at her hopefully. She had no more cakes, though. She and the man with no face looked directly at each other. She heard her father urgently yelling: "Hanako, hurry! We don't want to miss our train!"

She hesitated, frozen in place. "Hanako!"

"I have no more cake!" she shouted out. There was

nothing more she could do! Then she turned and saw throngs of people rushing toward a train. Papa scooped up Akira, and she and Mama joined the surging crowd. As she pressed forward, she realized she had shouted to the man in English.

And it turned out they were all running for a train going in the same direction they had just come from.

Papa seemed to be confused, wandered aimlessly for a few minutes, and then stood in front of a sign for a long time. He had been trying to be so American for so long! Was it possible he couldn't read Japanese very well anymore?

As Hanako waited, she thought of the two children dashing away with the cakes. They had not looked happy to get the *mochigashi*; they had looked absolutely panicked, as if somebody might steal the sweets from them. Would they even be able to appreciate how good the cakes were? Or would they just eat them all at once in a panic?

Mama approached Papa and laid her arm around his shoulder. He glanced toward her, then studied the sign further.

"Why doesn't he just ask someone?" Akira asked.

Seeing how confused Papa looked, Hanako started

to feel scared, almost dizzy. It made her dizzy to think that her father didn't actually *belong* here in Japan, and as a matter of fact, maybe her parents belonged nowhere in the world, not here and not there. This made her feel as if her whole family could float up and up into the sky, right up through the hole in the ceiling, like they had no weight. See, the law in America had always been that you couldn't give up your citizenship during times of war, but President Roosevelt had signed the law just to get rid of them. That's what Papa had told her. He had wanted them out, and he had gotten his way. One thing she had to admit about President Roosevelt was that he'd been a very powerful man.

And yet. And yet. To her personally, her father was a more powerful man, because the president had not taken care of her. He had not worked to feed her. That was her father. And her mother. So the fear started to drain. And see there! Papa was at last nodding confidently and said, "This direction!" He had read the sign and knew where they should go! Relief washed over her. Her parents would do everything they could. She took her brother's hand and said it out loud: "Mama and Papa will do everything they can. We'll be fine. We're going to have the best life ever. That's a fact. I *promise*."

## ELEVEN

And yet. And yet.

They were on the next train now. Was it possible for a train to be any more rickety? It felt like it might fall to pieces even as it chugged down the tracks. It might even tip right over at any moment, or jump off the rails. Akira, sitting next to her as he'd asked to do, had a look on his face of terror-delight, as if a part of him liked this wild ride and a part of him didn't. It was actually amusing.

And yet. It was hard to forget the children she'd given the cakes to.

"Mama! Remember those pictures you had from the Dust Bowl?"

Mama used to tear photos from magazines, photos of the Dust Bowl years in the 1930s in America, when a long drought had stricken the Midwest. She'd started collecting them even before Hanako was born, stuffing them into a drawer. Then when Hanako was just a toddler, millions of people had to leave the Midwest, where massive dust storms were creating dark, towering clouds in the fields, like the smoke from the biggest fire she could imagine. When Hanako looked at such pictures, and at the pictures of the people who'd left their homes behind, she felt in her heart that she knew those people. They were white people, but Hanako had a strong sense that she had met them, maybe was even related to them, though she hadn't and of course she wasn't. And that's how she felt about those two kids at the train station. She *knew* them. She had *met* them before today.

"Yes, of course," Mama replied.

"Why did you collect those?"

"Oh, what makes you think of that?" Mama paused to think. "I don't know why I started collecting them. I suppose those people reminded me of Nikkei I knew. Picking produce for a living. But today those people remind me of us. They had no home." She thought more. "I brought those pictures to camp, but I threw them away when we left America."

"You brought the pictures to camp? Mama, *why*?"

"Well." Mama got a pained look in her eyes. "The way the world drives you from your home, sometimes. I just like a predictable world, but it hasn't worked out that way for us or for them. Maybe for anyone . . ." That kind of scared Hanako. It made her feel she could be driven from her home again someday, when she was older. When she had a family to take care of. She wanted to talk more, but Mama's mind seemed to have drifted away. She was blinking, her mouth hanging open as she stared at air.

Akira was studying Hanako as if he were suspicious about something, as if he were about to accuse her of something. Then his face relaxed and he said, "It's all right that you gave those kids our cakes. I was mad for a minute, but it's all right."

"Don't worry. We'll eat a thousand cakes, Aki."

He looked excited at the prospect. "Then I could eat one every single day! For . . ."

"A thousand days."

"A thousand days!"

She didn't want to get his hopes up *too* much, so

she added, "Anyway, we'll find a few more somewhere. It might not actually be a thousand."

But she could see by the way he was smiling dreamily into space that he was thinking now of a thousand colorful *mochigashi*, maybe sitting in piles around him on the floor.

The train soon entered farmland. Here and there houses were clustered near one another against small forests and wild, disorganized fields, but they were *green*—nothing was destroyed! Everything looked perfectly peaceful, like there had never been a war and never would be. Sometimes you could see an expanse of farmland, the fields stretching into the distance, separated from any houses. In other areas the houses had small farm fields next to them. Not too far away were mountains—she had heard that just about everywhere you went in Japan, you could see a mountain. They were going to the place where Papa had grown up, and it didn't look destroyed!

Just seeing all the green made Hanako feel better, and her energy surged. Her eyes drank it all in. Green = Life.

They passed fields where Papa said wheat was growing. "Wheat is a winter crop—" he was explaining when the PA announced something. Papa interrupted himself to bellow, "This is it!"

What? Already? Hanako jumped up.

"Hurry!" Mama snapped.

"Hurry!" Papa yelled.

"Help me!" Akira called out, and Papa grabbed him rather roughly with one arm and took luggage in the other.

Hanako scrambled after them, tripping once and feeling so panicked, she cried out as Aki had, "Help me!"

But nobody heard her, and she scrambled to her feet. The train was slowing down, though, and then it stopped. For them. There was no conductor, and Papa pushed open the door. He threw down the suitcases and hopped to the ground to help each of them out. Then they all stepped back and watched the train pick up speed.

As it grew quieter, Hanako looked around. There was a platform, but it seemed like it was plopped in the middle of nowhere. Papa rubbed his face as he looked around.

Finally, Hanako asked, "Which way should we go? Papa?"

"Hmm," he said, like she'd just asked an interesting question. Hanako spotted a group of old wooden buildings, a couple of them almost shacks, in the distance, and Papa led them through the weeds toward that. Some of the weeds were taller than Akira.

The buildings were made of dark, unpainted wood, topped off with slanted roofs. One roof was bright red tile, but the others were grayish brown thatch or tile. There was no glass in the windows—most were covered with something white, either paper or cloth. The path through the village was dirt and pebbles. People walked through the streets, different kinds of people than in the city. These people were calmer, and a few times one of them caught Papa's eye and nodded as if they knew one another—which Hanako knew they didn't.

Papa paused in the middle of it, his head cocked, almost as if listening. "I'm trying to find my memories," he said, and kept cocking his head.

Silence, except for the wind in the trees beyond.

Mama shifted the luggage in her hands. "I don't like the weeds," Akira said. "They're scary." So Mama picked him up, ready to continue walking, still holding her suitcase.

"I can take the bag," Hanako offered, but Mama just shook her head no. Mama was the kind of person who would carry her youngest child until she collapsed. A lot of parents Hanako knew were like that.

Papa began moving suddenly, so they all did. "Do you remember where we're going, Papa?" Hanako asked.

"Yes. I just had to find everything in my memory."

Hanako pictured her father's brain like a bunch of shelves with boxes on them. He could search through the boxes until he found what he was looking for, and then he would have no problems remembering. Hanako's brain wasn't like that at all—it was just a big mash-up.

It felt quite odd walking and walking to wherever, to meet her grandparents for the first time, not having *any* of her things. Not even having a gift for her grandparents. She had packed so carefully: six skirts—three for summer and three for winter. Six white blouses. Twelve pencils with erasers and a notebook. Five toothbrushes and toothpaste. She didn't bring soap because Mama said they would have that in Japan. Her pajamas, of course. And a gift for her grandmother: a pretty, empty glass perfume bottle that her mother's only sister, Jean, had given her. Many Japanese Americans had both American and Japanese names that they used, but

Auntie only called herself "Jean," and Hanako didn't even know her other name. You could just barely smell the perfume that had once been in there. Hanako would sniff it in camp sometimes, and it smelled like another world, the world she knew Mama had lived in while she was dating Papa—Hanako had seen pictures of her all dressed up. Mama said that even if you didn't have a lot of money, you got to live in that world while your future husband was courting you. It was a world that had once been in Hanako's future for certain, before the war had broken everything in half. Now and then, even after they had kids, some of her parents' friends had gone dancing on Saturdays while somebody babysat their kids. But Papa always worked Saturday nights, and Mama stayed home with Hanako and Akira. Her parents had seemed happy, though—back then, a million years ago.

But she had to pay attention now; here beyond the village, the ground had grown uneven, and it was harder to walk. There were rocks and weeds, bushes and trees, everywhere.

"This is the land time forgot!" Akira cried out. "I read about it in a book!"

And so it was. Hanako had the feeling that she was

in a book, that she had stepped off the path of real life. And yet something felt good. It felt like nothing could hurt them here. A giant bomb had fallen, and even that could not hurt this special place.

As they walked, Papa moved as though he was sure where he was going. He even started humming! At one point he stopped and stared at a small wooden house with a slanted roof. In the yard surrounding it were two large pine trees and several others Hanako didn't recognize.

Papa was tilting his head, his lips pressed slightly together. "When I walked away last time, more than seventeen years ago, I never looked back. I just kept walking."

Hanako remembered that when they were leaving their own house for the last time, she had stared back the whole way. "Why, Papa?" she asked.

"Because I was scared it would make me change my mind."

Mama grunted as she let Akira slip to the ground. She was sweating, her hair sticking to her face.

Hanako realized she was sweating as well. She wondered if she looked sloppy. She wondered if her grandparents would like her. She wiped her face with the back of her hand, but then Akira said, "You wiped dirt all over your face."

Oh no! "Aki, will you clean it off?"

She knelt down, and he wiped his coat sleeve across her forehead. "It's worse now," he said. "Sorry."

But Papa had started striding quickly toward the house, and Akira ran after him. Mama started off as well, but Hanako was worried about her dirty face. She liked to make a good impression. She wasn't like Akira, who never cared what anybody thought.

Papa seemed to read her mind. He stopped abruptly and turned around. "Come on, Hanako. This is family."

He strode back for her. She let herself be pulled along by him, taking in all the details. Her grandparents' house! They had traveled across an ocean to get here! The house was square, with a narrow, covered *engawa* wrapped around it. Many of the farmhouses they'd passed were two stories high, but this was one story.

Papa knocked on the door, calling out, *"Otōsan, tadaima modori mashita!"* It meant "Father, I'm home!" Spoken politely and with respect. In Japan people had different ways of saying things depending on the standing of whom they were talking to.

Hanako heard noise from inside, and she quickly stepped behind her father as the door slid open. A little man was standing on the threshold, not nearly filling it.

And just like that, she fell in love with her *jiichan*! He took her breath away! He was so small, he was almost like a child, and he nodded his head yes over and over. His skin was wrinkly like a prune. Yes, he looked exactly like a sweet prune. He looked more like a prune than an actual prune did—sweeter and more wrinkly. Papa stepped forward, a look almost of awe on his face, and then he and Jiichan hugged tightly, which Hanako knew was unusual among Japanese people. But Papa was American.

*"Nyōbō desu,"* Papa immediately said, introducing Mama.

Mama bowed repeatedly and mumbled something over and over. She seemed overwhelmed.

"Hanako," Papa said to the old man, pulling Hanako from behind him. "Hanako, this is your *jiichan*," he added.

Before Hanako could bow and greet her grandfather, Jiichan cried out passionately, "I speak English! Yes, I do! It does a talent I learn in America many years before you." He had a funny, kind of high voice, almost like a cartoon character—like Akira's voice, except in an old man. He was Akira decades from now!

Hanako wasn't sure what he meant—before *she* learned English?—but she curtsied, then thought that was wrong, so she quickly bowed instead. Jiichan put out his hand, and he and Hanako very firmly shook. Still holding her hand, he pushed his face forward and looked at her intensely, startling her, but then he laughed. "That how I learn in America to shake hand. I take class. You supposed to look in eye, then shake firm."

Hanako giggled shyly.

"And this is Akira," Papa said. Akira had taken Hanako's spot behind Papa, peeking from behind him.

"Healthy children! I can see it! Much health happens in America, do you think?"

Jiichan was speaking right at Hanako! "*Hai* . . . Yes," was all she could think to say. She bowed again, just for good measure.

He laughed. "She likes to bow, *neh*? Is she always this dirty? I work in field, I like dirt! The cold! Come in, come in."

"*Arigatō gozaimasu,*" Hanako said, bowing yet again.

"You must speak the English. We have been practice it since we heard you are coming."

They carried their things inside. Hanako immediately took off her shoes.

"Such small feet. How do you balance?" Jiichan asked, laughing like an imp. "We will laugh at each other, and life will have beautiful!"

Suddenly, Akira ran up to Jiichan and threw his arms around him.

"Ahhh," Jiichan said. "American like to hug." As he hugged Akira, he glanced at Hanako's feet again. He lifted Akira with a big, big grunt, staggering sideways before finding his balance. "She inherit my feet, *neh*?" he asked Papa. "Look at my feet." He held up a tiny foot and almost fell over. As he set Akira down, he nodded modestly. "Yes, yes, for old man I have powers—my feet have traveled across the ocean until now this girl has my same feet."

"Absolutely," Papa said.

Then Jiichan's jaw fell as he studied Akira's wine stain. "Ahhh," he said. "Ahhh. *Ungaii!*" He touched Akira's stain and said, "This thing will give him much luck. It is good color, I like very much."

Akira looked like he would explode with pride.

"Otōsan, it's good to be here," Papa said. "You have no idea. And where is Okaasan?"

"She trying to buy futon. Every day after work she look for futon for good price. If she doesn't find, the children will sleep on floor. Sit down, I will make you tea. It will not be—ah, what's the word?—*fancy*, but it will be tea."

"Oh, let me make that!" Mama said.

"No, no. How long you have traveled? The energy is all mine. You will find that I am never tired." Then he nodded. "Ahh, well, as I am older, I am more tired some days. I cannot lie. I am old."

"Ah, you will never be old!" Papa said. "But do you have water? We drank our water on the train, and the children never complained."

Jiichan looked shocked. "You must let them complain when they live here!" he said. "When you are young and when you are old, you may complain. In the middle you have to—"

"Take your lumps," Papa finished.

"*Nani?*" Jiichan asked. That meant something like "Eh?" or "What?" But he left the room and quickly returned with a tray of water glasses. It felt so good to drink!

They sat at the *kotatsu* on the living room floor. A *kotatsu* was a low table frame, covered by a futon or a heavy blanket, which in turn was covered with a tabletop. Underneath was a coal-burning heater. You were supposed to sit on the floor and put your legs under the blanket. This would keep you warm during the winter months. They'd used a *kotatsu* at the barrack they'd lived in at Tule Lake.

Hanako gladly sat at the table and soaked up the warmth. A *kotatsu* was something comforting. She looked around the small living room. The floor was covered with tan *tatami*, and the walls were gray blue. *Tatami* were thin straw mats. A Japanese scroll hung on a wall; it was a picture of Mount Fuji. Fake orchids sprouted out of a planter next to a big basket in a corner. Everything looked old. Jiichan came back with the tea and said, "Nothing fancy. Nothing fancy."

As Hanako straightened out her skirt, she noticed how dirty her legs were. She looked like she had walked through mud! "I'm so dirty!" she exclaimed.

"You are very dirty! There is water in tub if you wish to clean!" Jiichan exclaimed back. He seemed surprised at how loudly she'd spoken. "I will show you!"

She followed him into a small kitchen and then to a tiny adjoining room. Everything here was small. But the square wooden tub with a fire underneath it was very big. Hanako asked, "Is it all right? May I take a bath?"

"Yes, of course you must take bath!" Jiichan said. "I insist you must! Do you know Japanese bath? You must clean off first and then get in tub to soak. There is *tenugui* to dry yourself." He indicated some plain folded cloths. "A bath is very good."

Jiichan put his fingertips to the sides of his forehead as if that helped him think, and then he said, "Yes, this is good idea." He brought his hands back down and smiled. "I'm very pleased tub has made your happiness."

Then he left.

Hanako paused, considering whether her parents might be mad that she was taking a bath instead of talking at the table. Also, she knew it wasn't her turn to bathe. At camp Mama had told her what life would be like in Japan. Everybody would take a separate bath one after the other in the same water in a deep wooden tub. The oldest and most important took their bath first, then the next oldest, and so on. Men before women. Mama had also told her that it would probably become her job to heat the bathwater, the same water night after night until it got too musty to use anymore. She looked uncertainly at the small fire underneath. She'd been warned that Japanese take very hot baths.

There was a pail and a big bowl. She undressed. It was the first time she had undressed in private in several years. Then she wetted a *tenugui* and washed herself with soap, rinsing by pouring the bowl on herself. There was a drain in the floor.

The side of the tub was actually quite high. Hanako climbed in and sank into the water. When she sat up, water came to her chin—Akira would need to stand while he bathed! *Ahhh*. The heat was not as shocking as she'd expected. That is, it was startling but not shocking. She hadn't taken a bath since before camp. For the Japanese, soaking in a bathtub was as important a daily activity as eating and sleeping, because it made you strong and healthy. She closed her eyes and felt the heat and water make her stronger, change her.

# CHAPTER
# TWELVE

When she heard laughter from the other room she stood up, eager to talk to her grandfather, who was different from anyone else she had ever met. She dried herself with a scratchy *tenugui*. As she reached her feet, she saw how dirty her toes still were. She rubbed on them with the towel. Then she heard more laughter and didn't want to take time cleaning herself further. She put her dirty clothes back on.

Back in the living room, everyone was drinking tea. But Akira jumped up when he saw her. "I was waiting for you! I have to make *shi-shi*!"

"Outhouse in back, but he want to go with you," Jiichan said.

"I'll only go with Hana!" Aki confirmed.

Hanako and her brother had used many outhouses. Back in California, when Papa wanted something really fresh for the restaurant, he sometimes took them with him to a farm, where he bought butter, milk, or meat. He did this whenever somebody booked the restaurant for a special occasion. The farms often had outhouses that Hanako and Akira would use. Akira hated them— he worried he was so skinny he might fall into the hole by accident. This was actually not possible because the hole wasn't big enough, but Hanako always had to go with him and hold on to both of his hands.

So they went outside and saw a small wooden build- ing with what looked like a sheet of tin on top. Right inside the door was a pair of slippers. When Hanako opened the door, she saw a wooden lid on the floor. "I guess you have to squat," she said.

"I don't want to."

"I know, but you have to."

"You do it first so I know it's safe."

Hanako thought this over. She put on the slippers and stepped carefully into the outhouse, then lifted the lid. She squatted over the hole, and when she was done, she took a square of newspaper from beside the lid and wiped herself. The paper was rough and scratchy.

"There you go!" she said to Akira. "I can confirm it's safe!"

So she stepped outside, where Akira put on the slippers. After he had finished, he pulled up his pants and said with satisfaction, "I like it. It's safer than American outhouses."

That made no sense, but she let it go, because Akira was Akira.

Back inside, there were now two teapots on the table, and when Hanako sat down, Mama poured her a cup. She knew it was barley tea for her and *sencha* for the grown-ups. She sipped at it and smiled. The tea was like the bath: it made her stronger. She slipped her legs under the blanket. She felt such a surge of optimism that she wondered for a second whether she'd been hallucinating when she saw Hiroshima.

But then Akira blurted out, "I saw a boy with scars and only one ear! He was in the train station! And I saw a soldier with no pants on the train! The boy's face was all pink! And he had a little sister or someone with him!"

Jiichan's face suddenly turned sad. "So you have seen Hiroshima."

Papa nodded. "It was hard to believe what we were

seeing, even when we were staring right at it. Was there really only one bomb?" he asked.

Jiichan filled his cheeks with air, looking for a moment like a round-faced doll. Then he puffed out the air and frowned. "Just one. Many air raid, but all false alarm. Let me say this even in front of your children. There were many thousand of dead body—floating on river, piled in field, lying in road. Everywhere. From far away they look black because covered with fly. I have seen this myself. So many fly buzz in city, I do not know where so many fly can come from. They look like dark cloud that move over the body. I travel to city every month with all my vegetable to sell in cart. But after bomb I walk with all my neighbor to city to give away our vegetable. I tell you something: I hear much that people help other people right after bomb. Their skin hang from body, but they stop to help. So you see? Maybe worst day in history. Maybe. But on worst day in history, people stop to help."

Hanako was leaning forward, her elbows on the table. "So were there a lot of bodies?"

"So many. One second alive, next second dead. I see this myself. I see a man alive, walking, then he dead. I think he die standing up."

"The pink boy had a claw for his right hand!" Akira blurted out.

Hanako hadn't noticed that!

"Many children like that. We call them *sensō koji*. Ahhh, how to translate?" He looked at Papa.

"War orphan," Papa said.

"Are they starving?" Hanako asked. She herself had been hungry a few times, but she'd never been *starving*. So she had no idea what "starving" truly, truly meant. But the way she imagined it was feeling like long nails were sticking into your stomach. She knew it must hurt. She clutched at her stomach, felt a stab in there.

"*Hai*, some starve." Jiichan was silent for a moment, then said to Hanako, "What thought did you have of city?"

Hanako paused. Then she said, "It was worse than the camps. I felt grateful I wasn't out there. Where we were was good compared to that!"

Nobody answered at first, but Jiichan nodded thoughtfully before saying, "I no expert—I never live in prison. But to compare lose freedom to get bomb and starve and die, there is no sense. If worse thing than jail, does not make jail good."

Hanako felt kind of rebuked. She slumped her shoulders, embarrassed. But Jiichan smiled at her, and then his smile grew. "You are right, I am wrong." He pressed the tips of his fingers into his forehead again, concentrating. "I mean to say . . . and it is, you must forgive America. I see and hear many bad in world, many bad. After bomb explode, black rain fall from sky. Big black raindrop. I don't see this one myself, but it is story I hear people say. I am sorry to tell these many thing in front of my grandchildren. Why I tell it, it is that I want to say, there is many bad, but there is also many good. So we move forward in life, *neh*? When we can, we move forward."

For some reason, Jiichan's words felt like a puff of air on Hanako's face. And it was funny how that little puff of air could blow away so much. She had this sensation that America was suddenly far away not only in distance but in time as well. The camps were a million years ago. The boat trip just ended but might as well have been decades in the past.

Just as quickly, she suddenly felt filled with doubt. "But how do we move forward?" She paused, knowing her father might be upset over what she wanted to say next. But she said it anyway. "Look at what the camps have done to Papa! Look how old he's gotten!" She didn't look to see her father's reaction.

Jiichan didn't hesitate. "The way to move forward is through *kintsukuroi*. Do you know this word?"

Hanako shook her head.

"When you break pottery, it is in pieces. Then you repair each crack with lacquer and paint the lacquer gold. It is very rare and expensive, but my father was given such a piece of pottery when he save rich man son. It is family legend. The boy ride off on his own on his horse. He fall to ground, and my father pick him up and run with him all the way to doctor house in next village. It is one of proudest moment in our family history."

Jiichan then waited, his face filled with expectation. So Hanako said, "Your father must have been very strong."

That seemed to satisfy him. "Yes, is so. So you see, in the end, bowl end up more beautiful than before it was broken. This is *kintsukuroi*. Thing break, you must fix with gold. It is only way to live your life. I will show you."

He walked to the kitchen, obviously trying to hurry but in truth moving quite slowly.

Papa stared after his father and said, "Children, you must promise to come see me at least once a year when you're grown. Hopefully, we will live in the same city. But you must not move to another country. I won't allow it!"

"But, Papa, you're the one who moved to another country!" Hanako said accusingly.

"I know . . . and if I hadn't, I wouldn't have met your mother, and I wouldn't have the same children." He thought for a moment. "I suppose you will both have to move wherever is best for you after all."

"I already told you I don't want to grow up," Akira said. "I don't want to. I want you to take care of me." He burst into tears, and Mama and Papa both immediately reached out for him, Mama getting there first and sweeping him into her arms.

"Aki, Aki, we're always going to take care of you, no matter if you're grown up or not. All right?"

Akira nodded tearfully.

Hanako looked forward to growing up and making her own decisions, but as soon as she had the thought, she had its opposite: The decisions she would have to make someday might be too hard for her! She didn't want to make them!

But then Jiichan was coming into the room whistling in a sorry fashion—he could hardly whistle, and he couldn't stay on tune at all! He was so full of joy, though, that the whistling was, well, it was *amazing*. It was the whistling of someone so full of joy, he was almost a madman. Hanako half expected him to jump into the air and shout in ecstasy. It made her suddenly not care at all about growing up or not.

He was holding two pieces of pottery: one a plain, boring blue-gray bowl, and the other an amazing blue-gray bowl with random cracks that were filled with shimmering gold. It was the most beautiful bowl Hanako had ever seen. Jiichan set them down side by side. "The rich man gave us two bowl, special bowl and plain bowl. He was very good man." It was hard for Hanako to take her eyes off the bowl with gold cracks. She wondered, *If this bowl had cracked a little differently and then been repaired, could it possibly be as beautiful?*

Jiichan said, "Hanako, while you are here with us, this will be your bowl."

He handed it to her. She felt like she was holding something remarkable, like the entire planet Earth, in her hands.

"Be careful with it," Mama said, and Hanako set it down carefully. Mama was leaning toward Jiichan, her face earnest, and laid her hand on his. "We don't know how long we'll need to stay. We're very grateful."

Hanako thought Jiichan felt a flicker of wanting to lean back—Mama often got so close to people's faces.

"AHHH!" Jiichan said. "No need to be grateful. Stay as long as you want, as long as you want. Please do! But we have not much. I wish we have more for you. Most of rice we must sell to who and where government says. But we happy for share. It is our delight. Many day people from city come knocking on door begging us for food. They walk all this way. Busy parent send out their children to find something to eat. Children as young as Akira come to our door. Food, food, food. It is all people think about. If you have never been starved, you cannot understand. But we cannot share with stranger again. Everything we have is yours now."

Hanako looked from her mother to her father. Would they have enough food? Would they have to walk the unfamiliar roads and knock on strangers' houses to beg for food? Would Mama and Papa send her out on such a mission? And Akira? She looked at the bowl with disappointment. It was still beautiful. But while *kintsukuroi* was fine for a bowl, she figured life was much more complicated.

Jiichan, however, did not appear worried in the least. He was sitting with his elbow on the table, his chin resting in his palm as he stared dreamily at Akira. He nodded, then nodded again. "I love this child," he said. "Yes, I do." Then he smiled so hard at Hanako that his eyes scrunched up. "This one too. I have not met them before, but they have my feet. His are small too; I have seen it." Then he thought that over. "Even if they don't have my feet, I will still love them. But it is good thing. My son leave, and then his babies have my feet. That is *kintsukuroi, neh?*"

## THIRTEEN

Jiichan!" Akira suddenly shouted. "We have no clothes! Tell him, Hanako!"

"We lost our bags," Hanako explained. "That is, somebody lost them. They're gone. They weren't there in the pile of luggage from the ship. One of my skirts was really cute too! And Akira had a baseball jacket."

She was surprised when Jiichan looked genuinely horrified. "A baseball jacket!" he cried out.

For a second she thought he might be making fun of her. But then he looked brokenhearted. "A boy should not lose his baseball jacket. We like baseball very much in Japan. There is no baseball during war. Everybody miss it." His face filled with pride. "I play shortstop when I seven year old. I play one season. Pretty good too. Maybe would have become professional one day if I have time."

"We can buy cheap clothes," Papa said. "What we need to worry about is food. All right, Hana-chan? We may not find you *cute* skirts, but we will find you skirts that are wearable."

"Yes, Papa," she said obediently. But she felt a little disappointed. In camp she had thought that when they got out someday, they might have a few nice things— not *very* nice things, but maybe a little house, their own choice of what to eat for dinner, and, yes, a couple of cute skirts. They could get Sadie back. . . . Anyway, she still had her coat. If necessary, she would never take it off.

Suddenly, Mama took hold of Hanako's braid and started stroking it. She leaned in very close and said, "Hana-chan, we will find you one cute skirt somewhere in Japan. But you have to make sure to hold your head high no matter what you are wearing."

Hanako could hardly hold her head up because Mama was clutching her braid. "Yes, Mama," she mumbled.

"Good!" Mama said passionately. Then she cleared

her throat dramatically and said, "I have forgotten something important to mention! I learned some good news on the ship. They said that we're entitled to two monthly rations of butter and sugar from the United States government, since the children are still American citizens. The American consulate in Kobe will distribute the rations for each US passport."

"Ohh!" Jiichan cried out. "The Americans have so much butter and sugar they can give away! Ah! It is hard to imagine."

That was wonderful and amazing! Maybe now they wouldn't have to beg for food. Could a person survive on just butter and sugar? Hanako wasn't even sure *how* to beg. Would she drop to her knees and say—what would she say? *Please, my family is very hungry, could you spare some rice?* She was so glad that Mama had kept the passports tied in a small purse to her waist with the sixty dollars!

"We can trade butter and sugar for rice. Everyone in Japan, they think of rice day and night," Jiichan was saying. "Rice has gripped their mind." Then he tipped his head toward Akira and said, "Do not worry, little one, all will be fine and you will eat every night!"

Just then there was a knock on the door. "Who is

that?" Jiichan asked. He made a long, loud grunt as he stood up from the floor. Hanako was so curious that she followed, standing behind him as he slid open the front door. It was an old woman, very old. Hanako started to cry out, "Baachan!" But she saw that her grandfather didn't know the woman.

The woman bowed deeply. *"Onegai desu. Zutto tabete inain desu."* ("Please, I haven't eaten for a long time.") Hanako could see that this was true, for the woman's clothes hung limply on her, and her shoulder bones jutted out from under her lightweight black kimono. Then the woman looked directly at Hanako and pulled up a kimono sleeve to reveal her very bony arm. It seemed to be only weird indents and veins. There was no flesh at all. Hanako gaped, then caught herself and looked up into the woman's eyes. The woman seemed glad that she'd made an impression. She added that she had grandchildren she must feed as well.

"Jiichan!" Hanako said. "We must give her something."

Then Jiichan pulled up his own sleeve to reveal his *own* thin arm. "This is so in Japan," he explained. "But I will give her potato my neighbor give me last week. *Hai*, I will give her if you would like it."

"Yes, please!"

He went to the kitchen, leaving Hanako to face the woman. She tried to think of something nice to say in Japanese and settled on *"Watashi wa Hanako to mōshimasu."* ("I am Hanako," said politely.)

The woman bowed deeply, murmuring, "Hanako-san." Then she closed her eyes for some reason and stood there like a statue, her arms slightly raised. Hanako just stood watching, unsure what she should say, if anything.

Then Jiichan returned with a single potato, telling Hanako again, "It is my special potato from neighbor." Hanako could see that he wanted to give it to her and Akira, but this poor woman was so old. . . . He handed the potato to Hanako, and she handed it to the old woman, who'd opened her eyes again.

The woman looked like she might cry with joy. *"Arigatō gozaimasu. Oh, arigatō!"* She gazed lovingly at the potato, as if that's what she was thanking, then hid it somewhere under her kimono before turning and leaving, walking directly toward a wooded area. Where was she going? And so quickly. Maybe she thought they would take the potato back?

Jiichan was gently tugging Hanako out of the

doorway. After he closed the door, he said, "I know it break heart, but it is important not to feel heartbreak every time someone ask you for food. Otherwise, you will not survive, *neh*? The woman is very old, but we must be careful."

Hanako felt obstinate, though—she opened the door to see the old woman again. She was now heading in a different direction, toward another house. Hanako watched as she knocked on a door. Then, as if she sensed that someone was watching, the lady turned slowly around and studied Hanako for a moment before turning away again. The other door opened, and she bowed deeply, then dropped to her knees. The man who answered did not take pity; he closed the door.

Hanako wished she had another potato to give her! She couldn't stand it! She shut the door and returned to the table, where everybody was talking and laughing except for Akira, who was staring listlessly into space. Then he raised his eyes at her and looked furious.

"That was my potato!" he said accusingly. He turned angrily so that his back was facing her.

"Aki, she was so skinny! You should have seen her arm." Akira didn't budge, though. He loved potatoes. He loved them fried, baked, and boiled. He loved them hashed and mashed and any way at all.

"You didn't even ask me!" he said.

That was true ... but hadn't she done a good thing? And yet. Was it good to give the potato to a hungry old woman, or bad to take her little brother's potato when she knew how much he would have enjoyed eating it?

And now her own stomach was rumbling with hunger. Mama started to comfort Akira. "There will be other potatoes, Aki-chan."

Hanako looked to Papa, but he was pressing his lips together sadly. "Papa, did I do good or bad?" Hanako asked.

"Well, it was good for the woman, Hana," he replied. "It was good for her. So that's something."

# FOURTEEN

J iichan threw his arms into the air. "Children! I can cheer you both up! I can!" Everybody looked at him. "Hanako first. You have lost your clothes, but I must tell you, I have surprise for you. Look what I have! Something we have saved for two month." He hustled to a shelf and brought down a single sheet of paper. On the paper was a picture of a girl about Hanako's age, wearing a plaid skirt. Jiichan showed it to her with an air of incredible expectation.

She didn't know what he expected her to say but finally came up with, "My best friend in camp had a plaid skirt. Her mom got the material from the Sears catalog."

"AHA!" Jiichan said so loudly that Hanako jumped. He rummaged in a basket in the corner and pulled out a couple of yards of plaid fabric. He looked like he might cry! "Your *baachan* found someone who knew someone who found an American with plaid cloth. The Americans have everything. It does not matter what it is, they have it. She searched for many long time, starting when she heard you would come. She traded her last kimono for this, the one she be save for you since she heard you are born." He nodded happily. "She think you love her kimono, but she think you love this more. She will make you skirt."

Before Hanako could say a word, Jiichan spun around to Akira. "And I have found something for you as well." He reached into the basket and pulled out an ugly rock. "This is geode—ugly on outside, beautiful on inside. If you break it open, you will see that inside it look like diamonds." He handed the rock to Akira.

Akira assessed it as if unsure—that is, was this old man pulling his leg? "Diamonds on the inside?" he asked suspiciously.

"It is up to you to break open or not," Jiichan said. "If you want my advice, I will give." When Akira didn't reply, Jiichan said again, "I could give you my advice, but only if you say you want. I don't want to push if you don't want."

Hanako piped up, "What is your advice, Jiichan?"

His face brightened. "I think it is too special to break open. Maybe someday. It will have to be right day. Not any day, but right day. This is good advice, *neh*?" He looked as proud as a peacock over this advice.

Akira held the rock. He still seemed unsure whether it was a miracle or a trick.

Just then the door opened, and an old woman with a severely stooped back entered. At first Hanako thought it was someone else begging for food. But then the woman's face lit up at the sight of Papa. She shuffled straight to him, hugging him hard and starting to weep. She mumbled in Japanese, but Jiichan said, "We speak English. I enjoy it very much."

"Every moment I work in field, I think of you," the woman said to Papa, switching to English, weeping harder now. "Every moment. Every moment in my day."

Papa reached out for his stooped, tiny mother—Hanako's grandmother!—and held her by leaning over. His own eyes filled with tears as well. He rubbed Baachan's curved back as if he could straighten it out.

Hanako wondered if Baachan's back hurt. And she wondered if her back got that way from working the fields and if it would stay that way even if she stopped.

As they pulled away from each other, Baachan's eyes landed on the plaid fabric. She seemed astonished, then angry, then as if she might cry. Her mouth fell open and her forehead wrinkled up in a pre-crying sort of expression as she turned to Jiichan.

He looked stricken as well. And then real tears began pouring from his eyes. Through his tears he kept saying, "*Suman, suman.*" ("I'm sorry, I'm sorry.")

Everyone was standing around them. "What is it?" Mama asked several times.

Finally, Jiichan hung his head. "I have got too excited. I have ruined her surprise. She has searched many month, then she has waited two month to surprise this girl." His head almost touched his chest as he nodded and cried. "I have got too excited. It was not my surprise to give to girl. The rock was my surprise for boy."

Baachan cried a little too. Hanako could not think of a thing to say! Then all she could come up with was, "It's fine. It's such a good surprise that . . . that I'm still surprised!" Did that even make sense? She stepped forward shyly and took Baachan's hands. Her hands were so wrinkly, and her face, too. More so even than Jiichan's. "It's very beautiful cloth. It's the most beautiful cloth in the world. I saw gold cloth in a museum once, and this is more beautiful." What was wrong with her? That was the kind of lie she would tell Akira! Plus, she had walked through fabric stores where there was cloth so beautiful, it was like magic. But then she picked up the material and said more firmly, "It's the most beautiful cloth in the world."

Baachan smiled now, very, *very* pleased. "I think so," she agreed. "I said same to myself when I see. I glad you think also. I will make you very nice skirt. I very good at sew. I want to be tailor when a girl, but I never get chance. But now you will give me chance to make perfect skirt. You will see. It will be perfect. It will be best skirt you will ever have."

# FIFTEEN

Jiichan had gone to sit at the table with his head in his hands, muttering to himself. "I try, I try," he said forlornly. "Not much happen to me most day. I wake up, I eat, I work in field, I come home, I eat, I take bath for hour, I go to sleep. I don't have to try be good person, because nothing happen. So today I disappoint with myself." He pressed at the sides of his head.

Baachan hurried over and slapped her hand through the air. "What you talk about? We move on from you tell about cloth. We talk about make skirt now!"

He looked surprised. "We move on already?"

"Yes." Then she shook her head affectionately. "We move on, *jijii*."

Hanako was a little surprised at that. *Jijii* meant "old man," as in "old codger." You might say it about an elderly man in kind of an insulting way. But Baachan said it like she really liked him a lot.

"Did you find futon?" Jiichan asked.

The old woman shook her head no. "I very disappointing, *gomen nasai*."

"Oh, don't apologize!" Hanako blurted out.

"Yes, please, the children will be fine. Here, let me introduce everyone properly," Papa said, laying his hand on his mother's arm. "This is my wife, Kagako."

Baachan swatted at the air. "It only me, no need for introduction. I could not even find futon. I have no bed to offer my grandchildren." Now *she* hung her head as if she were a terrible failure. Hanako had never met two such apologetic people!

"Baachan, please don't worry. I love to sleep on the floor!" Hanako said loudly. "It's my favorite thing to do! I don't even like beds." Another lie. She tried to avoid looking at her grandmother's stooped back.

"Oh! She speak so softly, and then suddenly she speak loudly," said Jiichan. "In this way she is also like me, *so da neh*?"

"*Hai*," Papa and Mama said at the same time.

"So then you've met Hanako," Papa went on. "This is Akira."

Akira bowed deeply and said, "I'm very pleased to meet you." Hanako felt a flash of pride for him. He must be so very tired, yet here he was using his best manners.

Baachan's face turned into something beyond happy. She looked overjoyed. She stood beside Akira and touched her own old face lightly, all the while staring at Akira as if she were touching *his* face. Then she stepped back suddenly and said, "What do I thinking? Let me make you dinner."

"Oh, let me cook!" Mama said. "Hanako, come help now!"

"It only me, no need to help. No help! Please! Dinner simple, boiled carrot top, potato, and rice. Not much rice."

But Hanako wanted to help this stooped woman who'd said "It only me." So she followed her into the small kitchen. "I can set the table," she told her grandmother.

"No, no, you are tired from travel."

"I'm not tired."

"No, no. No need to help a woman like me."

Hanako knew that the Japanese way was to say no even when you meant yes, so she persisted. "My mother will be mad at me if I don't do anything," she said honestly.

"Oh, then you must help," Baachan said. "Bowls in here, you take to table. We eat at *kotatsu* during winter."

The bowls were surprisingly pretty, colorful and matching but not identical, in the Japanese way. They came in sets of five, since four was bad luck.

She set the five colorful bowls on the table, then returned for *hashi* and spoons. Actually, she and Akira usually used forks, not chopsticks, but she doubted her grandparents would have forks. When she set the *hashi* in front of Akira, she saw him frown. "Can I use my fingers this once?"

"No," Mama scolded. "We're in Japan now."

Hanako returned to the kitchen. She felt so curious about her *baachan*. She sat on a stool and tried to think of something to say. "Is this what you eat every day?" was what she came up with.

"This good day," Baachan said. She nodded her head back and forth as she stirred the soup, almost as if she heard music in her head. "We have small amount rice we buy just for you. Many time we eat wheat when we cannot find rice. But we don't have many money left. We run out rice because someone steal some from house last year. It was very, how you say . . . ?"

"Infuriating?" Hanako guessed.

"Inful . . . ?"

"In-fur-i-a-ting. It's like when something bothers you and you feel like kicking someone."

Baachan laughed. "A word for when you feel like kick someone? Ah, I miss English! They have many good words!"

"Thank you for selling your kimono for me. You didn't have to do that."

"What use does woman like me have for beautiful kimono? But I always thought someday I would give to you."

"But you never met me!"

"But still . . ."

"Thank you for thinking of me," Hanako said.

"But you see what my thought worth. I have no beautiful kimono to give you."

"Your thoughts are wonderful!" Hanako said. She had never met anyone who thought less of themselves than Baachan!

Baachan looked pleased and suddenly reached out

and stroked the air right in front of Hanako's cheek. "I knew my son would have nice daughter."

Hanako blushed. "You speak English very well," she told her grandmother.

Baachan beamed. "I know you lie to old woman, but it nice lie, thank you."

"No, I mean it," Hanako insisted.

"No, no, no, it hard for me to do anything very well. That just my nature. I work hard, that what I do well."

Hanako swung her legs in and out a few times. "Is this the same part of Japan you were born in?"

Baachan looked surprised, and Hanako worried that she was being nosy. "Never mind," she said. "I was just asking, but never mind . . . please."

Baachan looked confused now. She turned back to the soup. "Food ready, you go sit down. No help me again. I want take care of you."

In the living room they were talking about taking the train overnight to Kobe to get the butter and sugar in the next day or two. Papa wouldn't come; he would be looking for work, maybe in Hiroshima. Hanako admired the gold-cracked bowl in front of her. The cracks were shaped like twigs on a tree. Jiichan was telling them about some Australian occupation troops in Hiroshima, that maybe they could hire Papa as an interpreter. The Allied occupation consisted of Western soldiers, mostly Americans, who were stationed in Japan to restore order and tell the Japanese people how to make a new government. General Douglas MacArthur, whose title was the Supreme Commander or something like that, was in charge. It was a little hard to comprehend how anyone, even a Supreme Commander, could create a whole nation from scraps. Hanako herself had problems just making a diorama for class, a tiny world with a few clay figures.

"Is General MacArthur a good man?" Hanako asked now.

"I don't know," Papa said. "He's a powerful man. That's all I know."

Baachan brought in the big pot of soup, and then set it in the middle of the table with a ladle sticking out of it. She left and returned with *shoyu*, a spoon, and a bowl of what looked like pulverized sprinkles of dry fish. But as Hanako looked closer, she saw little bits that looked almost like hardened eyelashes. *"Kore wa nan desu ka?"* she asked politely. ("What is this?")

"*Inago.* Dried grasshopper we save from summer,"

Baachan said. "Or locust. Not sure what American word. Some confusion about that."

Those were grasshopper legs! Hanako looked at her parents to see what they would have to say. Papa said simply, "Protein."

"I didn't know Japanese ate insects!" Akira practically shouted. "I don't eat insects!"

"It not Japanese tradition," Jiichan said. "During war, government said must eat insect to survive. Also, it will give you energy because grasshopper have many energy. They have almost as much energy as me when I your age, Aki."

Surely Hanako didn't have to eat grasshoppers! She had a particular dislike of grasshoppers. For one thing, they spit that dark stuff that looked like tobacco juice.

Baachan ladled out the soup, filling Hanako's special bowl. They all poured *shoyu* into their soup. Akira poured in a lot because he loved salty things. Jiichan used the spoon to sprinkle some *inago* into his bowl. Papa did the same. The spoon and grasshopper bowl were passed around. When it reached Hanako, she hesitated, then turned to her parents. They were both looking at her without expression, but somehow their lack of expression seemed like an expression of warning to her to behave herself. So she spooned in a very little bit of grasshopper. Jiichan was already slurping up his soup.

"Oh, it's not so bad!" Akira said happily, chomping down. "Hanako, don't be a sissy!"

Baachan hesitatingly placed her hand on Hanako's forearm and said, "Very good for you. Protein make you grow strong."

Hanako spooned some soup up, but she secretly kept her nostrils closed so she couldn't taste it too well. That didn't seem so bad. So for her next spoonful she breathed through her nose. The soup actually had hardly any taste, but at the same time it tasted really awful, because you knew that in it was a strange, ugly creature. She ate extremely slowly.

Then Baachan said, "I make her something else to eat?"

"No!" Hanako, Papa, and Mama all said at once. "No, I'm sorry, it's very good," Hanako added. "It's one of the best things I ever tasted. It reminds me of . . . Juicy Fruit gum!" That was such a stupid lie, she actually laughed out loud—how had that even escaped her mouth? But Akira seemed thrilled.

"Really?" he said excitedly. "Then let me have more!"

He poured the rest of the grasshopper into his bowl and munched happily. He probably thought it tasted like Juicy Fruit just because she had said so!

Baachan was quite pleased. "Everybody like the way I make grasshopper?"

"Mmmm," they all said at once.

Hanako realized that the only thing worse than this horrible hot soup would be the same soup when it was cold. So she quickly sipped the rest down and swallowed the grasshopper bits. She wished she had some *misoshiru* with seaweed and tofu, but this was obviously a case of *shikata ga nai*. "It cannot be helped."

*Shikata ga nai* was good, and it was bad. It was what many Nikkei believed about most any awful situation. That was why so many of them accepted it when they were imprisoned. They accepted everything that the camp administration wanted them to do, no matter how bad conditions were. In Jerome a couple of these "acceptgoats," as Papa had called them, were beaten, but it didn't stop them from accepting. Some people were concerned about their futures, but many others became obsessed with the present and held a never-ending parade of sports competitions, beauty contests, parties, talent shows, and dances. Hanako was in a talent show herself several times, doing really simple dances with her friends. It seemed like there were constant dances at Jerome. And the older girls curled their hair *just so* every day, and they walked giggling in their skirts through the rain and mud as soldiers with guns stood in the watchtowers. Papa used to say it was a way of living with no past and no future, just a "now," and you had no idea when "now" would end. Today Hanako could feel everything was different. There was a yesterday, and there would be a tomorrow.

# SIXTEEN

It turned out that her grandparents were giving them their big bedroom and were taking a tiny bedroom for themselves. After dinner Hanako and Akira rubbed their teeth with *tenugui*, since they had lost their toothbrushes with their luggage. Then they took off their clothes and lay down in their underwear on the *tatami* in the big bedroom. They shared a heavy blanket—the weight of it pressed against Hanako, but she liked it. And the floor, the floor was good. Even though you'd think a floor was a floor, somehow this one felt very comfortable and made Hanako feel cozy and at home. And as soon as she lay down, Hanako realized how tired she was. She wanted to stay up and contemplate meeting her grandparents, but she was too exhausted.

The pillows were stuffed with buckwheat—that's what they used in Japan, not feathers like in America—and they made a soft noise when they were moved. The blanket she and Akira shared was scratchy on her legs. That made her think of her pajamas. She decided to try to send a message through thin air to whoever had them: *There's money in the seam.* She did not want that money to go to waste. They had worked too hard for it.

She heard her father say, "Ahhhh . . ." as he lay down. He sounded extremely comfortable. He and Mama were sleeping on a futon. Also, her grandparents had given the nicest blanket to Mama and Papa, because Papa was the only son, so he was supposed to be spoiled.

This was the thing about being spoiled: you had to rise above it. Papa had told her this long ago when discussing how much his parents had doted on him when he was a child. He had not even had to clean his own room!

"Papa?" she asked suddenly.

"Yes, Hana-chan."

"Was this your bedroom, or did you have the small room?"

"Ah, this was mine."

"That's what I thought."

Maybe he had turned out well anyway because the family had been so poor. Maybe. Perhaps it was all right to spoil kids when you didn't have much to give them. If Hanako had almost nothing, she would give everything she had to her children. She knew that for a fact. Because she liked babies a lot. Apparently, they didn't always like her, but she liked them.

Somehow or other she slept until ten in the morning, meaning she slept thirteen hours straight. She only got up because Mama woke her. Papa was relaxing at the *kotatsu* and said he wanted to spend one day of vacation before looking for a job, because it might be his last day off for a long time. Jiichan had left to work in the fields, but Baachan was standing behind Papa combing his hair. She smiled peacefully at Hanako. "I comb his hair until he turn eighteen, but I have not done for seventeen year. It got messy!" She laughed as if she had made a great joke.

Papa seemed quite at home. Hanako stared. She had never seen him so . . . spoiled. He obviously liked it a lot. He looked like he thought he was a king!

Mama rolled her eyes. "He asked why I never comb his hair!"

Baachan reluctantly put the comb in a pocket and said sadly that she had to go work in the fields now too.

"I stay home only for you," she said fondly to Hanako.

"For me?" Hanako asked.

"Yes. This first morning I don't work in many long time. I get up early and wash clothes so you and your brother have something to wear today as soon as it dry." She closed her eyes, as if enjoying the moment. "It feel very good. I like go to work late." Then she gave her head a little shake, as if waking herself up. "But I go now. You bring me lunch, *neh*? I count on you bring your *jiichan* and me food."

"Yes, Baachan!"

After they left, Mama had Hanako press the clean clothes that were wrinkled from being in Mama and Papa's suitcases. Baachan owned an iron that you filled with hot coals from the stove. The ironing board had short legs, so she knelt as she worked inside the small bedroom.

She could hear her parents and Akira playing in the living room. They sounded happy. Hanako couldn't remember the last time she'd been alone like this for more than a few minutes. Before camp, she'd had a small bedroom of her own, so she'd been by herself in her room sometimes. Now she found she liked it like this. It felt good. That is, she liked being around her family and friends and even strangers sometimes, but being alone like this filled her with pleasure. She soaked it in, felt filled with independence. She felt like . . . *Hanako.* Then she did something she knew she shouldn't do. She put down the iron, glancing furtively at the door.

She went to her grandparents' closet and slid the paper door to the side, just suddenly overcome with curiosity about their lives. The wooden clothes hangers were straight across, not with slanted sides like American hangers. Jiichan and Baachan each had six outfits, plus the ones they were wearing. Plain clothes, but when Hanako looked closely, the sewing seemed perfect, each stitch nearly identical. Mama had always used a sewing machine, but it looked like Baachan sewed by hand.

There were boxes on the floor, and after another quick glance at the door Hanako opened one—greedily, almost. She unwrapped a piece of gray silk cloth, and inside was a small stuffed dog, white with black spots.

Around its neck was a ribbon, and on the ribbon was sewn "Tadashi February 2, 1910." That was her father's birthday—he would be thirty-six soon. He was born in the Year of the Dog. She held the dog pressed against her chest like something precious.

She picked up another box and opened it. It was a white rooster, and even before she looked at the ribbon, she knew what it would say. Then she did look, and that's what it said: "Hanako May 13, 1933." The Year of the Rooster. People born that year were deep thinkers and hard workers, just as she was. Papa said so.

Then she realized Mama was calling her, so she quickly returned the animals to their boxes and hurried into the living room.

"Are you finished ironing? Come help me make lunch, and then we'll bring it to the wheat field."

They boiled what was left of the rice in a steel pot on a charcoal stove. Akira began screaming at Papa for some reason, so Mama rushed out. Akira did that sometimes; he could get quite emotional. Hanako sliced vegetables, trying to make each slice attractive and perfect. Carrots and some grated white turnip to make it pretty. She found five wooden boxes with matching covers in a cabinet and filled all five—she and Akira would need to share. The boxes were maybe eight inches long and had two compartments. She placed vegetables in the small compartment. She didn't keep a good watch on the pot, and the *okoge* at the bottom got scorched a little darker than usual. Still, she loved the crispy brown part and knew Akira did as well. She placed fluffy rice in each box, and on top of that the *okoge*. She couldn't find any other food in the house, so she examined her work, thought it looked sufficiently pretty, and closed each box.

There was a basket in a corner, and she placed the boxes in there—they barely fit. When she went to the living room with the food, Akira was lying sideways on the top of the table. Mama and Papa looked tired.

"What is it?" Hanako asked.

"He's very hungry," Mama said. "He wants 'good food.'"

"I have rice."

Mama raised her eyebrows. "He wants peanut butter. He misses peanut butter. He misses 'good food' in general."

"But we only just got here," Hanako said. Nobody responded.

Actually, she could use something tasty as well;

they'd eaten *katapan* for breakfast and drunk barley tea. Mama leaned over the table until her face was very close to Akira's. "What do you think, should we go see Jiichan and Baachan?"

His eyes were glassy, and he didn't answer. But then he pushed himself up, and they all left for the fields, Hanako carrying the food basket. She had heard that Japanese houses were usually built north-south, but the houses in this little village faced every which way. They left the houses behind and stepped into a small woods.

She looked around, shifting the basket to her other hand. "Do we know where we're going?" Hanako asked.

"Your *jiichan* explained it to me," Papa said. "Keep your eyes open for a big pine tree, and then we'll take the path on the right."

"But . . ." There were many big pine trees! Yet Papa seemed quite confident, so she followed silently.

Here and there the bigger path forked into a smaller one. One time there was a kind of big pine tree at a fork, but Papa strode left as if he walked this path every day. Parts of the forest were quite heavy, but in other parts you could see the *komorebi*—the sunlight filtering through the trees. There were different types of *komorebi*; in this forest, at this moment, it was like beams from flashlights shining through the green. She had never been in a forest before, but she saw a picture once of *komorebi* that was misty like a cloud.

Akira, who'd been trudging, came to life and almost screamed, "A giant pine tree!"

And so it was. They turned right onto a narrow path and continued, sometimes needing to push branches out of the way. It took another thirty minutes before the forest opened up to fields below—it turned out they'd been on a hill. As they grew closer, she saw that Baachan wore a big straw hat, and Jiichan wore a white scarf wrapped around his head and tied under his chin and a red cap on top of that.

Her grandparents didn't seem to notice them. Mama had brought a blanket with holes in it, and they sat on that. Hanako watched her grandparents work, both bent over deeply, but sometimes Jiichan stood up and stretched his back. Not Baachan, of course; she was forever bent. Sometimes they both bent over so far that Hanako couldn't see them behind the wheat stalks. She wondered: Was this the kind of work like in a factory, where you did the same thing over and over? Or was everything constantly changing—the insects and the weeds and the wheat? And so maybe you felt alive and happy doing it? Was that possible? Back in America the government had let some Nikkei out of the camps to go to work, usually in factories. Hanako had known two former college girls, previously rich, who'd gone to work in a canning factory just to get out of the camps. Not the Nikkei who were sent to Tule Lake, however. They had to stay incarcerated.

It was not very cold out, maybe in the high forties— warmer than Tule Lake in January. The wheat was still mostly bright green, with touches of yellow at the top. The plants were not arranged in straight lines, but rather in slow, big curves, like a loose letter *S*. And of course in the background, at the horizon, rose mountains. Huge gray clouds hung heavily over everything.

Hanako's stomach was rumbling. She would like some toast with butter right now, and maybe some chicken. She could eat chicken because she had never befriended one. In camp she had to admit the pork was good until she befriended one of the pigs. She went to see him every day for two weeks, bringing him scraps she saved for him. Then one day he wasn't there, and she knew he'd been eaten. So she didn't eat pork ever again. She'd previously met a couple of pigs, but she never made friends with one. That made everything different.

Her grandparents had spotted them. They were waving and making their way between the wheat stalks. Akira was lying on his side again with that glassy-eyed look. "I have something for you!" Hanako said to him enthusiastically.

She saw a flash of curiosity in his eyes. From her pocket she pulled out a piece of butterscotch. "I was saving it." She waited for his excitement.

He started to smile, then replied, "No, it's yours, fair and square."

"No, it's for you."

He thought that over. "You can have it, Hana-chan."

So she put it back into her pocket. Maybe she would save it for a day when she was extremely, very, completely hungry. Then she would suck it for ten minutes.

Baachan wore an expression of eagerness as she got closer. Hanako knew this was because her grandmother was happy to see them. When she sat down, Hanako asked, "Are you pulling weeds?"

"*Hai*, weed drive me crazy, but it feel good to pull out. I feel very satisfy when pull weed."

"*Very* satisfy," Jiichan said. "It my happiest moment until you get here."

"Can you eat the weeds?" Akira asked.

"I don't know why," Jiichan said, "but in the world not so much plant you can eat. Most plant for to look beautiful. Make you happy. That important too."

Hanako felt that this was true. If she had looked out the train window at Hiroshima and seen even one green tree, that would have made her hopeful for the city's future. As it was, she didn't know if the city had any future at all. How could it?

She took the food from the basket and handed out the wooden boxes. She had forgotten *hashi*! "You have to use your fingers," she said sheepishly. "I'm sorry."

"*Daijobu!*" Jiichan and Baachan said together. ("It doesn't matter, it's all right.")

Hanako noticed that her grandparents ate seriously, not in the cheerful, social way people in the restaurant used to have their meals. No, her grandparents ate like people who needed to eat so they could have energy to work. Akira was taking a lot of the rice he was supposed to share with her, but she didn't say anything. She wanted him to grow tall. But then he stopped and looked at her slyly. "I know, we're sharing," he said, grabbing two carrots before handing her the box.

The rice was a little overcooked—her fault!—but it still tasted very good, and even the vegetables seemed delicious. She left two carrots for her brother, and he gobbled them up gratefully.

And then she just felt happy, like she hadn't felt in years. She was still hungry. One thing about camp was that they did get enough food. She realized she might not have food like that for a long time. And yet she felt happy, here where her grandparents were eating so seriously, where the clouds hung like heavy fruit, where the wheat curved into the distance. She felt like she could eat five more boxes of rice, and yet somehow it felt perfect, a perfect moment. She wished she could stay right here, forever.

# SEVENTEEN

As much as Hanako could see that her grandparents enjoyed sitting with them, she noticed that soon they were gazing worriedly at the fields, and for the first time they didn't seem to be very interested in Hanako and Akira. Then Jiichan pushed himself up. "We stay long time to eat."

"But it's only been about half an hour!" Hanako said.

"Usually we take half that," Jiichan said, worriedly eyeing the field. "We must raise food. There is not enough food in Japan."

"What are you doing? Mostly picking weeds? We can do that," Hanako replied. "Can we help?"

Jiichan gazed at her thoughtfully. "Maybe someday we need you to help. Not every day, but maybe we will need you two or three time when we work on rice. But you are children, and you just arrive to Japan. You must enjoy to rest today."

As her grandparents trudged back through the wheat, Hanako gathered the boxes. There wasn't even a single grain of rice in any of them.

On the way home Akira ran ahead, sometimes leaping up to slap hard at low branches. The forest was a mix of evergreens and leafless trees. She'd never been through a forest in the winter before. It seemed empty and quiet, except for the noise of Aki's movements. Then, when they were almost out of the forest, he leaned over as if out of breath. Hanako caught up with him and laid her hand on his back as he breathed hard. He stood straight and turned his palms upward—they were bloody from hitting the branches. "I wanted to forget how hungry I am," he said simply. Just as he said this, they heard arguing in the distance.

They looked toward the voices, and there was a gathering of children, some of them teenagers and some of them quite small.

Akira elbowed Hanako. "It's the boy!" he said, his voice low. "From the train station."

The boy with the pink face. He wore a jacket now, and so did the little one. Some of the older boys he was with looked tough and scary.

Papa laid a hand on Hanako's back to push her along, while Mama picked up Akira protectively and rushed off.

*"OI!"*

Papa and Hanako paused, but Mama moved away even faster. It was the pink-faced boy, and he was calling to Hanako!

*"OI!"* he shouted again. He picked up the little girl and started running toward them.

The little girl was screaming, *"Neh, chotto! Chotto!"* over and over. ("Wait!")

Hanako glanced to her left to see that Mama was already out of the woods with Aki. Papa looked from the boy to Hanako. "Do you want to leave?" he asked her urgently.

But the boy didn't scare her. "No. Maybe he just wants to say thank you for the cakes."

Papa rested his arm around her shoulders. The boy approached and set down the girl.

"*Oi!*" That meant "hey." The boy studied her for a second, then asked almost with disbelief, "America-*gaeri?*"

"*Hai.*"

The little girl reached out and touched the purple coat sleeve, first tentatively, then curiously.

The boy said in casual Japanese that the cakes weren't very good, but *arigatō* anyway. At least they'd filled their stomachs. The girl asked for more.

The whole gang of kids was now moving toward them. Papa pulled Hanako away firmly, and they strode quickly out of the forest. She heard steps behind her but didn't look back. Then, out of the trees, she turned around and found herself face-to-face with the pink-faced boy and the small girl.

The boy seemed to be thinking hard, and finally he came up with, "*Mochigashi?*"

"Papa, do we have more *katapan?*" Hanako asked Papa.

"I have three more bags." He paused. "But Akira is hungry and will be hungry again." He looked torn, unsure what to do.

"But just one bag?" Hanako begged.

So Papa went ahead to get a bag. Hanako excitedly bowed to the boy and asked in Japanese, "Is that your sister?" Maybe he would be her first Japanese friend!

The boy hugged the toddler with alarm, as if Hanako would steal her. She quickly reassured him. "I just meant . . . you're both so young . . ."

"Our parents . . . they were killed. We live at the train station . . . some days."

"Oh! How did they die?"

"From the bomb, of course! My dad used to make *geta* and sold them in a little shop in front of our house in Hiroshima."

*Geta* were Japanese sandals.

"My sister was here in the country—my dad gave a family many *geta* to take care of her because the cities weren't safe. But I had to stay in the city because my whole class was mobilized by the government for labor. The lucky classes were mobilized to grow food in the country. I worked hard!" he spoke this last part proudly, then added defiantly, "I'm taking good care of my sister. She's not starving!" He had sharp black eyes, like he was constantly thinking and evaluating. Maybe scheming. The scheming look actually made Hanako a little nervous.

"But why doesn't that other family take you in?" she asked.

He laughed, not in a mean or bitter way, but just like he thought she was funny. "Because there are no more *geta* to pay them with. It's nothing personal—they have their own troubles." Then he said, "Sometimes we are at the station, and sometimes we are wanderers."

The word he used was *watarimono*. Hanako wasn't sure, but she didn't think that was a bad word. Maybe kind of like explorers? Nomads? She wasn't positive.

She reached into her pocket and shyly offered the piece of butterscotch. The boy looked at it, curious, but didn't reach out. "What is it?"

"It's candy!"

He let Hanako drop it into his hand.

"You suck on it until it disappears," Hanako explained. The little one reached out, but Hanako said, "Don't let her swallow it, even though it's very delicious." She knelt and said, *"Ochibi-chan."* ("Little one.")

The boy opened the wrapper eagerly. He chomped off a bit for his sister, then pushed the rest into his mouth. He chewed with interest but not the joy Hanako was expecting. But the little one's eyes opened wide, and she let out a chortle. Then her eyes got a sly look, and she gulped.

Hanako giggled. "Oh, bad girl, you swallowed—"

But the boy took the candy out of his mouth and threw it far into the distance. "I don't like it! It's not food. It's . . . it's like it's making fun of me." His face twitched in anger and turned away. Now Hanako could see the side of his head and a red, raised scar in the place where his ear had been. A lump. She wondered how much it would hurt to have your ear ripped off. Probably it would hurt so much that it would be the center of your life right then. There would be nothing else at all in your mind, not even your family who you loved a lot.

Hanako had to stop herself from reaching out to touch it. And then she did, resting her palm on it. The boy started but then didn't move. It felt like a lump of clay. And she knew it was not ripped off; it was burned off, exploded off by heat. She knew this, just by laying her hand on it. And she knew he wasn't specifically thinking about his ear at the time, because his whole body would have been in pain. Yes, you could learn a lot by laying your palm on someone's scar. Finally, she lowered her hand.

And for a moment the boy didn't look tough, not at all. He looked like he might cry. Papa showed up with the crackers, and the boy was immediately back to being tough again. He threw the bag into the air, said "*Arigatō*" a little rudely, kind of like a smart aleck, then said, "Next time I'll bring you something. Maybe a kimono? And then you'll give me rice." He stated it as fact.

Her grandparents had a little rice left, but it was not for Hanako to give away. She tried to get things straight in her head: She had touched this boy's scar and understood the pain he had felt. But her grandparents! Her family! So she simply said, "We don't have any rice."

He just laughed like he saw right through her. "I'll find a pretty kimono, you'll see!" He sauntered off like those American teenage boys, his little sister chasing after him.

Hanako turned agog to her father. For some reason, talking to this boy made her feel almost feverish. "His family had a *geta* shop," she said. "Before the bomb dropped and killed his parents. . . . Did you see his ear?"

Papa didn't answer, so she looked at him. He took

a big, loud breath and stared at the sky. He got quite involved in studying the clouds. Hanako searched to see what he was looking at, but the special quality of the sky from earlier had faded, and now it was just overcast and gray, such as you might see on any day. It was just the sky.

But her father didn't move. She looked up again but didn't see anything. "But, Papa," she finally said. "There's nothing there!"

He wasn't even listening.

She looked back at the boy. Her heart went out to him! And yet. As they disappeared behind a house, she felt a sudden stab of guilt, like maybe she shouldn't have offered him crackers that Akira could eat when he was very hungry. She needed to take care of Akira, just like the boy took care of his sister. Guilt for giving away food swept over her, through her—her heart was filled with it. She felt almost sick to her stomach. There was not enough for everyone here. She had never seen anyone beg for food in America, but over there if she had given a beggar food, it would not have made a whit of difference. The restaurant had been awash in food! Every day more food arrived! Even in camp, all they had to do was show up at the cafeteria, and the food was there.

She turned back to Papa and waited. After a few minutes more, he lowered his head and said seriously, "Some people, maybe they do many great things. But for other people, in a certain time and place, maybe you do *one* great thing. You save someone's life somehow out of the blue—right place, right time—and . . . I think that restaurant I started out of nothing, that was a great thing. That was a great achievement. It was like building a ship as big as the USS *Gordon* because I built it out of nothing. . . . Or maybe you have a shop where you sell *geta* you make. Maybe you spend two hours painting beautiful dragons or trees or calligraphy on each pair. And then a bomb drops on your store." He rubbed the top of her head. "So you see? Here we are. No chance for me to do something great in the world again. I just need to help my family survive." He closed his eyes, and his head sort of shivered before he opened his eyes again. "*Do* you see? We have nothing else to give a boy like that. This is a fact."

She stood still, concentrating. She concentrated very, very hard. Then she hardened her heart. Even if the boy begged, even if his little sister cried next time, even if he brought her a gorgeous kimono, Hanako would not share food that Akira could eat. Even if

Hanako herself cried, she would not share. There was not enough; this was a fact. The world was filled with facts that could not be changed. She had learned this during their camp days. There were many, many, many facts.

# EIGHTEEN

When Jiichan and Baachan got home from the fields that night, Jiichan cleared his throat over and over, and also shook his head a lot without saying anything. Finally, he blurted out, "We will need to have more rice!" He stopped short, as if surprised by his own outburst. "I am mean to say . . ." He looked very sad. "I know you are just arriving here, but we will run out of rice because now we are very many. We have many vegetable. We have all the vegetable we will ever need! We thought we had many rice, but today we feel worry. . . ." He stuck his lower lip out as if he were four years old. "I wish I was better *jiichan* so I could give you many rice."

"Otōsan!" Papa said almost angrily. "Don't blame yourself!"

Then everybody started talking, and Mama tapped the table for attention. "We will go tomorrow to Kobe for butter and sugar. That will help."

*"Hai! Hai!"* Jiichan said. "We will trade butter and sugar on black market for rice!"

But it turned out that Hanako's grandparents had discovered this afternoon that the wheat was being attacked by insects, so they did not think they could go to Kobe. And Papa needed to look for work tomorrow; besides, they did not want to spend extra train fare for him to go to Kobe. Train fare was not expensive, but Mama insisted that they should not waste money.

So it would be Hanako and Akira with their precious passports, and Mama, whose Japanese was merely passable. Everybody sat sadly at the table, not saying a word. Then Papa and Mama silently held their eyes on each other for about three whole seconds, like they were having a conversation without talking. Papa's face brightened. "How about if Kagako works in the fields? Okaasan can show her how to kill the bugs, and, Tōsan, you can go with the children to Kobe!"

Mama had suddenly started energetically picking

up tiny bits of dust or dirt from the *tatami*. She didn't seem to have heard because she was concentrating so hard. "Hana, you must shake out the *tatami* when you are back from Kobe!" she exclaimed, as if Hanako had been remiss.

"Yes, Mama."

"Kagako, you can help out in the fields, then?" Papa asked gently.

"Yes, of course, I can do anything at all, you know that!" She frowned at Hanako.

"Mama, I didn't know the *tatami* were dirty!"

Mama's face softened. "Yes, Hana, I know, you're a good girl."

Everybody was cheerful now that Jiichan would be traveling with the children. Papa seemed very pleased with himself. "I'm the idea man," he said modestly.

"You take after me!" Jiichan said. "You don't remember, but when I young, I have many idea. Now I only have idea about weed and bug." He leaned very close to Akira's face. "I will take you to Kobe, do not worry, Aki. We will not get lost."

Baachan's mouth started to open, and it stayed open. Then she said, "No, I cannot say." She shook her head, *then* added, "But I must say! I am think the children stand out very much. They look America-*gaeri*. It very cute, but it never good to attract attention if you have precious thing like butter and sugar. I have not seen butter or sugar in many year. Maybe it been ten year. In truth, I cannot remember. Maybe I have never seen, and only *think* I saw once." Her eyes got dreamy. "I wonder what it taste like?" She smiled sadly. "I will never know."

"In America you have tasted!" Jiichan said with annoyance. "Remember? We buy butter from friend who have farm. But sugar I have no memory of. I may have tasted sugar, but I have no memory of." Hanako could tell he was looking back into the past. "No, no memory. I have heard sugar taste like fairy tale."

Baachan nodded. "Why you annoy with old woman? *Hai*, I remember butter now. I fry vegetable in butter for one week. That very good week. Not best week ever, but very good."

Hanako remembered that Papa used to buy fresh butter for the restaurant twice a week. She used to cut off slices to eat like cheese. The restaurant had pounds and pounds of butter and sugar. Butter was special even when they'd owned plenty of it, however. Now it seemed like it was better than gold. Her mouth watered over the butter that they would be getting soon but that she would not be allowed to eat.

Baachan groaned. "Nobody listen because it only me. But I say again. My grandchildren are very cute. I cannot imagine before I see them how cute they will be. But now they will have precious things, and many will be looking at them."

Mama seemed to be listening closely. "What do you suggest?" she asked.

Baachan went, "Ahhhhhh. Ahhhhh." She looked quite concerned. "I am wondering about Hana-chan braid. I have not seen such a braid during the wartime. . . ."

*Oh, no.* That was the only thought in Hanako's mind upon hearing that. She didn't think of her braid as something that could be cut off, if that was what Baachan was suggesting. It was *attached* to her.

"No, she must keep her braid!" Jiichan protested. "Otherwise, she will not be Hanako."

"Maybe, maybe. I am only me, no need to listen."

Hanako laughed nervously. "It's my braid! I've always had a braid!"

"No need," Baachan repeated.

Then, to Hanako's relief, everybody dropped the subject.

ooooo

It turned out there was only one train straight to Kobe, and it would be leaving at ten that night, to arrive in Kobe at eight in the morning. So they ate dinner, and Jiichan took a bath. Hanako and Akira both laughed, but Akira positively *cackled*, because they could hear their grandfather loudly singing a silly song about *fresh snow, fresh snow, it goes where it goes, where does it go?*

"It melts!" Akira cried out. "It melts, Jiichan!"

While Baachan took her bath next, Hanako cut vegetables, which she put in three boxes for herself, Akira, and Jiichan. Mama and Baachan would need two of the boxes for work in the fields the next day, so she stuffed the three boxes as full as possible and put them into a basket. She did not know what Papa would eat, but he insisted she not pack him anything.

It was decided that Jiichan would carry the passports. "I will fight for them if anyone try to take," he said, taking a fighting stance.

Hanako agreed to wear ugly, puffy pants called *monpe* and a plain white blouse of the sort that Baachan wore in the fields. Also, Baachan took her measurements so she could start the plaid skirt. "I will not stop working while you are gone. I hope you will like skirt when you see."

"Of course she will love it!" Mama said. She pulled Hanako in close. "Hanako loves everything I've ever made for her."

"Yes, Mama," Hanako replied obediently, although in truth, Mama had gone through a phase when she thought flowered drapery-type fabric made pretty skirts, and she had sewn herself and Hanako matching outfits that made them both look like walking curtains. Hanako felt embarrassed just thinking about walking around in those clothes!

Then Mama said fondly, "Remember those flowered skirts we used to wear? So pretty!"

"Yes, Mama."

"I don't remember," Akira said.

"You were just a baby," Hanako said, then added, "They were actually the prettiest skirts in the history of the world!" She paused. "But Baachan's will be just as pretty . . . or prettier . . . or just as . . ." She did not want to insult anybody.

"Time to go, time to go!" Jiichan said, pacing excitedly.

Baachan said shyly, "Maybe you like my black jacket?"

"Thank you very much, but this is my really special

coat," Hanako said, putting on her purple one.

Papa picked up Akira. "Now, will you behave for your *jiichan?*"

"But, Papa! I don't always like to behave!"

Papa frowned.

"Yes, Papa."

"Make sure he behaves, Hanako."

"Yes, Papa."

Hanako was not that much shorter than Jiichan. It felt a little strange to be going out into the dark with such a small grown-up. In truth, she was a little afraid of the night. It used to seem like an adventure just to sit outside after dark in their backyard in America. They would bring out a blanket, and Mama would make popcorn, and they would listen to the crickets. That was pretty much the extent of Hanako's experience with being outside at night.

But she took Akira's hand and said, "I'm very brave."

"I know," he said.

Everybody said their good-byes, and the three of them stepped out into the cool air. Hanako and Akira followed Jiichan, with Hanako so close, her feet almost touched his as she walked. She clutched her brother's hand. With her other hand, she carried the basket of

food. Jiichan was carrying the passports in a money belt at his waist. He'd said it was where he kept money after he sold his vegetables in town. He also held an oil lamp. It was mostly ceramic, with a metal knob to advance the wick, and it looked ancient. It looked magic, too, like you could make a wish on it.

"Stay close so can see ground, don't trip," Jiichan said. He looked around furtively. "We save oil before war start, but we are almost out. Your *baachan* had this idea because she believe war will grow very big. We already at war with China, but she think we will be in even more war." He lowered his voice so that Hanako could hardly hear. "In general, we do not want anyone to know we have oil."

Akira hurried to keep up and immediately tumbled over a rock. "Ohh! Ohh!" Jiichan cried out almost in despair. That was probably because he was so old, he didn't remember how often kids fell down. He knelt next to Akira, shining his light.

Aki gazed at his knee, where his pants had gotten dirty. He looked ready to cry. "These are my only pants!"

"Baachan will make you more!" Hanako assured him. "Any color you want! Won't she, Jiichan?"

"*Hai*, any color. Purple, blue. We will buy cloth . . . somehow."

Akira seemed to be deciding whether he should go ahead and actually cry. Finally, he said, "All right. I want brown, please."

"Brown is very good choice!" Jiichan said fondly. He looked very pleased. "I proud you make such good choice. Very smart boy make good choice in life!"

Now Akira looked pleased. "Thank you."

They continued on their way, more slowly this time. The lantern didn't give off a lot of light. It was like a big, single firefly.

They moved silently. Hanako was concentrating hard on making her way in the darkness, and she knew her brother was too. Jiichan seemed almost an expert at what he was doing. He was not a normal person, Hanako thought. In the daylight he sometimes appeared awkward, but now there was something almost graceful about him. And he was wearing straw sandals, which did not look easy to walk in.

She'd been concentrating so hard that she was surprised how quickly they seemed to reach the village, which was almost completely dark. They walked between the huge, black shapes of buildings. A couple of homes did have light shining through the rice-paper doors—probably people lived at their shops.

When they reached the train tracks, they sat on the platform and waited. "Sometime train come early, sometime come late," Jiichan explained. "I go to Kobe three time on train. I had cousin there, but he die when he seventy. So I understand train. We wait, and train will come when it come."

There was a rustle nearby, making Hanako's heart rush. But Jiichan didn't even seem to notice. Then an eerie voice sounded, halfway between a house cat and something wilder. Akira jumped to his feet with a screech, knocking the lamp over. Hanako and Jiichan jumped up as well. Jiichan immediately wrapped his arms around Akira and held him hard. "Is only *tanuki*!"

But Akira was crying.

"What is *tanuki*?" Hanako asked, picking up the lantern. Oh no! She could see a wet spot on the ground where oil had spilled.

Jiichan knelt over the spot. "Ahh, that too bad. Always too bad to waste." But then he cheered up. "Is only raccoon dog, Aki-chan. Many *tanuki* in Japan. Very famous animal here. They can change shape, but will not hurt you. They bring good luck. Now we will have good luck finding rice at good price, this I promise you."

Akira shook his head quickly a couple of times. "They change shape?"

"Ah, I admit I have not seen this, but I have heard. They are famous for to change into human. That is legend from many year ago. But they mean no harm. Very cute. You would like, Aki. Someday we will see one, and if we have food, will feed it. It will eat out of your hand, you will see. Then your luck will come."

Akira was thinking this over, sticking his lower lip out. Just like Jiichan had! Then he said, "All right," and sat back down.

The lantern flickered and sputtered out right then. It was very dark. Hanako reached out to touch Akira, then sat down.

Jiichan struck a match and tried to relight the lamp. But it wouldn't light. "Ah, I cannot light again. Wick is dirty. Will not work. When we see train, we will need to wave and shout. Cannot hold up lamp." Yet he firmly held the lamp as if it were as important as butter or sugar.

So they sat in the dimness, the only light from the night sky. Hanako felt as if she had never been so alert. Akira was leaning on Jiichan, not her, and she felt oddly lonely, but just for a second. She tried to listen as hard as she could, a little worried that the train would pass them by if they didn't have a light. She couldn't hear anything.

"The *tanuki* brought us bad luck," Hanako said. "Now we have no lamp."

"We do not know our luck yet!" Jiichan said. "We have not had our journey. When we are home again, then we will know good or bad luck. It is hard for children, but must be patient. I cannot be patient for anything when I am child. When I child, life move very slow, and yet now I am old man."

There it was—she could hear the train, but she couldn't see its lights yet. "Stand up, but do not go on track," Jiichan said. "As train get closer, we must wave and shout. They will see us."

Suddenly, the lights were there, and they were growing quickly. Hanako was surprised at how fast the train was barreling down on them. Then she saw its lights. She waved her hands wildly and shouted, *"Tomatte!"*

*"Oi! Tomare!"* shouted Akira and Jiichan.

Hanako jumped up and down and screamed more loudly than she'd ever screamed. And the train slowed down! And stopped. A man in uniform opened the

door but didn't bring down a step—he said someone
had stolen it. Akira boarded first, the man lifting him
by the arms. Then Hanako, then the food basket, then
Jiichan last. He grunted loudly as he pulled himself up.
The man tried to help, but Jiichan said, "I am strong
for age!"

The car was quite full, but they found a seat they
could all squeeze into. Akira closed his eyes and seemed
to be instantly asleep. This time he leaned on Hanako.
Jiichan as well had already closed his eyes. Hanako held
tightly to the food basket, then reluctantly let it slip to
the floor in front of her. She closed her eyes too, suddenly tired. In her mind's eye she could see the lamp
bobbing along the path.

She remembered the time in Jerome when she and
Akira had been standing at the barbed-wire fence,
and in the forest beyond they could see what seemed
like thousands of fireflies. Akira had stared through
the fence. It was a very beautiful sight. "That means
everything is going to be fine," she had told Akira.
"We're going to be fine. We have a good future! This
is proof."

He had believed her, of course. But shortly after
that they were transferred to Tule Lake, where there

were turmoil and violence and arrests, and now they were here, traveling ten hours for butter and sugar. She opened her eyes, studied the peaceful faces of her grandfather and brother. And then she thought, *But I'm fine now, at this moment.* And this was true.

# NINETEEN

T hen, right when Hanako had fallen asleep, Jiichan was suddenly crying out, "I have forgotten! Even with my amazing memory! We must change train in Hiroshima!"

The train was just slowing down. So they rushed off with their belongings, and then hustled through the station until they found a new platform to catch a train to Kobe. When they were finally settled on their new train, Hanako was not sure if all the rushing had been exciting or awful. Akira didn't seem to care. He was in one of his moods where he allowed himself to be led wherever and whenever.

But right before he fell asleep, he looked suspiciously

at Jiichan. "Are we on the right train now?"

"All is well," Jiichan said confidently.

So Hanako and her brother went to sleep. When she woke up, it was very bright out, the sky outside cloudless, the sun white.

Jiichan was saying, "Hanako! Hanako! I cannot wake up your brother!"

Hanako was not surprised. "You have to scream near his face. Sometimes that's the only way."

Jiichan leaned forward until his nose almost touched Akira's. Seeing their faces so close was funny, because they looked so much alike. It was like seeing old Jiichan an inch away from young Jiichan.

"AKI!!! YOU MUST TO GET UP!"

Akira opened one eye first, then the other. Jiichan leaned back with relief. "It very hard to wake you up. I try many time. You worry old man; no good will come of it." He seemed a little vexed at them for the first time since Hanako had met him.

Hanako and Jiichan ate half their food, but Akira ate all of his. Nobody had the heart to tell him to save some for later.

Jiichan got directions to the consulate from the ticket window, and they stepped onto the street.

Hanako didn't know what to expect, but she saw that Kobe was a mix of flattened ruins and damaged buildings as well as many undamaged ones. "Ahh, Kobe bombed," Jiichan said seriously. "I read in newspaper."

"An atomic bomb?" Hanako asked.

"No, regular bomb. Only two atomic bomb. The other in Nagasaki."

After the shock of Hiroshima, seeing the damage of Kobe did not seem surprising at all to Hanako. People walking around them didn't seem to notice a thing; they were just going on about their lives. Here and there a middle-aged or older woman wore a heavy, colorless kimono, and a couple of somewhat younger women wore colored ones. Many of the women wore *monpe*. The men wore plain, casual jackets and baggy pants, and all of them had caps on top of their heads. She didn't think the bagginess was a style like with Pachucos; they were probably wearing whatever was available. A US serviceman walked with a Japanese girl in heavy makeup. They were laughing and seemed quite happy. The streets were crowded. It was odd to think: not that long ago, bombs were dropping here. But she could see that you just accepted such things had happened, then got on with your life. Survival.

They strode silently along the busy street. Hanako spotted a bustling outside market, right next to a single broken concrete wall and a big pile of rubble. The sellers, and many of the buyers, looked like very tough people. There was a girl, too, with bangs and hair to her ears. She looked very tough as well, and very mean, like maybe she would kill Hanako for five US dollars and a meal. *Survival.*

Akira was holding one of Hanako's hands and one of Jiichan's as he looked with fright upon the market. She squeezed his hand. "They're not mean; they're just hungry," she told him.

"I think they're dangerous!" he said.

"Maybe," she admitted.

"They mean *because* they hungry," Jiichan clarified. "So you must be careful. Black market not good place for innocent children. I heard black market are run by gangster. Some children not so innocent; they may go."

The consulate turned out to be a solid-looking stone building. Strong, like America, Hanako thought. The inside reminded her of a bank. There were several simple armchairs around a square coffee table with a fake plant for a centerpiece. Mama, who had decorated the restaurant, did not believe in fake plants. She bought plants called philodendrons from a Japanese man who had one hundred thousand plants in his nursery. Hanako used to water the philodendrons. But then, as her family was closing the restaurant down, she had forgotten, and they had all turned dry and brown. She heard later that the man had sold his nursery and one hundred thousand plants for five hundred dollars.

A wooden counter stretched across the room, and behind it stood a woman. She was Japanese, but there was a white man at a desk behind her. He had that look of "I'm the boss." Papa had told Hanako that one of the main purposes of an American consulate was to help and protect Americans in a foreign country. That's why the consulate was giving butter and sugar to Americans.

Jiichan approached the counter like he was an important man. "I am grandfather of two American," he said to the woman in English. "I have their passport and come for two butter and sugar." As he spoke, he made his squeaky voice lower and firmer than usual.

"Of course," the woman said. She took the passports and walked away. Jiichan winked at Akira like they were pulling a fast one.

Then Jiichan broke out in a huge smile. "It worked! I admit I had a doubt!"

"Yay! I want to eat a lot tonight!" Akira said happily.

The woman returned with four bags and handed them to Jiichan. "Ahhhh," he said. "You are good woman. America is can do." He bowed his head to her. "We thank you. My grandchildren will eat well tonight."

"You're very welcome." She had a heavy accent, so she wasn't American Japanese. She smiled at someone in line behind them, and Jiichan furtively hid the bags in the food basket, which he now took from Hanako.

Outside again, they were back in the powerless world of Japan. In Tule Lake, Hanako used to feel the power of America constantly, beating them all down. Before the camps, Nikkei were trying to ride the American power like some surfers she saw once at Manhattan Beach, muscular men balancing on long, colored boards atop the rushing waves. It was beautiful to watch the surfers. Back then a feeling would well up in her sometimes, like she just really, really loved America.

But Jiichan was talking: "Must go to market for rice, and then catch train." Three men suddenly accosted them, asking loudly all at once if they wanted to sell their rations for yen.

Jiichan cried out like an animal: "EEYAHHHH!"

He looked like a wild thing! The men seemed surprised, and then Jiichan snapped at Hanako, "Come, bring your brother and follow me!" He was holding the basket with both arms as he pushed through the men.

After they'd quickly walked a ways, Jiichan explained, "We don't sell for yen. Yen is paper. You cannot eat paper."

Akira leaned over and threw up, out of nowhere. "Oh, no, Akira!" Hanako said.

He shook his head. "Those men scared me!"

Hanako had a handkerchief she kept in her coat pocket, and she wiped his mouth with it. Then she hesitated. What should she do with the handkerchief? She could not throw it away; that would be wasteful. But she could not put it in the pocket of her precious purple coat. So she stuffed it into Akira's pocket, and he didn't seem to mind.

When they reached the market back by all the rubble, Jiichan paused to think. "I cannot bring you into market, but I cannot leave you here by yourself."

Hanako thought it over, and she did not want to go into the market, but she also did not want to remain here without a grown-up. She waited obediently for Jiichan to decide.

"Come with me," he finally said.

They moved through the crowds as Jiichan studied all the tables. People bargained and haggled loudly, while others hung back, as if waiting for their chance to strike. It was so noisy and crowded. Sometimes the seller would just laugh at the buyer, but Hanako didn't know if that was just to get the buyer to offer a higher price. One seller yelled at her to get out of the way; shocked, she stepped quickly behind Jiichan. It was such a different way of shopping than going to a store with price tags on the products! There were pots and pans, spoons and *hashi*, cigarettes and lamp oil, tea and leather. There was one table with nothing on it but what looked to be used, uneven pieces of wood. There were coats, candy, and a few items that she had no idea what they were. Jiichan spotted some wick that he could use in the lamp, so he bought that. Much of the oil had spilled, but there was still some left.

One lady screeched at Hanako in Japanese, "I will buy your coat!"

Then Jiichan spotted a man selling rice. Immediately, Jiichan transformed into a different person. He barked in rude Japanese, and the man barked back, calling Jiichan *jijii*, which was the disrespectful word

Baachan had used to call him "old man." Jiichan didn't seem to notice the disrespect. He was like a bulldog.

"*Jijii*, you ask too much! The answer is no! Go away now! I don't like *jijii*. *Jijii* are too cheap!"

This went back and forth, until finally Jiichan shook his head to Hanako. "No can get fair deal from here."

Hanako felt a stab of disappointment—in her mind, their precious goods would get them anything. They started to leave, but all of a sudden the seller called out, "*Oi, jijii!*" When they turned back around, he nodded yes. "I do it for the children," he said. But he said it as if he didn't care a whit for them or anyone in the world, for that matter.

But honestly, Hanako didn't care a whit what he cared a whit about—after all, this was not the time to be sensitive. In exchange for the butter and sugar, the man gave them two bags that looked like about fifteen pounds of rice each. Jiichan checked inside each bag, then nodded.

He changed back into his sweet self as he handed Hanako one of the bags, which he placed in the basket for her. Then he said solemnly, "You must guard this as you would guard your brother." He thought that over and added, "Never mind. Your brother always come first. But you must guard very well. If you cannot, I will carry both."

"I can do it!"

Akira looked worried. "Hana, let him carry it. Someone might take it from you!"

"Aki, I'm one of the bravest people in the world!"

"Oh . . . okay, then."

They wandered around the market for a few minutes searching for anything else interesting to eat—they'd brought two American dollars—but they didn't find anything Jiichan wanted. Then Hanako spotted something that *she* wanted.

"Jiichan, please!" She pointed to a table covered with *mochigashi*. "This is the best cake in the world! Have you ever had it?"

Akira jumped up and down. "*Mochigashi!* Please, Jiichan!"

Jiichan looked like he had a sudden headache. "Ahh, ahhhh! It very hard to say no to grandchild! Even though this is not useful food, *neh*?"

"Please!" Hanako and Akira begged.

Jiichan slumped over. "I lose. I must say yes." He walked with slumped shoulders to the seller. The seller's face came alive at the sight of one of the American dollars, and as Jiichan bargained, Hanako and Akira eagerly picked out five cakes apiece, just as they had in the train station. Hanako felt as excited as she had the first time she'd picked out cakes. These were prettier than the others, if that was even possible! She held on to them, just staring.

"Put in basket. We will save for later," Jiichan said. "When you save treat for one hour, it will taste better! I learn this from my mother many year ago."

"But, Jiichan!" Hanako and Akira both exclaimed.

"It is trick I learn!" Jiichan exclaimed back. "I learn from my own mother!" He seemed as excited as they were. His face was actually turning red, he was so excited.

Hanako thought this over. If they waited, it would taste even better. It was hard to say no to that. So they obediently put their beautiful cakes into the basket. She leaned over and touched her nose on Akira's. Then she crossed her eyes at him until he laughed.

"I know many trick," Jiichan said, "and I will teach you everything I know. We have many long time until you grow up! Many long time!"

So they went to the train station carrying their precious items, and after boarding, Hanako and

Akira sat patiently in their seats. The basket was on the floor under Hanako's feet, and her grandfather had pushed the other bag of rice under the seat in front of them.

Then, as the train chugged along, suddenly Jiichan announced showily, "NOW you may each eat a cake! It is time!"

Hanako rested her eyes on his face for a brief second, just because she was so amused by how red with excitement he was. Then she opened the basket, and she and Akira stared at the colors. "*Jan-ken-pon* on who picks first!" Akira said.

So they did rock-paper-scissors, and Hanako won. She leaned over the basket and studied her *mochigashi*. There were pink, lime green, and yellow. She only had the one yellow, so if she ate that, she would have no more yellow. Therefore, she decided to save it.

"Hurry!" Akira was pulling at her coat.

"You're not supposed to pull at my coat!"

"But you're taking too long!"

Then she hesitated. "Jiichan, do you want to pick one first?"

"What?" He thought this over. "Children should pick first. But I very thank you for asking. All right, I will take one." He gazed into the basket. "Hmmm. This one . . . no . . . maybe . . . no . . ."

Hanako and Akira glanced at each other.

"Ahhh . . . I don't want to choose wrong. . . ."

"Jiichan, they will all taste the same!" Akira half shouted.

"You think? Then I will take green. I have not eat a green cake before."

Hanako selected pink for herself and waited for her brother to choose his—he took a tan one with green sprinkles. Then Hanako bit eagerly into her cake and . . . it tasted like . . . nothing.

She turned to Akira. He was leaning over with his face twisted up. She took her vomity handkerchief out of his pocket and let him spit out his food. She spit out hers as well.

Jiichan nodded thoughtfully. "I was tricked. Yes, I was. I saw the pretty color and believed it was sweet. I know there is no sugar in Japan for cake. But I saw the pretty color." He thought more. "Maybe my mother wrong this one time. Treat did not get better in one hour. All these year, I think my mother never get anything wrong. Very smart woman." He was babbling, like he was trying to figure out what had gone awry.

He seemed more upset than Hanako and Akira!

"It's all right, Jiichan," Akira said, looking worried. "I can eat one if you want."

Hanako added, "They're very pretty. We can put them on the table for decoration!"

But Jiichan was still sad. "All my life, that trick always work. How come it don't work today? Now you disappoint." He shook his head again, but then sat up extra straight. "But I think . . . before you come, every day is same. Now everything very emotion. So this is good. It is very good. I will grow old and have many emotion, *neh*?"

But he still seemed a little sad, so Hanako said, "Your mother was right. But the whole world just had a war, and when there's a war, all the rules change. So maybe there's new rules now."

"Ahhh, yes, make sense. We will find out the new rules together then. *Ii ne?*"

"*Hai*, Jiichan."

"We have had good luck with rice, brought to us by *tanuki*. We cannot complain."

"How does that man stay in business?" Hanako asked. "Doesn't everybody know his cakes are phony?"

"I should have realize," Jiichan explained. "Maybe to some people this cake is good. Probably baker use sweet potato to make it a little sweet. Maybe to some people they like to get something pretty and a little sweet for their children. Who am I to say that is not good idea? Maybe same thing make you sad, make Japanese children happy."

And there was Akira, doggedly eating the rest of his tan, fake *mochigashi*. "I won't waste it," he said.

That made Jiichan nod with a grin, then laugh. He turned delightedly to the man across the aisle. "That my grandson. He good boy." The man nodded politely, and Jiichan settled back, well pleased.

# TWENTY

In a station in the middle of the night, a few bare-foot children—maybe orphans?—ran onto the train yelling and laughing. They ran down the aisle shouting, *"Banzaaaaai!"* One of them stopped and pointed at Akira's eye and shouted, *"Banzaaaaai!"*

"Leave him alone!" Hanako shouted back.

"No!" Akira barked out, hiding his face. Then he turned and snarled, lifting his sharpies.

"No!" one of the boys barked back. But they seemed surprised by the sight of his sharp nails—to Hanako he looked exactly like a little wild beast. The kids ran off laughing, a conductor chasing them.

Everybody in the car settled down, and Hanako

went back to sleep. She awoke to find the conductor leaning over them saying quietly, *"Sumimasen."*

It was still dark. Jiichan took both the bag of rice and the basket, and Hanako grunted as she lifted Akira. She didn't want to awaken him, because that would require yelling on the train. Jiichan seemed reluctant to let the conductor touch the rice and basket, so he simply threw them down and quickly jumped off. Hanako handed Akira to the conductor, who held him while she stepped down. Then he handed down her brother and bowed before closing the door.

"Akira!" she shouted. "Aki!" She set him down, and he fell over as the train rumbled off. "AKI!"

He sat up and jumped to his feet, holding out his hands in the same funny fighting stance Jiichan had used before they left for Kobe. "Oh. Are we home?"

"We have to walk."

"Can you carry me?"

"You're too heavy."

"On your back?"

"I have to help carry the rice."

On the train Jiichan had put the wick in the lamp, so they had a little light. All around them they heard strange calls, but this time Hanako knew it was *tanuki*, maybe the very same one that had brought them luck. There was a rainbow halo around the moon, partially cut off by dark clouds. Then it was cut off entirely as it started to drizzle.

It was very dark, but Jiichan's seemingly supernatural eyes could see with just the lamp, and he didn't lose his balance like Hanako and Akira kept doing. Hanako could make out his dark form moving slowly, stopping every so often to make sure they were behind him. It started pouring. She took off her coat and rolled it into a ball that she wrapped around the bag of rice she was carrying. She was very worried about the rice, and also about her beautiful coat. Otherwise, she was fine.

Walking through a downpour. In Japan. Her eyes were open wide; she felt once again as if she had never been so alert, so *here*. But Akira was crying.

"Aki, are you cold?"

He didn't answer.

"Aki?"

"I'm freezing," he said at last.

She unwrapped her coat from around the rice and draped it around her brother, even though it was soaked. But he kept crying. Strangely, she did not feel like crying at all. Instead, she remembered something her teacher in Tule Lake had told her one rainy day. They had been standing in the mud surrounded by the ugly barracks, and Papa had been locked up in the stockade. And a flock of big birds had flown over the camp, like magical beings. The teacher hadn't tried to cheer her up or say "Look at the beautiful birds," but instead she'd spoken of feeling the sad beauty of human suffering and seeing the beauty in nature and how you're here and feeling all these things at the same time and . . . Hanako hadn't really understood. But she was sure she understood now, watching the torrential rain that was barely visible in the darkness. Here, in the most unlikely place, in the pouring rain in the middle of the night, she understood her teacher. It was dark and beautiful out. It was mysterious. She was here. In the mud. Just here.

Then she tripped and fell into the mud, smashing her chest against the basket, and the moment was gone. Jiichan rushed back to pull her up. Akira came close. "Don't touch me, I'm all muddy. Don't get my coat muddy!" she shrieked at him. She heard a hysteria in her voice. Her coat, her precious coat! The feeling from before was completely gone. She had no idea now what her teacher had been talking about. She trudged behind Jiichan, suddenly completely exhausted. If she was exhausted, how must Akira and Jiichan feel? One so much older than her, one younger.

It seemed like a *long* walk home. She grew so tired, she barely even recognized the house when they arrived, just trailed after Jiichan. She stripped down to her underwear on the porch, so as not to get the inside of the house muddy. Akira took off his pants and his shoes.

Inside, Baachan was asleep by the *kotatsu*. Waiting for them. Jiichan set down the rice on a *tatami*, murmured, "We must not wake her," and went straight in to bed, as did Akira and Hanako. Hanako knew that if she hesitated for even a second, she would fall asleep right where she was.

In the bedroom she lay down with Akira clinging to her like a baby monkey—it felt like his arms were extra-long, wrapped all the way around her. Both of them had soaked hair. She suddenly cried and cried—it felt like forever—as she let the tears wash away all the years in camp. Those years were gone, and they weren't coming back. She knew that now. She had worried before about when all the bad things would end, and now she somehow knew that they had. Her family might not rise higher, but they would no longer sink lower. She shivered from the cold, here in the middle of this tiny house in the middle of the countryside in the middle of Earth in the middle of the universe. She was *here*.

# TWENTY-ONE

In the morning Hanako could smell soup as she entered the kitchen. Baachan rushed to the doorway to greet her. "You have good trip!" she said breathlessly. "I making you rice now!"

Hanako loved the way you could always tell rice was cooking, and yet it had no smell. It was just one of the qualities about rice that made it different from every other food. "I'm so hungry!" she said.

"We will see how long last this rice," Baachan said. "If it last long, maybe next time we keep some butter and sugar." She placed both hands on a rice bag, her eyes closed. "I feel spirit of rice!"

"Can I try?" Hanako asked. Baachan removed her

hands, and Hanako placed hers on the bag. But she didn't feel anything, just a bag of rice. Still, that felt very good—it filled her with satisfaction.

"Where is Papa?" Hanako asked. He hadn't been in bed when she got up.

"He still look job," Baachan replied. "He don't come home yesterday. But you eat now. Also, you feed everybody. I need leave. Your *jiichan* already left for field. I just wait for you to get up. I want to say good morning. But I cannot be late so much. Many thing to do in field. When I return later, I have surprise!" She looked at Hanako with an expression of fervor. In fact, she was beaming so hard, she looked almost crazy.

The skirt! "Oh, Baachan!"

"I go now. We will have fun later!" She left with one childlike skip before returning to her shuffling step.

Hanako ran to the front door to watch her, headed toward the woods in the light drizzle without an umbrella. Would she catch cold?

Then she sat at the *kotatsu* and ate rice and carrots in her pretty bowl. Her feet were toasty, and her fingers were cold. Mama came out and announced that Akira was running a fever. "Hana, will you make him *ochazuke*?" That was rice with green tea, with a topping or two, like seaweed or dried fish. They probably didn't have any toppings here except for the grasshopper.

Hanako hopped to her feet to boil water for tea. Green tea was very healthy; still, Akira didn't usually get to drink it. He drank barley tea. So he must be very sick to get such special treatment. She put the *ochazuke* in her own special bowl with the gold cracks and took it into the bedroom with a porcelain spoon.

Mama lifted Akira and held him up while Hanako fed him. His lids were very heavy, and sometimes his eyes fluttered shut. Then they would flutter open, and he would take another bite. He ate half the bowl before he closed his eyes, and Mama laid him back. Hanako loved taking care of him the way she had when he was a baby. She used to sit in the big chair, Sadie beside her and Akira in her lap, while Mama made soap in the kitchen or took a bath or cooked dinner.

Mama spent the entire morning in the bedroom with Akira. Hanako had to leave because Mama was so intense when one of them was sick that Hanako could not stand to be there. Mama did not like it when Aki or Hanako got sick. It worried her so much that you could feel her worry no matter where you were, even if you weren't at home. Sometimes she acted like they might die from a simple fever! She would stay up all night just because one of them had a very stuffed nose. "What if you suffocate?" she once asked when Hanako was congested. That didn't make sense—Hanako would simply breathe out of her mouth. But when Hanako suggested that, Mama said, "What if you get something caught in your throat?"

When Hanako left the bedroom, her mother was just sitting there kneeling and watching Akira like she was a statue, frozen in time.

Hanako shook out the *tatami*, then cleaned up the kitchen. The house was very neat but surprisingly dirty. When she ran a damp rag once across a small section of the kitchen floor, the rag turned black. But then other parts were quite clean. Probably cleaning the floor was not a priority for an old woman who worked all day in the fields. Survival. *Priorities*.

For Jiichan and Baachan, work was probably the number-one priority. Her grandparents had returned to Japan when Papa was nine, more than twenty-five years ago. Twenty-five years of working the fields as Baachan's back warped and she grew old. Hanako wondered how it worked in Japan: Did you just keep working until you died?

The kitchen grew dark and light again as the clouds

covered and uncovered the sun. Then she heard the front door open—Papa!—and rushed into the living room. But it was the pink boy with his sister! She just gaped—they had walked right in!

The boy looked just as surprised to see her. "I thought nobody was home!"

Hanako couldn't think what to say and could only come up with, "I'm home."

The boy quickly opened a package—quickly despite the injuries and scars on one of his hands. She hadn't noticed before, but two of his fingers looked like they were sort of welded together. With a cry of triumph, he threw the cloth wrapping to the side and exposed a beautiful kimono, red and orange with white birds and white flowers. Other colors too. It looked expensive. "I was going to leave this! In case you had rice I could take. I wasn't going to steal; I would leave you the kimono. It's worth a lot."

The little one glared as if she thought Hanako was a bad person.

Hanako did not know what to do. She thought of Akira and how hungry he got. And yet this little girl no doubt got hungry as well! But Akira . . . She hardened her heart. "We have no rice." She hesitated. "I could give you carrots. You don't have to give me anything in return."

The boy bowed his head, then raised it slowly, suspicion in his eyes. "No rice?" His eyes flashed angrily for a moment.

"Mama!" Hanako shouted. "Mama!"

The boy looked startled as Mama came out of the bedroom. "What is it?" Mama asked.

"This boy—I was going to give him carrots. He wants rice, but I told him we have none."

"I will get the carrots," Mama said. She looked angrily at the boy. "We have no rice!"

While Mama went to the kitchen, he quickly wrapped the kimono up again. The fire left his eyes, and they turned pleading. "If you have rice, I would be so grateful! What is it that you eat every night?"

"We eat many carrots," Hanako said.

The boy bowed his head sadly, but when he raised it, his eyes were angry again. This time the anger was hidden. But Hanako could see it, lurking behind his false smile. The little one was staring glassy-eyed into space, the way Akira sometimes stared. Hanako turned her face away because the child seemed so sad. She thought suddenly of the fake *mochigashi*. "I have more cakes for you!"

But Mama had had the same thought! She came out with two bunches of carrots, as well as the cakes in a bowl. "Do you have somewhere to put these?" she asked.

The boy did: his big pockets. He seemed quite excited, and Hanako thought of Jiichan saying that some children would be happy to eat these cakes. She worried briefly, because what if she and Akira became children like that soon? What if they ran out of rice and regretted giving away these cakes that tasted like nothing?

The boy was looking around the house, at the walls and floors and *kotatsu*, then said bitterly, "It's warm here." He left then, without saying *arigatō*.

"He came right in without knocking!" Hanako exclaimed. "I got scared."

Mama seemed worried. "That's bad. . . . Still, he's just a child. Not much older than you."

Hanako was feeling guilty now that she hadn't given them just a little rice, or even asked him to stay and warm up. But Akira was calling, and Mama hurried to him.

Hanako followed, kneeling next to her brother. When she felt his forehead, it was very hot. Worry blazed through her heart, and the guilt fell away. She would do anything for her brother, whatever she had to! She would not share with strangers. Not now or ever. They simply didn't have enough. "Life is filled with facts," she murmured. But the guilt abruptly washed like a big wave over her again.

"Where did he get the kimono?" Mama asked.

"He probably stole it," Hanako replied. "Where else would he get it?"

Mama paused. "It's not his fault. I would do the same for you, and more," she said.

Hanako did not know what "more" Mama would do, but she thought that the boy would also do whatever it was. For the little one. Hanako wept, blinked back hot tears of frustration.

"But, Hanako," said Mama. Hanako looked up. Mama's face was hard, her eyes like stone. "You did the right thing. If it happens again, don't forget that. You may cry. But don't forget that you did the right thing."

# TWENTY-TWO

When Jiichan and Baachan came home, they ate quietly at the *kotatsu* with Hanako while Mama stayed in the bedroom. There was a pall in the house because Akira had hardly moved all day, except to wobble his head and groan softly. Mama had mashed up rice to feed him, but when Hanako had gone in to check, he hadn't eaten anything at all.

The soup that night was nearly the same as the first time: rice, carrots, carrot tops, and grasshopper. Everyone ate like they were starving. For some reason, as she ate, Hanako felt electrified by the grasshopper. It was like she needed to eat it very badly. She chewed the way she would chew something that actually tasted good.

In short, she was very, very hungry, and maybe anything tasted good when you were that hungry.

Then there was no more, just a big bowl's worth left for Papa in case he came home tonight. After helping to clean up, Hanako decided to put on Mama's coat—hers was still damp—and wait outside for him so they could have a talk when and if he arrived. She wanted to ask him if Akira would be all right, and maybe some other questions. She stood near the steps, trying to see. It was dark out—it must have been seven or eight. The world was completely quiet except for the ringing of the *Fūrin*—the Japanese glass wind bell—that hung in a tree. The front door slowly opened, and Baachan came out with a blanket. "It cold?"

*"Hai, arigatō gozaimasu."* Hanako wrapped herself up in the blanket.

Baachan lingered and looked into the darkness. "Your father good man, *neh*? He miracle baby. I have when forty-two."

"Yes, he told us. He talks about you all the time."

"Oh? He say nice thing?" She laughed shyly. "I hope so."

"He says you were so pretty and petite."

"No, never pretty. What is . . . ?"

"Petite. That's when you're small and slender."

"Oh, he call me skinny? I have talk to him about that!" But Baachan laughed and laughed, like she was having the best time she'd ever had. Her laughter washed over Hanako. Her parents loved her a lot, she knew that, but here with Baachan was something different. Her grandmother had just met her, yet *adored* her. She hadn't done anything to deserve it; it was just there, in the air around them, like something shimmering. It made her feel like some kind of *amazing* person. It made her feel like being here in this bombed-out, impoverished nation was the best experience she would ever have in her life and like her hungry stomach was just an *adventure*.

"No, not skinny!" Hanako replied. "Slender is like . . . well, it's different from skinny. It's good."

Baachan's head dipped as if she was embarrassed by the compliment.

"And he said you never yelled at him once, but you did scold when he misbehaved."

"Sometime he bad like any child. But I don't yell at miracle baby. That bad luck."

"Do you have photographs?" asked Hanako.

"I show you tonight!" Baachan said eagerly. "I have three. We save our money to get photograph three time when your father growing up."

Suddenly, Papa called out from the road, "Okaasan? Hanako? Why are you out here? It's too cold!"

"Papa's home!" Hanako ran and hugged him. "We got white rice! First we got the butter and sugar, and then Jiichan sold it at the black market!"

"Congratulations! Great work!" He picked Hanako up and twirled her around once. "Now, aren't you going to ask if I found a job?"

"Did you?"

"I went to find an interpreter job, and I ended up in an office with the occupation army." He lowered his voice. "I think they're doing some illegal things. I know they are."

"Like what, Papa?" she asked as he set her down.

"Some of the soldiers are taking items from the commissary to sell on the black market. They had me sell some cigarettes today." He reached into his pocket and pulled out two packs of cigarettes. "They paid me with these. Maybe if I get a few more, we could get some fish, or something good."

"But, Papa, you told me once never to steal!" Then

she thought of the boy, and of Mama saying, "I would do the same for you, and more."

"I will keep looking for a better job. But in the meantime, I *will* feed my children."

"Akira is sick," Baachan said. "To feed him is more important than not to steal. I do not steal my whole life. For myself, I would starve first. But Akira must eat."

Papa kissed his mother gently on the top of the head. "He *will* eat."

As Papa and Baachan chatted, Hanako took one of the packs of cigarettes and smelled them. She had never held a pack of cigarettes before. Here in Japan, maybe this pack was valuable, like butter or sugar. She had heard a lot of people loved these things, and at times they'd been hard to get even in America. And yet the smell was kind of sickening; it made her head reel. Nevertheless, she cradled the cigarettes in her hands as if they were money. Actually, they were more valuable than money, probably like a lot of things were right now. Money was for places like America, places that war had not destroyed, places where people bought things at the market—organized places where people agreed that a one-dollar bill was just as valuable as a pack of cigarettes or a stick of butter. She thought about how in school she had learned that there had once been a civil war in the United States. Out in the field, after a battle in Kentucky or Virginia or Georgia, a dollar bill in your pocket would not be worth a can of beans. Neither would a hundred-dollar bill. When she was younger, she had asked Papa about that war, and he said he doubted it would be the last battle fought on American soil. "That's the way of the world," he said. "But I will keep you safe forever." She had believed him, but thinking about it now, she suddenly no longer believed him. There were things in the world he could not protect her from, or Akira, or Mama. But he would do everything he could, she was sure of that. He would steal, and more, just like Mama would.

# TWENTY-THREE

They all went in to see Akira, but he was sleeping. Mama said he felt better, though. She couldn't explain how she knew this. "I know my son" was all she could say as she sat cross-legged staring at him.

They all cheered up a bit after that. But Mama remained in the bedroom as everyone else went out to the *kotatsu*. Papa gobbled up his soup, which must have been cold at that point. Baachan disappeared and reappeared with a weathered envelope. She sat next to Hanako. "Here my three picture." She carefully opened the envelope. Her hands were tan and gnarly, and the top joints seemed as permanently bent as her back. She set three black-and-white photographs next to each other on the table with the bottoms of the pictures perfectly aligned. The first was Papa in what looked like a little army outfit, complete with matching cap. He was leaning on Baachan, and Jiichan was on the other side of him. Baachan's back was straight, and her face . . . it was filled with joy. It made Hanako realize that even though Baachan was extremely happy that they were all together in Japan now, her face today had something sad in it. Even right this second. It made her quickly touch Baachan's arm and say, "It's all right." Baachan looked confused, and Hanako said, "I mean . . . we're all here together!"

Baachan was looking at the picture again. "He six year old," she said fondly. "He very attach to me."

"He so attach to his mother," Jiichan said, joining them. "He attach to me too, but when he little, he attach most to his mother. He howl like a dog when she go to take bath, so she have to take him with her. She set him on floor while she take bath. I very serious. He sound just like dog in pain. Even he nine year old, he sit outside bathroom wait for her to finish."

"That's not true!" Papa protested. "I don't remember that."

"Don't be embarrass you attach to your mother," Jiichan said, chuckling.

Papa chuckled too. In the picture his eyes looked large and gleaming.

The next photograph was of Papa at about Hanako's age now. "We take this photograph because he still boy, but we know he be man soon," Jiichan said. "When he twelve, she cry all time because he grow too fast."

"He grow very fast," Baachan said. "Very, very fast." She wiped a tear away and gently patted the picture. "We think sometime maybe we get frame for these and keep on table, but then maybe I cry more if I see all time."

In the next picture the three of them were sitting down. "This right before he left for America," Baachan said. She got teary again. "I proud of him, but I miss him too."

In the photograph Papa looked confident, and his eyes were gleaming here also. Baachan's back was somewhat bent. That made Hanako so sad. She touched the first photograph, then touched Baachan's arm again, and she said, "You're pretty and petite, just like Papa said."

Baachan nodded her head in agreement. "All

right," she said. "All right." Her eyes were alight, like she rarely accepted a compliment, but would accept just this one time.

Jiichan was the opposite—Hanako already knew how much he loved compliments. Now she said to him, "You were the handsomest man in the world when you were young!"

He laughed with delight. "You very smart girl! I quite proud of your smartness!"

Then Baachan stood up, clapping her hands three times in slow-motion applause. "Time for your surprise, smart girl!"

Hanako stood up with anticipation as Baachan went to the big basket in the corner, lifting a few items up and then pulling out the plaid skirt!

"Oh, it's beautiful!" Hanako shouted, running over and reaching for it. "It's gorgeous!"

And it was too; she wasn't lying. She felt shy for the first time in years and ran into the bathtub room to change. The skirt fit perfectly—snug but not tight, and right where she liked skirts to fall, in the middle of her knees. She half ran back to the living room.

Everybody exclaimed about how perfectly it fit and how beautiful it was and how beautiful *she* was. Her grandparents didn't have a mirror, but she was absolutely positive the skirt made her look like a girl in a Sears catalog, if they ever had a Japanese girl in the catalog. She had a moment of regret that she couldn't see herself, but then it didn't matter. She could just feel how perfect this skirt was; she didn't have to see it.

Baachan said shyly, "I work a long time at night, hardly sleep, but next day I don't feel tired." She was happily bobbing her head up and down, up and down. "I had to finish your surprise. I wanted to. It look very nice. I wish I had more money, I make you many skirt. More skirt than you can wear."

"Then it wouldn't be special like this one is!" Hanako exclaimed. "This is the best skirt that was ever made since the beginning of time!" And she was pretty sure that this was true.

# TWENTY-FOUR

The next morning, when Hanako woke up, Mama was singing with Akira like he was a baby. *"Up, up, up goes the little red bird."* He watched her, his eyes strangely reflective instead of deep. It was Saturday, a workday for Baachan and Jiichan. They had already left for the wheat field, while Papa had gone to his new job. After Hanako ate rice and carrots and had cleaned the kitchen, Mama left Akira and called her to the table. "We need to talk," she said.

Hanako didn't like the sound of that. She sat down. Mama touched her face, then said, "There's a school only twenty minutes away. Hanako, we're going to start you in sixth grade, and you'll be in seventh when the new school year starts in April."

Hanako was stunned. A school? She had to go to school already?

"My Japanese isn't good enough for school here!" she said. "I can't read and write well! Will there be a bus? Or do I have to walk by myself? Will the other kids like me? Are they mad at America for bombing them? What are the teachers like?" She took a breath. She didn't know anything about Japan!

"Baachan will go with you the first day to show you the way. She says it's very easy."

"But I'll be different from them. They won't be nice!"

"Hanako. Hanako . . . ," Mama said. "This is where we are, and we just have to accept that. There is nothing for you to do all day, and anyway, Baachan says there is a rumor that the Americans will be insisting on compulsory school at least until after ninth grade."

"Why do we always have to do what the Americans want?"

"They're in charge now. That's the way of the world. Somebody is always in charge."

Hanako tried doing what Akira sometimes did when he was mad: She turned around so that her back was facing Mama. Then she crossed her arms over her chest. "When do I have to start?" she said into the air.

"Well, Monday. Baachan especially would like you to go to school and study hard. That way . . ."

"That way what?"

"Well . . . one day you will have to return to America, and we want you to have an education."

She whipped around to face Mama. "I thought I was Japanese now!"

"Hana, we haven't thought everything through yet. But we have nothing now—we own nothing. I think . . . I think your father felt that since we had nothing, and since Roosevelt took us prisoners of war, since our friends were beaten in camp, and other reasons, he wanted to renounce America when the goverment pressed him about it. It wasn't his idea, but when the government came to him, he realized he wasn't sure if we would be safe in America. So your father and I *did* give up our citizenship when they brought it up. But even on the ship, he was changing his mind—because of you and Akira." Mama leaned in so suddenly that she almost knocked heads with Hanako. "Do you understand?" she asked loudly, as if Hanako were hard of hearing. "Your grandparents are tenant farmers. They will never own land. Nobody will have anything to leave you, so you will have to make your own future. Making your own future will be easier in America. That was why Papa originally left his parents. But for a girl in Japan . . . and from tenant farmers . . . tenant farmers are peasants here. They have little to no future, because they pay so much to rent their land, it's impossible to get ahead. Oftentimes you not only don't get ahead, you begin to owe your landlord more and more money. And then you have a bad crop one year, and suddenly you owe your landlord your entire future. There is no escape at that point. You know, it's similar to the way it is in the United States for tenant farmers. The landowners make the money, the tenants struggle to feed their families. Like the Dust Bowl people I had pictures of." She paused. Then she gave her head a shake, stood up, and hovered directly over Hanako. "Do you understand?"

Hanako hung her head, then asked, "I thought those people owned their land?"

"They were tenant farmers. Your papa didn't want his children to have that life. That's why he worked so hard at the restaurant. And now he has brought you back here, so . . ."

"But why can't I go to college here and then open up a restaurant?"

"It's not the same for girls here as it is in America."

"But I don't know if you want me to be American or Japanese. Mama, I don't understand!" Hanako felt very small as Mama hovered over her. She felt like an ant.

"Papa is trying to figure out in his head what your future should look like. He's concentrating very hard on it. He is in charge of your future. I am in charge of your life *now*. And I say you are going to school Monday."

Hanako squeezed her knees with her arms. "Then I guess I'm going to school Monday." Her voice sounded as small as Akira's.

Mama sat down in front of Hanako and squeezed her own knees. Hanako didn't look up, but she could feel her mother staring at her in that intense way she had, trying to claw her way into Hanako's brain. "Hana . . . your father told me a long time ago about your *baachan*'s back. Sometimes you can slightly fracture your back, if you bend over wrong in the field, or anywhere, really. So there was a day that Baachan suddenly had pain in the field, but she kept working, day after day and year after year. And her back kept bending worse and worse. Papa figured this out."

"That's not true! She said she didn't even notice it happening!"

"It *is* true. She knows the day it happened, but she ignored it and didn't tell anyone."

"Does her back hurt her?"

"Yes, I asked. It hurts her very much sometimes. Sometimes if she sneezes it hurts. She hates to sneeze. But it mostly bothers her, not hurts. It feels very, very, very stiff and uncomfortable. I'm not saying this will happen to you if you're a tenant farmer someday, but I'm saying tenant farming is not like owning your own land. It's a very difficult life. Owning your own land can be a difficult life too, but you have a better chance. And you have something to leave your children. You'll see someday. Having something to leave your children will be so important to you. Your father was obsessed with that, but he understands it will no longer happen."

Hanako could not imagine spending her life bent over, always looking down unless you made an effort to raise your eyes. She had noticed that Baachan often stood just staring down at the floor, as if that was a more comfortable position for her.

But Mama needed to return to Akira, so Hanako got to work draining the tub water, cleaning the tub, refilling it with the pump, and starting the fire beneath it. The pump was in the kitchen, with a rubber hose attached. The hose went into the kitchen sink or the bathtub as needed. There was a small window between the kitchen and tub room to put the hose through. The whole time she worked, she thought of school. In truth, many kids at Tule Lake didn't take school very seriously. It wasn't really like school was before camps. It was more casual, and the children didn't behave as well.

Shortly before dark, Jiichan and Baachan came in from the wheat field. Baachan was holding a cabbage. "I pulling weed, and I thinking, my grandchildren need cabbage be healthy. Come. We cook soup."

Hanako followed her into the kitchen. "You sit," Baachan said. "I make soup."

"Oh, I'll help you!" Hanako said.

"No worry about me. I don't mind."

"I don't mind," Hanako replied.

"I do it every day. It nothing."

"But I want to help you." And she did.

"I do it. You go to *kotatsu* if you not feel like talk to me."

"No, I want to talk to you," Hanako said. "Unless you don't want me to."

"No, I want, but only if *you* want."

Baachan filled the pot with water and put it on the burner, then turned to Hanako.

"Why your forehead wrinkled?"

"I'm worried about school," Hanako blurted out.

"You go to school important," she said. Then, all in a rush, she went on: "I never go, I not rich enough to go, and look at me. Your back straight; you don't go to school, maybe you end up like me. You get it from me." She looked like she wanted to cry. "It my fault you might be like me!"

"But, Baachan! I'm *me*!"

Baachan studied her. "You don't look so much like Aki. He look like his *jiichan*. Maybe you are more like other grandparent. But we must be careful with your back. We will fight to stop this." She patted her own back. "Who know, maybe if I go to school, my back never bend. Maybe I be smart enough to work as maid for rich person. If world perfect, I can even be tailor. I not complain, I just telling you." She shyly touched Hanako's face. "I know, I know it different from America here. That why you worry?"

Hanako dipped her head. "I don't read and write well in Japanese," she admitted. "I have nice hand-writing, but I don't know many *kanji*."

Baachan looked truly concerned. Hanako studied her grandmother. She was beautiful, not beautiful like "pretty," but beautiful like "good." She took Hanako's hand and set it on her back. "You feel my back." Hanako wasn't sure why Baachan wanted this, but she swept her palm up and down her grandmother's curved back. Her spine felt like gnarled wood. Bumpy. "We must fight so this is not your future," Baachan said. "Don't forget that. That all I say."

Hanako glanced at her bare feet, then looked up at her tiny, hopeful grandmother. "All right," she said.

"Good!"

Then Hanako stared at Baachan's back and asked, "Mama says it hurts sometimes?"

Baachan nodded slowly. "Yes, sometime it hurt." She swatted at the air like she did earlier. "Believe me, you don't want. I don't complain, I just want you know. So you see?"

Hanako nodded.

"Good, then I cook now!"

Baachan placed the cabbage into a pot. She looked fondly at the pot. "I receive this pot when I get marry. It gift from my mother. It only gift I get when marry." She smiled at Hanako. "When you get marry, you will have many present. I will get you myself! I will sew you hundred skirt. Somehow I will find money for cloth."

"Did you wear a kimono at your wedding?"

"*Hai*, of course! I wear purple kimono my mother make."

"I love purple! Where is it now?"

"Oh, I sell many year ago, a few year after marry. Then, when my aunt die with no children, she leave me her kimono, and I want to give to you, but needed to sell instead. But I have something I can give you. It is purple silk wedding flower I put in my hair." She looked extremely shy as she continued. "I want to ask you, will you wear these flower when you get marry?"

"Of course I will! It's my favorite color!"

Baachan bowed her head a few times. "Mine too."

While the cabbage and rice cooked, Hanako and Baachan perched on stools to wait. Baachan said thoughtfully, "You get slowly from old place to new place. You accept now. It funny, even my back. It sound crazy, but I accept it as it happen. Nothing I can do, so I accept. That Japanese way."

"People never complain in Japan?"

This time Baachan swatted the air with both hands. Then she did it again. "Oh, many people complain.

Oh, yes, we complain. But we accept, too. At least, that my way. Then war come and people think about how survive. So hard for many people to survive. Think about survive, not complain."

"So what did you feel like when the war started? Did you vote for the war?"

"We no have vote in Japan," Baachan said. "We still no vote. We just try to recover from war."

"So do people . . . do they have dreams? Do they think about the future?"

"Oh, yes, think about future! All I want every day is see my son, meet his children. I want to meet his wife to make sure she good enough."

"Do you think Mama is good enough?" Hanako asked, curious.

"*Hai.* You are my granddaughter, so that mean she is my daughter. So I work in field every day, whole time I imagine see my son. Rice grow, we harvest, we plant wheat, wheat grow, we harvest. We grow vegetable, we pick weed, we destroy bug. This my life. We pay many money for fertilizer is one of my biggest worry. So fertilizer, vegetable, weed, bug, this my think about future. Many time I dream we have good crop. What you dream?"

"I used to dream exactly the same dream as Papa.

I dreamed we would work all the time, and then we would own three restaurants. And then he would send you a million dollars! That was my dream!" That wasn't true; she had never dreamed that. But if she had ever met her grandparents before, she surely *would* have dreamed that!

Baachan laughed. "What I do with million dollar? I make you many skirt, that what. You may as well keep money and buy skirt. That save me some time." But she suddenly turned sad. "Your father miss us, but he have to go to America." Her eyes went far away. "It very hard to be in different country from your child. I never tell him this when he leave, so he don't feel guilty." Her eyes came back to the kitchen, and she beamed at Hanako. "Someday you do like your father. You go make new life, like American way."

Hanako watched her grandmother stir the soup, then remove the pot from the stove, her thin arms sticking out from beneath her rolled-up sleeves. Those were old arms, wrinkly and spotted—arms that had worked hard for decades.

"Baachan . . . may I ask? What was the war like here? Did you ever get bombed here in the country, even once?"

"No bomb in farm country," Baachan said. "But war is here. Everybody get poorer and poorer, and more boy get sent to fight. My neighbor boy hide. He don't report for war. The police come for him, and he hide in our closet. We very surprise when he run into our house so fast, but we see his face very scared, and we hide him without ask question. As soon as he run in, my husband say, 'Hide in closet!' We don't even know what we hide him from, but we can see he need to hide."

"What happened to him?"

"He don't leave our house until night. Then we never see again. We don't talk about to neighbor. It better not to know."

"In America we don't really understand why Japan bombed Pearl Harbor."

"Ahh. No free press in Japan. We don't know many thing. I know long time leading to war, there many assassinate in Japan. Military want big Japanese empire, like country in West have big empire. We have only one leader, Takahashi Korekiyo, who many people have told me don't want this. He want rich country, prosperous people, but many other leader want rich country, strong army. He want cooperation, not empire. But Takahashi got assassinate. So many assassinate in Japan. Can't keep track who is in charge."

"Papa says the history of the world is a lot of people fighting for power, within each country, plus between countries."

"If your father says, then is true. But too complicated for me and your *jiichan*. We are tenant farmer. I can see right or wrong in my house and in my field, but for country is very hard."

"Baachan, were you sad to leave America? That was 1919, right? Papa told me."

"I worry when I return, but we have duty. My mother-in-law old and sick. But 1918 many problem in Japan. They have *kome sōdō*. Many big *sōdō*."

*Sōdō* was "riot," and *kome* was "uncooked rice." So many big riots over rice.

"I hear many city in chaos. Also many people die from flu in 1918. And then when we come back to Japan, country have powerful people who want military state and powerful people who want socialist state. Even though my country may have many hard time, these year with coup and assassinate is very unusually bad time for my country. If people kill for socialist or if people kill for military, result is same. Then all the war.

People kill and fight and kill and fight, and I work in field, and my back bend more every year. This is my life after your father left, until now." She gazed lovingly at Hanako. "So I thank you for come back. I thank you very much."

Hanako blushed. "I wish you had just stayed in America! Couldn't someone else have taken care of your mother-in-law?"

"Oh! Hana-chan, you don't mean what you ask!" Baachan looked quite taken aback. "Jiichan has duty to his mother. More important than stay in America."

This, Hanako knew, was true. Then she had a happy thought. "But then all the chaos ends, and it gets better."

Baachan seemed to be thinking this over. "Many people die first. See . . . people who make decision never think it will end the way it end. People think everyone else is wrong. Maybe almost everybody is wrong. Maybe you have only one person who is right, and then he is assassinate because nobody realize he is right." Then suddenly she cheered up. "But I think more than one right person in world, *neh*? World to get better. Yes, I believe world to get better." She looked at her hands, her knobby knuckles. "My life is work. I work if war,

I work if no war. I *kill* someone if he try to hurt you, but I don't kill anyone else. My husband and I have no want to kill. Our whole life is work. But now we work for you, so is very different." Hanako was surprised how *vicious* Baachan momentarily sounded when she said, "I *kill* someone if he try to hurt you." But now she was back to her peaceful self.

But something occurred to Hanako. "Am I bothering you, asking so many questions?"

"You ask many question as you want. Even though it hard work answering your question!" She had completely cheered up as she stirred the soup.

"Well, what do you think of America now?" Hanako asked.

"I live in America eleven year. America very strong. You can feel how strong is America."

"Papa has a friend whose father used to beat him. So the man wanted to love his father, but it was hard because of the beatings. Papa says that's how he feels about America."

Baachan's brow furrowed. "I like for your father to live in America. America very strong, country can protect, you can be safe. But I like him here too. I like him here for me, not for him. When I see my grandchildren, happiest day of my life." And suddenly, Baachan was crying. *Sobbing*.

Hanako shot to her feet and quickly moved to where her grandmother was stirring the soup. She reached out her hand and let it hover for a moment over Baachan's back, then laid it firmly on the curved spine. Baachan tried to stir the soup as she sobbed.

"What is it?" Hanako asked.

"I just think of day I sell my wedding kimono! I did not want to sell!" She spoke through her tears. Then she half shouted, "You go! You go! Now! I don't like cry over something so stupid!"

Hanako hurried out of the room, feeling panicked. She could hear Jiichan talking with Mama in the bedroom. She sat alone at the *kotatsu*, her face in her hands. She would go to school, and then she would get rich, and then she would find a kimono just like the one Baachan had sold, and she would buy it.

But Baachan had shown her the only three pictures she owned, and none of them was of the kimono. So Hanako would not find one that was just the same. That one was gone. All the money in the world would not get it back, nor get back Baachan's straight spine.

# TWENTY-FIVE

Hanako was alone.

But the thought of Baachan selling her wedding kimono just—it just made her suddenly want to be even *more* alone. It seemed so hot at the table! She got up and slid open the front door before climbing down the steps and walking cautiously into the yard. She went as far as the path in front of the house and looked around the darkness and saw nobody. Maybe this was the actual most alone she'd ever been. The half-moon hung over the pines, partly hidden by small, glowing clouds moving slowly across the sky— the sky changing each moment. She knew that Japanese were obsessed with the way everything was temporary, the way everything was always changing. You celebrate each precious moment in your changing world. That was the Japanese way. Probably during the war, this had all been forgotten as everybody suffered. It was certainly not something she herself had thought about in the camps. But it turned out that the camps, which had seemed to go on forever, were, after all, temporary.

Hanako looked back up at the sky and was surprised to see that the clouds had already disappeared! Faded away? Moved somewhere else? She would never know.

She thought suddenly about how the woman they'd given twenty-seven dollars to, to take care of Sadie, had never responded to the letters Hanako had written to her.

So she didn't know what had become of her cat.

So there were some things that she, too, just couldn't have anymore: they were simply gone. But what was it Jiichan had said? "So we move forward in life, *neh*?"

And she had her grandparents now. It was what she needed to concentrate on as she moved forward.

She heard Baachan calling out, "*Gomen nasai*, Hana-chan! I hurt your feelings?"

Hanako spun around. "No, not at all! No!"

"I don't mean to yell at you."

Hanako began walking toward the house. "It's all right. I was just thinking."

When she arrived at the door, Baachan seemed embarrassed, then said, "Well, I very sorry. You eat now? Not hurt your feelings?"

"Yes, everything's fine!" She slipped her arm through Baachan's. "Nothing ever hurts my feelings!"

They ate dinner before Papa got home again, because he told them that he wouldn't be home until eight each night. Surprisingly, Mama came out for dinner with Akira. He was wrapped in the heavy blanket and plopped down at the table, declaring, "I'm hungry! Hana, how come you didn't feed me?"

Mama petted his head, saying, "I will feed you, Aki-chan!" She spooned food into his mouth like he was a toddler, which he seemed to enjoy a lot. He ate all his soup, then looked longingly at Hanako's bowl. She gave him what was left.

The dishes were washed, and everyone was sitting at the *kotatsu* talking when the front door slid open and Papa stepped through. He held up his rucksack triumphantly. "I've got some things!"

He took his time making his way to the table,

teasing them. Then he took even longer to open his bag. Hanako was ready to burst. At last he held up a big green-bean can, grinning in a way that Hanako could not remember ever seeing before. Like a pirate or something. "Bacon grease!" he exclaimed. "They gave it to me instead of cigarettes today."

Jiichan stood up and took the can excitedly, opening it up and inhaling deeply. "Ahhhh! Ahhhh! The children will need this. My mother said children need fat and oil. She was not educated, but she could feel that this was true. She fed us fish whenever she could get." After closing the can again, he set it carefully on the table. Then he looked very proud of himself, as if he had obtained the grease. "I raise good son. Yes, I very satisfy about that. I did good job."

Akira grabbed at the can, and he and Hanako sniffed at it. Then they both dipped in a finger and sucked the grease off—delicious!

"I have more," Papa said. "I have *boku zukin* for Hanako and Akira."

Hanako and her brother looked at each other. *Boku zukin?*

"What's that?" Hanako asked.

"All the children wear them, even now. They wore

them during the war to protect themselves from bombs."

The *boku zukin* was a quilted cloth hood with a short cape. It had a tie at the neck. Hanako had no idea how this would protect anyone from a bomb, especially an atomic bomb like the one that had destroyed Hiroshima. It would not be possible for this little hood to stop a bomb, would it? No, it wouldn't. She picked it up and tied it around her neck anyway.

"I brought it so you could wear it to school," Papa said. "You'll fit in better."

"Yes, Papa," Hanako said obediently.

She wondered yet again what school would be like here. School in the camps had been simple and disorganized, and Hanako hadn't learned much. After they moved to Tule Lake, she changed from American school to Japanese school. Unlike many of her classmates, she hadn't gone to Japanese school before the war, which was why she couldn't read and write the language. The *sensei*—or teacher—had conducted class in Japanese, and while she could keep up with the spoken language, she couldn't keep up in the reading and writing. No, she was not looking forward to school at all.

But Papa wasn't done. Now he was holding up his

bag like an insane Santa Claus, a ridiculous smile on his face.

Akira jumped up, screaming, "I know, I know! I can smell it! You got fish!"

Papa turned his bag upside down on the table, and out fell a package wrapped in newspaper. Akira and Hanako ripped it open: a mackerel! It smelled maybe a day too old, but at the same time Hanako did not think she'd ever smelled anything better.

"I passed the fish seller on his bicycle," Papa said. "Let's eat it right now!"

And so Baachan cooked it alone, because she said she had a secret way of cooking old fish so that it didn't taste old. "Someday I will teach you secret," she told Hanako. "But tonight it will be something special I do. I am only person in world who know this secret." Her face was red with excitement.

And she cooked the fish in secret. And it tasted like it had just been caught an hour ago. The best fish in the history of the world!

# TWENTY-SIX

When it came to the first day of school, not having a mirror was truly a catastrophe. And there was not even a glass window where Hanako could see her reflection. She'd dressed in a white blouse and her new plaid skirt. And she'd let Baachan do her braid, even though she really wanted Mama to do it, because she knew Mama could braid her hair just right. But Baachan had insisted, and Mama gave Hanako the stink eye when she started to protest.

Hanako stood in the living room, with Akira, Mama, and Baachan evaluating her. Then Baachan placed her hand on her heart and said, "This sound like something your *jiichan* will do, but I have to brag. I have to say, I make perfect skirt for perfect girl. I very proud with myself." She lowered her hand and shrugged modestly. "All right. All right. I stop brag now. Make sure put on coat, very cold today."

Hanako fingered her braid to make sure it felt like it did when Mama braided it. It seemed to feel normal. And she knew the skirt was perfect . . . although if nobody had ever seen a plaid skirt before, they might not understand how perfect it was. Did people from all different countries think the same things were perfect?

But it was time to leave—Baachan was putting on her own coat. Hanako hesitated. She did not like first times very much. First times made her shy, even scared. First times made her ask, *Why?* As in, *Why do I have to do this?* She started to feel a little annoyed. Why wasn't she being given more days at home? What was the rush to get her to school? She suddenly stomped her foot, but Mama and Baachan happened to be looking at Akira at that moment. So then she stomped again, but nobody paid any attention.

So she resignedly put on her coat, and on top of that she wore the *boku zukin*. She didn't know if that was how you were supposed to wear the cape, but Baachan suggested it. On her feet she wore her leather shoes. None of the girls at school would own leather shoes, purple coats, or plaid skirts, so she wouldn't fit in the way she liked to do. But how could she not wear her special things for the first day of school?

Mama was staying home with Akira, so it was just Hanako and Baachan walking together. Right before they went out the door, Akira pulled at her sleeve.

"You pulled at my sleeve!" she accused him.

He screwed up his face angrily. "You and your coat!"

"Oh, stop," Mama said. She leaned in until her nose was touching Hanako's, and then she rubbed back and forth a couple of times. "All right?" she asked, as if she had said something more.

But Hanako didn't like first times! So she said, "Maybe. We'll see."

Then Baachan took her arm and pulled her gently outside. They strode down the narrow road through the village, past people bustling about. *"Ohayō gozaimasu!"* someone called out to Baachan.

*"Ohayō gozaimasu!"* she called back.

Hanako was clinging to Baachan's hand like a little child. Baachan's coat was old with frayed sleeves, but it looked heavy, so she was probably warm enough. Because of the curve of her spine, she had to kind of tilt her head back so she could see where she was going.

"Thank you for walking me to school," Hanako said.

"I enjoy. I use walk your father to school every day. He use go to same school you be going! You bring me good memory."

"Was he a good student?"

Baachan chuckled. "No. You be better, please. I appreciate."

"Then he grew up and started a fantastic restaurant. I wish you could have seen it."

"I see up here," Baachan said, pointing to her head. "I see everything in your father world up here." She pulled her coat tight; the top button was missing.

"Are you cold?" Hanako asked.

"I use to it. No worry, just me. There!"

Hanako followed her grandmother's eyes and saw a plain, one-story building. The dark wood looked like it was a hundred years old, chipping and discolored and cracked. Like the houses, there were no glass windows. Children milled about. She half expected to see the pink boy, but he wasn't there. She looked around. Did he go to school in the open air in Hiroshima? Did he go to school at all? Some of the kids dressed colorfully, and some quite plainly. But if you looked closely, you could see even the colorful clothes were old and thread-bare. The girls wore their hair cut above their chins, with bangs, and had plain skirts or *monpe*. A few of the children were barefoot, a few of the boys wore *geta*, and the others wore straw sandals. Hanako felt instantly regretful that she was dressed differently from every-body else. Still, she was very pleased with her outfit.

"I remember where office," Baachan said. "I never forget anything about your father. Come, please."

Hanako and Baachan took off their shoes and went into a small office attached to another small office. The inside looked as old as the outside, all brown and dark and discolored. Baachan spoke Japanese to the woman at the front desk, explaining who Hanako was. She bowed, and the woman gave a slight smile. The woman called to someone in the other office, and a man came out. Baachan explained who they were. "Ooooh, America-*gaeri*," he said. "Aaaaah." He looked at Hanako with open curiosity, almost as if waiting for her to do something American-like.

Then Baachan turned to Hanako. "I go now. I be here pick you up when school over. Wait if I late."

"What? You're leaving already?"

"You fine. You will learn many thing. I see you later."

As Baachan headed out of the office, Hanako felt a pang of worry over how bad her Japanese reading and writing were.

"*Kinasai,*" the man said to her. ("Come.")

She followed him to a classroom where kids were just entering and taking their seats. They were all wearing what Hanako knew were their straw sandals that they used just for inside. Baachan had told her she would need these, but she had not had time to make any. Indoor sandals and outdoor ones were exactly the same, except you must never get them mixed up!

There didn't seem to be any heat inside, so the kids were still wearing their coats. Actually, some of the kids didn't have coats at all, just their *boku zukin.* The man explained to the teacher that Hanako was an America-*gaeri* who'd just come with her family to Japan to live. He spoke loudly enough that the whole classroom was suddenly muttering, "America-*gaeri*!" To Hanako that seemed to mean "America come-backer." They stared as she walked toward the seat the teacher indicated. The empty seat was in the back, and every single person turned around to continue to stare at her. One girl cried out, "*Murasaki!*" That meant "purple."

Hanako felt self-conscious in her outfit. And then she didn't. She took off her *boku zukin* so everyone could see her coat better. After she sat, she folded her hands on her desk and gazed straight ahead. Back straight. Head high. Like the teenage boys: not scared of anything, at least on the outside.

The man left, and a boy stood up and yelled, *"Kiritsu!"*

Everyone popped to their feet. Hanako quickly stood up too.

The boy called out, *"Rei!"*

Hanako and the rest of the class bowed.

Then, in perfect unison, the other students said, "Takahashi Sensei, *ohayō gozaimasu!"* The *sensei* was an older woman with mostly gray hair and a no-nonsense manner. She held a stick in her hand for some reason. She turned sharply and began to walk out, everybody following her in a straight line.

They went into the schoolyard to do light exercises: bending, stretching, twisting, swinging, and a little bit of jumping and running. The entire school came out, all the children hopping around in their bare feet. She'd never twisted and stretched like this before; it felt good. The running felt good too. She felt like she might possibly fit in because she could jump and twist and stretch as well as the other kids.

Then everybody went back in. Takahashi Sensei, waving her stick, announced that the first subject was going to be math. Hanako was glad about that, because she was good at math. But when everybody took abacuses out of their desks, Hanako gaped. Abacuses? She had seen one once before but had no idea how they worked. The teacher quickly noticed that Hanako didn't have one and found an extra. She called it a *soroban*. As the lesson proceeded, Hanako could hear the other kids' beads clicking away. She looked at the teacher, then at her abacus, then at the other kids, who were already starting to giggle at her confusion and were murmuring "America-*gaeri*" to one another. Hanako's face grew hot. Math was the last subject that she'd expected to be behind in. Her humiliation lasted the entire hour—by the end, even the teacher was laughing a little at her. But the teacher wasn't laughing meanly, and suddenly it seemed like nobody was trying to be mean, just having a giggle. In fact, Hanako got the feeling the *sensei* liked her.

Next the teacher handed Hanako a history textbook that had whole sections blacked out. She tapped on the book with her stick. The pages reminded Hanako of the censored letters she had gotten from her father when he was in North Dakota. She couldn't read the *kanji*, and her leg started twitching impatiently. The *sensei* talked about the samurai and the feudal period in Japan, but she didn't use the word "samurai." She used the word *bushi*, a word Hanako had never heard. So it took her ten minutes just to understand that the teacher was actually talking about samurai . . . or that maybe samurai were a type of *bushi* . . . or vice versa. Anyway, they were *kind of* the same thing . . . or something.

It seemed that in the thirteenth century, Mongolia sent a huge fleet of ships to invade Japan. The Japanese were outnumbered and suffered huge losses, but then a typhoon blew in, pounding and sinking many Mongolian ships. So the Mongolians retreated. A few years later they tried again, but by this time the Japanese had built a wall to help repel invaders. Then another typhoon struck, again destroying most of the Mongolian fleet. So the weather was called *kamikaze*, or "divine wind." Hanako tried to take notes in Japanese, but she couldn't do it quickly enough, so she switched to English.

By the time the history session was complete, Hanako was exhausted from trying to quickly translate in her head. Reading came next. The teacher called on her, and the other kids seemed delighted when she couldn't read many words. One boy shouted out "America-*gaeri!*" Sensei seemed to take pity on her and called on someone else.

Since it was only mid-January, Hanako knew she probably had to suffer through at least two more months of school—her mother had said the school year ended in March, and then the new school year started in April . . . or something. Maybe. She was starting to realize that "maybe" and "or something" were going to be part of her life here in Japan.

During recess, she stood alone. She had expected everyone to be curious about her, but instead everybody seemed to have forgotten her completely. She took a piece of lint out of her coat pocket and pretended to be studying it. She actually got kind of involved with it, because it was red, and she didn't know where it had come from. So that entertained her for a few minutes. Every time someone sort of looked her way, she eagerly tried to catch their eye by holding her hand up in a small wave. Maybe she should target someone and try to be their friend. So she tentatively approached a group of girls. They gazed at her blankly as she hovered just outside their circle.

Some wore plain *boku zukin*; others' were quite colorful. There was a tall girl wearing a bright blue one with many white and yellow flowers.

"Your *boku zukin* is pretty," Hanako ventured in Japanese. "Did your mother make it?"

The girl studied her, ignored the question, then asked, "Why did you come back to Japan?"

"I didn't really come back. I was born in America." Everybody seemed to be waiting for more, so she added, "My parents came to Japan because . . . they wanted to open a restaurant here like they had in America."

The girls mumbled to one another, and then the tall one said, "Thank you" in English. The girls moved off, as if to get away from Hanako.

The bell rang, and they all went in to write haiku— special poetry—and Hanako decided to write about eyes, because that just seemed like a good idea. It seemed original—everybody else was probably writing about nature, like most kids had done when they wrote haiku in the camp school. She wrote about eyes looking left and right. She had to read her poem out loud, and everybody laughed, which really pleased her, as that's what she'd hoped for.

For lunch she had brought rice and cabbage with a touch of bacon grease on the rice. The teacher announced that a couple of mothers would be cooking *misoshiru* soup for them in the school kitchen. She seemed to be explaining this just for Hanako. When the miso was ready—complete with grasshopper bits in the broth—the *sensei* led the children in a song.

> *Yoku kande itadakimasu*
> *Kobosanu yoni itadakimasu*
> *Sensei arigatō*
> *Otōsan Okaasan arigatō*
> *Minasan arigatō*
> *Itadakimasu*
>
> I will chew well and eat
> I will eat without spilling
> Thank you, Teacher
> Thank you, Dad and Mom
> Thank you, everyone
> I will eat now

After lunch came more singing. Hanako didn't know any of the words, but she got quite involved swaying back and forth just like everybody else. It was funny how, when you were doing the same thing as other people at the same time, you felt different somehow—like part of the group instead of just yourself. Next they read out loud again, which was painful, and afterward they studied science, which was fun as far as she could understand it. After studies, Hanako was surprised when the teacher told them to clean the wooden floors of the school building, both in the classroom and out. Hanako was assigned to a team with five others. The five all watched her curiously as she carefully cleaned a corner, blew on it to help it dry, folded up her coat, and set it there. Then she joined them. Cleaning pads—part cloth and part rough plant husks—were handed out along with buckets of soapy water. The six of them got on their hands and knees at the end of the long hallway, and they pushed their cleaning pads into the wood. Afterward they oiled the floor. Hanako had cleaned many floors in her life, so this, at least, was nothing new. Except she'd never cleaned a floor in *school* before.

Then finally they were finished! The students put on their shoes and lined up. When the bell rang, some

of the boys shouted and ran out even as the teacher scolded them, but the rest of the kids walked outside in an orderly fashion.

Baachan was waiting as Hanako exited the door. "I couldn't understand the reading and the math, but everybody laughed at my poem," she said first thing. "And I'm supposed to practice with the *soroban* tonight. The *sensei* gave me one."

Hanako's *sensei* had also given her a list of math problems that she was supposed to use the abacus to figure out. Why couldn't she just write out the problem and solve it that way? That would take her two seconds.

"Homework good," Baachan said. "You work twice as harder as other student, then you catch up soon. Maybe three time harder. Even if four time harder, you must do."

They walked quietly for a few minutes before Hanako asked, "What did you do all day?"

"I pull weed. But today I happy working, because I get to quit early to come get you." She looked immediately worried. "But after while you need come by yourself. I cannot be away from the field too much—it would be tragedy."

"I understand."

"Did I use right word?"

"A tragedy is something really horribly awful."

Baachan nodded. "Yes, that exactly what I mean. If weed and insect win, would be tragedy. We would starve, so would others. So I must not take break. *So deshō.*"

# TWENTY-SEVEN

Every day after school, Hanako sat in the cold living room practicing her *soroban* and *kanji*. They had decided to use the *kotatsu* only for dinner, as they were running low on coal. Akira got slowly better, but he was never himself again. Truly never. He had become very subdued and fussy about how hungry he always was. He missed pork. He missed meat. He missed peanut butter. Apples. Bread. He would soon turn six and would not start school until April. So Mama took him for walks and made up stories and sang to him. She became like a regular performer. Papa managed to find a couple of children's books, including one of haiku by a famous Japanese poet from a long time ago. Akira liked this one best:

Cool melons–
turn to frogs!
If people should come near.

That poem made Akira SO HAPPY. He would just sit by himself and say he was imagining melons turning into frogs. If anyone bothered him while he was imagining this, he would get annoyed. Sometimes he would just sit off in a corner with a half smile on his face, imagining. Hanako did not know if he imagined the same thing over and over, or if maybe he sometimes saw green melons and sometimes orange ones, all different colors. Big frogs or little frogs? She didn't know, just saw that he was happy all by himself in his little melon-and-froggy world.

But he was losing weight. He said he wanted "real food." Papa bought another fish, but this one was even older than the last, and even Baachan couldn't make it taste good. So far they had spent parts of their sixty dollars on a few things: train fare to Hiroshima, train fare to Kobe, fake *mochigashi*, two old fish, and various items that Mama had purchased in the village to replace those in the missing duffel bags. Maybe other things—Hanako couldn't quite remember. Everybody gave Akira their carrots, but it wasn't enough. As he sat in the corner, Mama wouldn't sit so close that it bothered him, but she would sit about ten feet away, with her knees folded under herself, waiting in case he needed her.

When Hanako had nothing to do, she started a new game. To herself, she called it "the day game" if it was light out and "the night game" if it was dark out. Every day she would take more steps, by herself, away from the front porch. Fifty steps more each day and three steps more each night. During the day, toward the village. During the night, toward where Papa came from after work.

One night when she reached twenty-seven steps from the house, a middle-aged man with a lantern startled her. She had heard a noise behind her and turned swiftly around. "Oh!" was all she could think to say, her heart pounding.

He bowed quickly and apologized for scaring her. "You are the granddaughter?" the man asked in Japanese.

"*Hai!*" She bowed. "*Watashi wa Hanako desu.*" ("I am Hanako.")

He stepped closer, bowing slightly. Then he said furtively, "Our son came back tonight. I was coming to

tell your grandparents. Will you tell them? It is secret
to all but them. Please tell them thank you!"

"*Hai.*" They both bowed at each other, and the man
walked toward the farmhouse next door.

Hanako hurried back home, burst into the living
room, and exclaimed, "Their son came home tonight!
A man—I think he lives next door—said their son is
back, and it's a secret!" She felt like a spy!

Everybody was in what had become their usual
place around the *kotatsu*. They all stared at her for a
moment.

Akira said, "If something is a secret, why are you
telling us?"

"Ah, our neighbor," Jiichan commented. "We have
hidden his son one night."

"I have told her!" Baachan scolded. "You must not
bother her with tell again."

"I tell my way!" Jiichan said with passion. He turned
to Hanako. "I think he is safe. The war has ended, and
country is starting over. I think he is safe, yet we will
not tell."

Oh, it was the man . . . or boy . . . who had run
into her grandparents' house in the middle of the night!
Hanako started to speak, but Mama lifted a finger to

her lips to shush her. "We won't talk of it, even if he's safe now," she said.

"But the country is starting over, Mama!"

"We cannot know yet which direction our country will take," Jiichan said. "We hope for good, but we cannot know yet."

So Hanako sat down to concentrate on her *soroban*. Her abacus had twelve columns. Papa had taught her a little about it the night she brought it home, right before he went to bed, which he often did directly after dinner. The bottom beads, called the "earthly beads," were worth one, and the top beads, called the "heavenly beads," were worth five. The beam dividing them was called a "reckoning bar," and the only beads you counted were the beads touching the bar. You used your thumb to move beads up, and you used your pointer finger to move beads down.

Next on the *soroban*, she'd learned about the complementary numbers up to five: (3, 2) and (4, 1). She'd gotten pretty fast at addition problems using the complementary numbers, but her fingers still didn't fly like the fingers of the other kids. She was determined that someday they would—she decided she was going to fit in so completely that nobody would even know she was American. She was sure this was the secret to making her first friend. But then she thought of her purple coat and her plaid skirt that she wore almost every day. And her warm leather shoes, while everybody else wore handmade straw slippers, or even nothing covering their feet at all. And there was also her braid—the other girls all wore bowl cuts.

Baachan had moved everybody into the kitchen. She always insisted that Hanako have the *kotatsu* while she studied. If the others wanted to be warm, they had to be quiet. If someone wanted to talk, they had to leave the room so that Hanako could concentrate. Baachan wanted Hanako to return to America one day far in the future and become a businesswoman, and she would need to know math to add up all her money.

That night Hanako felt a little evil because she was thinking about how different she was instead of thinking about her schoolwork. But she had to admit, she also enjoyed sitting here relaxing, her feet and legs toasty, the whole household doing whatever she wanted! If she was thirsty, she knew they would fall over themselves to help if she called out for water. But she never called out; she just liked knowing that it was true.

Papa came home and kissed the top of her head. "Good! Hard at work!"

"Hi, Papa!" She got up to hug him. "Papa! When you were a child in Japan, did you fit in?"

"No, not for a long time. And then I did. And then I left."

Baachan was suddenly in the room saying, "Tadashi, she try to study. You must eat in kitchen!"

He shrugged jokingly at Hanako and said, "I'm being kicked out."

"But I'm finished studying!" Hanako said. "Please, Baachan?" Baachan crossed her arms in front of her chest, but Hanako could see she was melting. "Please?"

"All right, it good for Akira to be in warm room. Your father can eat at warm table. This is good too."

Hanako placed the abacus on a shelf that had been cleared off just for her. Akira had his own shelf too, filled with "Japanese" rocks and "special" dirt and "nice" grass that he collected during the day. Hanako and Akira sat on either side of Papa as he ate. They didn't get to see much of him.

"Papa?" Akira said. "Tell me the truth. Do you think I'm smarter or dumber than Hanako?"

"Hmmm, what an interesting question. Let me think . . ." Papa slurped his soup in an exaggerated fashion. "I believe you're both exactly as smart as each other!"

Akira jumped to his feet excitedly. "That's what I think too!"

"That settles it, then," Papa replied. "If we both think it, it must be true."

Akira leaned over and held on to Papa's right arm so that he had to use his left to finish his soup.

"I told you so, Hana," Akira said.

"You never told me that!"

"Yes, I did!"

"Uh-uh!"

Baachan pushed herself up with a groan and a grunt. "Must not fight! I do not like!"

"I'm sorry, Baachan. I'm sorry, Hanako. I'm sorry, Jiichan. Mama, I'm sorry! I'm sorry, Papa." Akira paused. "Sometimes I like to fight with Hanako. But not with anybody else."

Mama looked with embarrassment at Baachan. "When I'm tired, I do let them fight."

Jiichan said, "Not to matter! Let the children to fight!"

"No, I do not like!" Baachan exclaimed.

Jiichan and Baachan scowled at each other, but then Jiichan said, "Ah, well. She is in charge of house. I always say I do not argue with my wife over house matters. So there will be no fighting, then."

But he stood up and winked at Hanako and Akira, then announced, "I will take my bath now!"

Hanako could hear him chuckling all the way to the door.

# CHAPTER
## TWENTY-EIGHT

These days Hanako was walking to and from school by herself. It was funny. She had never realized before that growing up would mean being by herself more. She liked this, because it was the first time in her life that she looked around herself and saw . . . everything. It was just her and whatever was around her. Walking to school by herself was kind of breathtaking and kind of scary, kind of lonely and kind of fun. Some of the trees were enormous, and she liked to pause to imagine how long they had been growing—probably hundreds of years, for some of them. There was one tree that seemed to be twenty times taller than she was. No doubt it started growing long before the camps, long before the

Second World War and the First World War, probably
before the Civil War, and maybe even before the United
States was a country. Maybe. Japan would have been a
country, though—it was more than a thousand years old,
at least.

Sometimes she paused on the empty path in the
middle of all those tall trees and felt a bit scared, but in
a good way. She knew she was safe because pine trees
were scattered here and there, and they warded off nega-
tive energy. Back in California, Papa had asked their
landlord if he could plant a pine in the backyard. The
landlord had said yes, so Papa planted one. For a long
time he'd never told Hanako that Shintoists believed
pine trees were full of spirits and that that was why
he'd planted it. He hadn't wanted her to know, because
believing in spirits in the pines wasn't American. Not
at all. So she had thought it was a bit of a joke when
he told her about it. Now, however, she felt certain it
was true. She could feel it every day on her way to and
from school.

Then one day, after meandering home from school,
the house was completely empty—Mama and Akira
weren't there like they usually were. After trying to
study for a few minutes, Hanako decided to walk to the

fields to see if Mama and Akira were there. She sliced two carrots for a snack and wrapped them up in a cloth.

She shivered in the cool air as she walked past a couple of old farmhouses—and there, sitting on the steps of a two-story house, were the pink-faced boy and the little one. Hanako hesitated, then moved toward them. She stopped a few feet away.

"Good afternoon! I thought you didn't have a home?" Hanako asked in Japanese.

"We're just resting. We've been walking all day and haven't gotten any food."

Hanako took two steps closer. "What's your name?"

"Kiyoshi."

Hanako thought that meant "saintly," but that couldn't be right. Or maybe he had been saintly before and the war had made him something else. "I'm Hanako."

Kiyoshi nodded without a lot of interest.

"What's your sister's name?"

Now Kiyoshi perked up. "This is Michi-chan. I call her Mimi."

That meant her name was probably Michiko, since girls' names usually ended with *ko*, which meant "child."

Mimi was staring glassily into space, as she had

been the last time Hanako had seen her. "Is she well?"

"She's hungry. You won't give us rice," Kiyoshi said accusingly.

Hanako kicked at the ground.

"Nice shoes," he remarked.

He was wearing muddy straw sandals. But when she'd first met him, he'd been barefoot, so this was an improvement.

Hanako's shoes were black with shoelaces and the slightest heels and sort of pointy toes. The pointiness was her favorite part. The leather had grown scratched and wrinkled, but they were very comfortable and still pretty. She remembered spending an hour looking through the catalog in camp when she needed to order a new pair.

Kiyoshi was really studying her shoes. "I could get food for those. I know a girl who would like those, and her family has rice."

Hanako could feel his eyes boring into her toes— her feet actually seemed to almost warm up. He raised his eyes to look into hers, as if he was pretty sure he could get those shoes from her. She steeled herself to say no. But what if he tried to take them from her? Should she run now?

But then his face turned sweet. He picked up his

sister and hugged her tightly. "She's so hungry, I feel sorry for her. . . ."

Hanako thought that over. It wasn't as if Akira could eat her shoes, right? So if she gave them away, it wouldn't hurt him. Right? And yet . . . what would she wear to keep her feet warm? She tapped her toes together. She liked these shoes a lot, but she didn't absolutely *love* them the way she did her coat. Well . . .

She reached down and pulled off her shoes, holding them in her hands, looking at them for a few seconds. Then she handed them to Kiyoshi.

*"Arigatō gozaimasu!"* he said solemnly, bowing. "You're very kind." Then his eyes seemed to be evaluating her. "If you should ever have any rice, I could get you something special. If you don't like the kimono I had before, I could get you something else. What would you like?" he asked sweetly. "I might be able to get it for you. Would you like another skirt?"

Hanako hesitated. She certainly would like another skirt—she only had two. She highly doubted that Baachan would be able to buy fabric for a new skirt for a long time. But then she said firmly, "I can't give you rice." But she thought again of Baachan. What she specifically thought of was Baachan sobbing and chasing her out of the kitchen. And she had an idea that was pretty brilliant. "I wonder, could you get a purple kimono?" she asked.

Kiyoshi's eyes lit up like pure fire. "Purple?"

"Yes. Silk."

"You have rice?"

Hanako hesitated once more, glancing over her shoulder and then back to Kiyoshi. Mimi seemed to have heard and was now gazing seriously at Hanako. *"Ettoooooo,"* Hanako said. That was the way Japanese said "ummmm." "Maybe if you found a really pretty purple kimono, I could see if I could find you a little. It must be pretty, though. Very pretty."

Kiyoshi was evaluating her again. Mimi said, "I want rice."

Kiyoshi stood up. "I'll see you soon, then," he said confidently, and walked off with Mimi on his back.

Hanako looked around again, feeling rather mixed up. Had she just done a good thing or a bad thing? That is, it was a bad thing . . . but it also might turn out to be a good thing. Kiyoshi and the little one would get rice, and she would get a special kimono for Baachan. It was a good trade for everyone, wasn't it? She could give it to Baachan for her next birthday, whenever that was. It would be a wonderful surprise! And would everyone truly be mad at her if she said she simply had to feed two children? Would they?

But her heart was very, very heavy as she continued to the field. She didn't feel right about this at all. She had spoken too quickly! She hadn't thought long enough! As she stepped into the woods, she considered rushing back to see if she could find Kiyoshi, and finally she decided to do it. But Kiyoshi and Mimi were gone now. She saw a woman carrying a baby on her back, a man with a wheelbarrow. And nobody else. So she turned once more and headed for the fields.

When she arrived, she didn't see anyone at first. Despite how beautiful everything was—the curving wheat that was more yellow than the week before, the sky that was cloudless today—she felt a stab of loneliness. She felt like the last person on the entire Earth. But then she spotted some wheat moving unnaturally. She shouted, "Jiichan! Baachan!"

The wheat started to sway, and soon Baachan emerged from the plants. In a moment Jiichan emerged as well. They weren't moving quickly, but she could feel their urgency. They looked worried, maybe because she was here and shouting for them!

She hurried forward, saying, "Everything is all right! Everything is fine!"

"You scare me!" Baachan said.

"I almost have heart attack!" Jiichan said, but he wasn't mad.

"You just come to visit?"

"Mama and Akira weren't home," Hanako explained. "I thought they might be here."

Now Baachan looked even more concerned. She glanced at Jiichan, who seemed to be deciding something. "My feeling is not good," he said. "We must go home!"

What? "What do you mean?"

"I don't know," he answered. "Let me feel in my body." He closed his eyes and held his hands slightly raised, then dropped them and opened his eyes. "No, feeling is not good. We go home now."

Hanako carried her grandparents' food basket as they hurried back home. She ran a little ahead, plunging into the forest alone, because she realized that she had a bad feeling as well. In fact, she left them far behind. When she reached the house, the sliding front door was slightly open. "They're back!" she cried out, but there was nobody behind her to hear.

She shoved the door hard all the way open. "Mama! Akira!" The doors to the bedrooms were open. But when she went into the big bedroom, it was empty. She got scared suddenly and ran outside. But she could see her grandparents in the distance, and that gave her courage. She went back inside.

She girded herself and walked into the kitchen. The cupboard doors were open! She rushed forward, saw the cupboard floor was empty. She stared at the barren stone floor and let out a soft screechy noise.

"What is?" Jiichan gasped, behind her now. She turned and saw he was out of breath.

"Nothing! It's just . . ." There had been rice there this morning! She had seen it herself!

"What is your unhappiness?" Jiichan asked urgently.

"The rice . . ." Kiyoshi had stolen it, Hanako knew it. She had let him know they had rice, and he had stolen it. "I should have stayed home and guarded the house!" She burst into tears.

But Jiichan wrapped his arms around her and said, "No, no, not your fault. You cannot know. You were look for your brother." He lifted her chin with his fingers. "Not your fault, no, not," he said firmly. "We will think what to do. We may have to spend, your father have money. Not quite sixty dollar anymore. But we will be fine." He let go of her then and searched the cupboard, even running his hands over the shelves, though he must have been able to see there was no rice. He sighed. "I know your father want to buy you food, but he also want to save for your future."

Hanako knew that Papa had received ten American dollars as a tip one day. He wouldn't say what the tip was for, but it must have been pretty bad, or good. She thought he was probably dealing with black market vendors every day. She wondered if he became a bull-dog the way Jiichan did when he was bargaining.

Baachan finally arrived and was saying, *"Nani, nani?"*

Hanako thought about telling them the whole story, but she couldn't. She just nodded through her tears. Then she ran to the big bedroom and lay on the floor sobbing. She was not a good person! She was not a smart person! She was not much of a person at all!

Her grandparents let her be, or she thought they did, but then a while later she happened to open her eyes, and it turned out they were sitting there quietly, kneeling next to where she lay. She hadn't even heard them come in.

Jiichan looked extraordinarily sad, and even guilty, as if *he* had done something wrong. "I wish I could give you better life," he said, rubbing the thin hair on top of his head. Rubbing, rubbing, until it was standing on end. "It my fault." He lifted his hands, let them fall. "Maybe if I work harder . . ."

"It's my fault!" Hanako interrupted. "I should have stayed home!"

"You are child," Baachan said. "Not your fault. We do not worry. We will use your father money. He will understand. He worry about future, but I will explain he need to worry about today. . . ."

"We have bacon grease," Jiichan said hopefully. "Ahhh, let me check. I saw in there moment ago, but let me check." He pushed himself up.

If the bacon grease was gone, Hanako would . . . something . . . She sobbed more.

"We will fry carrot tonight," Baachan said. "Carrot in bacon grease is best food. Akira will like."

Jiichan came back into the room. "Bacon grease is there! We have good luck!"

"I love good luck!" Baachan exclaimed, then began stroking Hanako's hair and cooing, "Good girl, good girl, you are good girl."

The cooing and stroking was like warmth moving through Hanako's veins. It felt so good! It was almost hypnotic. *Kiyoshi left the bacon grease,* she thought with satisfaction. He had come only for the rice. Possibly he didn't even know what bacon grease was. And she had noticed two jars on the shelves, which she knew were filled with miso that her father had gotten. She felt the despair from the stolen rice exiting her body, almost like smoke escaping. "Good girl, you are good girl . . ."

Jiichan was standing in the middle of the room holding out his arms with his eyes closed. Then he opened his eyes and said "Ahhh" with satisfaction. To Baachan, he said, "Akira is fine, I can feel. They will come home soon."

He cleared his throat and stood up extra tall. "I don't like congratulate self, but can I say one thing?" Jiichan said. "I could feel bad in my body. Yes, I could. I knew was something bad in house. But it was stolen rice, not about Akira." Then he looked at Hanako. "When you and your brother are older, I will teach you to feel good or bad inside your body. It is talent I learn during this war. The village have council meeting to support war. Every village in Japan, I believe. Everybody scared not to go. And then one day I see that some friend I can trust, and some friend I cannot. I can feel in my body who I can trust. It is good talent to learn for survive."

Hanako thought about what Jiichan was saying. "But, Jiichan, if you can't trust them, they're not your friends."

"Ah, child," he said. "In war they are not my friend. But before war they are my friend. And after. One man from village loan me his ox before war for no money because I had none. He did not ask for grain when I harvest because he know I will not have extra. He ask for nothing. So he is my friend. He will always be my friend. But during war, he is not my friend. He report anyone who try to keep extra food for their own hungry child. He report anyone who try to hide their son from army. But if same person who try to hide son ask him today, he will loan them his ox even they have nothing to give him in return."

Baachan was sadly nodding. "He lost his own son in war. He love his son the way I love you. But your *jiichan* is right, he will loan you his ox for nothing if you have nothing."

It was getting darker in the room, but for some reason, even in the dim light that hid their wrinkles, her grandparents looked older. More tired. Exhausted,

even. Today Hanako had made life harder for everybody in her house. People who only wanted to make
her own life easier. Papa always said there is no point
in your bad experiences except to learn from them. But
she had a whole trail of bad experiences behind her, and
she didn't think she had enough time even in the rest of
her life to figure out what she might have learned.

# TWENTY-NINE

It turned out Akira had wanted to see the nearby river that day, so Mama had taken him. Then he had slipped on some rocks and said he'd hurt his ankle, and Mama carried him most of the way back home. But she had to rest a lot. Then at some point he said that his ankle had healed, and he walked the rest of the way.

Mama appeared almost dazed with fatigue as she explained all this, but Akira just calmly twirled his thumbs.

"Akira!" Hanako snapped. "Why did you make Mama carry you?"

"Never mind, Hana, I'm not in the mood for

fighting," Mama said tiredly. She lay back on the floor, murmuring, "Ah, Aki, Aki, Aki . . ."

Akira drove everybody insane sometimes, the way he could make a fuss, and then it turned out to be nothing. Hanako wanted to kill him sometimes, but then she'd look at him, as now, with his big, beautiful wine stain that nobody outside of the family thought was beautiful, just playing calmly by himself. She'd had to carry him herself once, when he was three. They had walked to the edge of camp, and he didn't want to walk back because he was tired. It was summer . . . she'd been so hot. But she had done it. And for some reason, these things made her love him more, not less. She just wanted him to play with his little toys all day if he wanted.

But all of a sudden, everybody was looking at her dirty, bare feet. Just looking.

"My shoes!" she cried out. She paused: Lies or truth, which was best? "My shoes . . ." Truth! "I gave them away because—because a girl needed them more than me!"

"But Hanako! Which girl?" Mama asked.

Hanako cast her eyes down before looking up again. "Mama, I don't know the girl. It's a long story. . . ." She clutched at her stomach dramatically. "I'm hungry!"

"I'm hungry too," Akira agreed.

But Mama was weeping. "Your shoes. Your beautiful shoes."

Baachan pushed herself up. "I go cook now. I fry carrot in bacon grease! Taste good! Not worry. I will cook, and after dinner, I will make straw sandal for Hana. Not to worry!"

As Baachan left the room, Hanako knew she had to tell her mother and brother about the stolen rice. Her heart sank a little. She looked down at her dirty feet and started to talk.

"I think we ran out of rice," she told Akira. Saying that completely erased all of Baachan's stroking and cooing. She felt like an awful idiot person again.

Akira lifted his head. "I thought we had some from the butter and sugar we traded."

"We ran out because . . . I guess we just ate it all. . . . Actually, maybe it was stolen. I think it was stolen."

"Was it stolen or we ate it?"

Mama was frowning. "Hanako, we have rice. What are you trying to say?"

"It was stolen," she said. "That is . . . I think . . . I'm pretty sure it was. Nobody was home, and it got stolen!"

Mama looked stricken, so upset that Hanako had to look away. But she could hear Mama huffing as if out of breath. She had to look back then, because she'd never heard her mother breathe like that. "It's my fault," Mama said. "We should have just stayed home."

"It's my fault for wanting to go to the river," Akira pointed out. "Everything's always my fault!" He burst into tears, but for once Mama didn't comfort him. She looked too flabbergasted that the rice was gone.

Jiichan had been pacing back and forth. He stopped now. "Nobody fault!" he said. "If you get robbed, it is not your fault."

"I'm a bad person!" Hanako blurted out. She burst into tears too.

"It's my fault!" Akira screamed.

"It's my fault!" Hanako screamed back.

"Oh, Hanako!" Mama carried Akira over, so she could hold both of them at once.

Jiichan surprised everybody by laughing. "These children have many fault, *neh*? I forget children tears. I ever tell you your father crybaby when he little? *Hai*, you would not believe it today, though."

That made Hanako and Akira stare at him. Papa a crybaby?

"Only his mother could make him stop cry. I thought he grow up and still cry all time, but he stop when he twelve. I don't think he ever cry again! First we worry that he cry too much. Then we worry he never cry anymore." He shook his head. "All parent like to worry, but your *baachan* and me special because we worry all time. We never stop! He cry, we worry. He don't cry, we worry. So you see?"

Hanako didn't see, actually. "See what, Jiichan?"

"You cry, is your job. Your parent worry, is their job. So everything is fine tonight. As should be." He crossed his arms over his chest and stood proudly, almost triumphantly. "I understand many thing!"

"Yes, Jiichan," Hanako and Akira said together. And they had both stopped crying.

"Aki, I'll help fry the carrots extra-special," Hanako said. "I'll use a lot of grease."

"Thank you."

"I go get onion from neighbor," Jiichan said, his face lighting up. "Onion make everything taste good."

Hanako headed for the kitchen while Mama lay back on the floor—she said her spine ached.

Baachan had already cut a lot of carrots in three different ways, to make them look pretty. Into sticks, into round slices, and into triangles. And they did look very pretty. Baachan could make any food look pretty. Then Baachan spooned two big globs of bacon grease into a pan and set it on the stove before lighting the fire.

"Oh, you can't cook it yet! Jiichan went to get an onion from your neighbor. He said onion makes every- thing taste good."

"Onion!" Baachan said. "One time during war we run out of food and eat nothing but our neighbor onion for three week. I never like onion after that." She con- tinued to cook, with a stubborn look on her face. "I don't want to smell onion!"

Hanako liked onions a lot. She liked to put them on sandwiches, and in spaghetti, and fried in tempura batter. But she didn't say so now. She asked, "Would you have starved if you didn't eat onions?"

Baachan nodded over the food. Then her face soft- ened. "Our neighbor have baby granddaughter. They mash up onion to keep her alive. . . . Yes, I have many memory of life. When I die, will be gone. *So deshō.*"

"You can tell me all your memories. Then they won't be gone."

Baachan looked amused. "What you want with memory of onion in your head?"

"Well . . . If I write them down, then if people are starving and they find my notes, they'll know they can live on onions."

"No need to write down. When people are starve, they eat anything. Many people eat sawdust to keep stomach from feel hungry. I try myself once, but it hurt my stomach." Baachan spooned the carrots into a bowl. But when they took the carrots to Akira, he had fallen asleep on the floor.

Jiichan was just coming through the door. He held up a big onion triumphantly, but his face fell when he saw the carrots were already cooked. "But this make it taste better!" he said crossly to Baachan.

Baachan glanced at Hanako, shaking her head. "Old man and his onion!"

Baachan and Jiichan stood looking annoyed with each other. Were they actually going to argue over an *onion*? But then Jiichan tossed it in the air. "Some people eat this like apple during war," he said to Hanako. He set it on the table, then shrugged at Baachan. "I try to help, but you right, you right. I am old man with onion."

Mama stood up and pushed the bowl toward Hanako. "Hana, you eat this while it's hot. Don't let it go to waste." Then Mama pressed her palms on

Hanako's cheeks so hard it was actually uncomfortable. "I'm so sorry I didn't stay home so that you could have rice tonight." She gave her hands a little shake, rattling Hanako's brain.

"It's not your fault, Mama."

Hanako didn't actually like soft carrots, but she ate every mushy bite. She wished there was some . . . fried onion on it. But she didn't say so—it might start a war in the house! She imagined her grandparents' lives during the war: working, eating onions and sawdust, bathing, sleeping, working. And they were two of the lucky ones.

That night, after everybody had gone to sleep, Hanako lay alone next to the *kotatsu*, which had cooled off. Papa had not come home yet. It was just like the old days when he didn't get home from the restaurant until late. Hanako knew that everything he used to do—all his long hours—was so that he could afford to send her and Akira to the best college that would take Nikkei when they were old enough, if that's what made sense. If it would have made more sense for Hanako to just take over the restaurant rather than going to college, then Papa would have decided on that instead. He said you had to be flexible so that you could make the right choice. Of course, that was back when they might have expected to have choices one day. She used to think of her future as a big plate of choices, and when the time came, she would choose from the plate. Now, maybe, she was back where Papa once was. So maybe—maybe—what she should be thinking about now was making sure that her own children had choices someday. And yet.

And yet . . . it was very disappointing the way things had gone. She had been spoiled, actually. Here in Japan, she could see there were no plates of choices. She wondered how it was in other parts of the world.

The house was so quiet! Where was Papa? But she knew where he was: out selling items to black market merchants. Hanako wasn't exactly sure why some of these sales had to be made late, but she didn't ask, because the words "black market" scared her a little. Japan seemed to have a sort of orderly lawlessness. That is, the black market and life in general seemed orderly and organized, and yet the markets were illegal . . . but totally in the open. And sometimes run by "gangsters."

Once, Hanako overheard Mama and Papa discussing a vehicle that some soldiers had gotten ahold of to sell. "It's a crazy life!" he kept repeating. "It's the Wild

West, except in Japan." Sometimes she thought he was embarrassed to have fallen this far, but other times he seemed to love the wheeling and dealing.

She felt a sudden pang of hunger in her stomach. Despite all the grease she had eaten, she longed for more food. She wondered where Kiyoshi would cook the precious rice he had stolen. Did he own a pot? Did he have matches to start a cooking fire?

Sometimes it was very hard to tell the difference between right and wrong. For instance, now Kiyoshi and Mimi would eat well for perhaps a few weeks. So was that wrong? But family was the most important thing, Papa always said that. He told her once that she should always believe that Akira was more important than she was, and he told Akira that he should always think that Hanako was more important. And she had let Akira down. So was that wrong? Yes, it was.

And then she felt it again, what her teacher had talked about, the sense of being *here*. Except it was more like the *here* of pain, like if you were standing in the most beautiful place in the world, but someone you loved had just died. Like the way her mother had described it when she went to see the place where her mother had drowned, off the dazzling coast of Hawaii.

For the Nikkei from America, the grown-ups accepted this kind of pain for their children. Papa would accept any humiliation or pain or risk any scandal to get some rice and bacon grease. At the same time she knew from history books that it was not just them. It was so many people across so many centuries across so many continents. It was people in every race and of every age who had felt this pain.

When Hanako had been confused, her teacher had said, "Someday you will understand, and then you will be almost grown up." So, maybe that was now, these past few weeks here in Japan. She was growing up. That was what being hungry, and seeing your brother hungry, brought you.

CHAPTER
# THIRTY

Papa was buying two-day-old fish once a week. He'd discovered that the occupation forces had bags of salt. And the Japanese wanted salt. So he'd been getting paid with salt and then "buying" fish with this. But somehow even the fish didn't make Akira happy. He was just different somehow. To Hanako it seemed as if he'd had some energy sucked out of him. He wasn't tired, exactly. Maybe "lazy" was the word. Hanako, Akira, and Jiichan went to get butter and sugar another time, and Akira had sat in his seat and shook parts of his body almost the whole time. Sometimes he shook his head, other times a leg, and sometimes he even shook his hands quickly in the air.

And then sometimes at home he would stare at Hanako—or even just at a wall—in a way that was strange. It made Hanako's stomach hurt, actually. Could she be getting an ulcer from worrying about him? He would stare at a wall, and Mama would stare at him. Unlike Hanako, Akira couldn't remember the restaurant and that whole life before camp. Sometimes she thought maybe he had nothing to look forward to, because he couldn't remember being free and getting plenty of food at the same time. He didn't understand that it was possible to have both in your life.

Sometimes all that staring made Hanako happy to get out of the house and go to school in the mornings. She would feel relieved to stroll in the cool breeze, away from any worries for the duration of her walk.

Except for on the first day of school, the other kids hadn't seemed that interested in Hanako's Americanness. But then one day, during recess, the girls crowded around her as if by plan. "Why is your hair so long?" a round-faced girl asked in Japanese. She was even taller than Hanako, with shimmery skin and a curious air.

Hanako touched her braid defensively, though the girl didn't seem to mean any harm. "I like it this way," she replied.

"But nobody else here has hair like that," a smaller girl said. This particular girl never wore shoes, and like Hanako, she seemed to own only two skirts. "Aren't you loyal to the emperor?"

Hanako didn't know what a braid had to do with loyalty to the emperor; she didn't know much about the emperor. She knew he was the one who had made the radio announcement to all of Japan declaring that the nation was surrendering to the Allied forces. And she knew he was revered by the people and even the military. He lived in a palace. But US General Douglas MacArthur had stripped him of his divinity, so now he was a man, not a god. The general must have been an extremely powerful person to change someone from a god into a man. She could not fathom it. When she used to see the directors of the camps she had lived in, they had seemed powerful. But General MacArthur must be at a whole different level of power.

"I don't know much about the emperor," Hanako admitted.

The other girls seemed confused. "So why did you come to Japan if you aren't loyal to the emperor?" the small girl scoffed.

Hanako thought that over. "My father decided we should come here."

"So then your father is loyal to the emperor?"

Hanako squirmed and finally lied. "My father loves the emperor. He hopes to meet him one day."

All the girls giggled at that. "Nobody meets the emperor!"

Hanako remembered suddenly that the emperor's name was Hirohito, but she was sure this little snippet of information wasn't going to impress these girls. Then she felt a sudden burst of defiance.

"What does my hair have to do with the emperor?" she asked.

"It has to do with respecting *us*," the small girl said. "You were just in a war with us less than a year ago! I don't think you respect us."

Hanako started to say she was locked up, but that would open up a whole new line of questioning. So instead she simply said, "I respect everybody." That is, she was polite to everybody, even to President Roosevelt, whom she had never met. But she *would* have been polite to him if she'd ever met him. Was that the same as respect?

A girl named Ayako, who was the ringleader, hadn't

spoken yet. Her brows were furrowed, her head tilted. The other girls glanced at her. "All right," Ayako said at last. "As long as you respect us."

The bell rang, and Hanako felt like the ringing was a blessing.

Papa had taken some of his cash and bought a bag of rice at the black market in Hiroshima. He came home early just to bring the bag to them. Hanako felt incredibly relieved. She knew she'd still done a bad thing, but she felt free now. Absolved. That was really what having money could do. Like if you lost a dollar, you might get in trouble, but it wasn't a big worry if your father had another dollar to give you. She knew this because she lost a dollar once, and even though Papa scolded her, she could see he wasn't *that* upset. Not like he would be if that happened today.

So now there was rice again. As Hanako cooked with her grandmother, Baachan whistled. She whistled so much better than Jiichan could! Everybody was in an extremely good mood—she could hear Akira squealing in the other room. He used to do that a lot when Papa would take his arms and twirl him around. Papa only did that when he was in a very, very good mood. In general, he was a somewhat serious person and didn't do a lot of that kind of monkey play even before the camps. But once they were imprisoned, he was serious every second.

Hanako asked, "Baachan, was Papa a big crybaby or just a crybaby sometimes? And was he always serious when he was a child?"

"Oh, no! He silly boy many time. I cannot tell you how silly."

"Did he become more serious after he left or before?"

Steam rose from the soup, and Baachan brushed sweat from her face. "Before. Once he decide to go to America, he change. He very determine. But he happy serious." She paused and looked wistfully toward the living room. "Not like now. He very different than last time I saw him."

"Do you miss how silly he was?"

Baachan stared down at the floor, then raised her eyes. "It make me love him more now because . . . because I know life has been hard for him. I cannot stand to think of it." She wiped away a tear. "He stay in Japan, maybe life be even harder. But we try very much to make his life easy. We spoil him. Sometimes he had to work in field. Many time he had to. But then we get home from work all day, and we let him take bath first. We give him warmest blanket, we give him most food. We give him everything we can give him." She lay her hands on her heart.

Hanako took the ladle from her and stirred the soup. She thought she should change the subject, because now she had made Baachan remember . . . something. Her eyes were wet, her hands still over her heart. "Baachan, is the emperor a good man?" she asked.

Suddenly, Akira ran into the room with his shirt pulled over his head. He had his hands out in front of him and ran right into a counter. But he just laughed while Hanako pulled his shirt straight. He hadn't acted like this since they'd been in Japan. In America he used to have a kind of chipmunk-like energy, always scuttling here and there. Here he'd mostly sat still, like the old people in the restaurant used to.

Baachan nodded, then frowned, then nodded again. "Some say yes and some say no. The military cause war, not emperor. He everything, and then he nothing. He god, and then he have no power. It very hard to explain the emperor. He part of *kokutai*. You know this word?"

Hanako shook her head.

"It is spirit of Japan. No, 'spirit' not right word. I don't know right word. It is what make Japan Japan. Many people worry surrender to America would mean Japan lose *kokutai*."

"I think I understand," Hanako said. "I can tell Japan is different. You can feel it even when you're just walking down the path. I can feel it now!" She'd just realized that.

"You study emperor today?"

"No, some girls were asking if I respected the emperor."

"Girls be mean to you?" Baachan asked with concern, peering up at her.

"No, they weren't being *mean*, exactly. They kind of ganged up on me, but then they weren't mean. I think they were curious."

"Yes, you very different from Japanese girl." Baachan smiled affectionately. "But I like you that way."

"You didn't ask me if *I* know anything about the emperor," Akira suddenly piped up.

"You know about emperor?" Baachan asked in surprise.

"Yes, the name of his era is Shōwa, and that means

'bright, enlightened peace.' But there was a war, no peace," Akira said proudly. "Did you know that, Hanako?"

"No, I didn't," Hanako admitted.

"Oh, you already learn," Baachan said, looking like she'd burst with pride. "How you learn this?" She suddenly looked like she might cry again! "Only five year old and already you learn. You may be genius! We will see, but you may be!"

"Mama is teaching me. And I'm almost six." He held up his hands for no reason, admiring his sharpies. "Baachan? Do you like the emperor?"

Baachan looked left and right, as if someone might overhear, then said in a low voice, "I have not met emperor, so I cannot like. I cannot respect. There was a time, maybe I get arrested if I say such a thing as this. But to you I can say: I cannot judge someone I have not met. If I do not know how they are in their home, how can I say I like? How can I say good or bad? If I know someone, I can judge." She held her hand to her forehead as if trying to see something in the glare of the sun. "I cannot see far. I cannot see past this house, my fields, my family. That is not my life to see that far, to understand the emperor. That is not my fate. My fate is to see you, to take care of you, to cook your dinner. That is all I want."

"But, Baachan," Akira said, "don't you want to know what the emperor is like?"

She shook her head. "Maybe when you grow up, you will see beyond your home, you will know people like that. Maybe that will be your fate. It is not mine." For a moment an unexpected look almost of envy passed over her face. Then it was gone, and she said, "If that is your life, I will be proud of you. So proud." She paused. "If that is not your life, I will also be so proud of you. So you see? I will be proud of you!"

# THIRTY-ONE

In early February, for his birthday, Papa brought home a little bit of salt, and Hanako and Baachan made *onigiri*—rice balls—at dinner. Baachan also obtained a little seaweed from a neighbor, as well as what looked like about a hundred tiny sesame seeds. She cut the seaweed into different types of strips, which she wrapped around the *onigiri* in pretty ways. Then Hanako sprinkled several seeds atop each rice ball. When they were done, Hanako stared at the rice, because she wanted to remember forever how pretty it all looked. She wanted to remember forever how good it felt to make the *onigiri* for Papa. She wanted to remember forever how fun it was to watch Baachan design this

simple food like an artist. It was such a happy evening
that she could hardly sleep later that night.

A couple of weeks later they went to Kobe and got
more butter and sugar to trade for rice. But Akira and
the whole family knew some hungry hours before then.
Papa occasionally used some money to buy more rice
and once even surprised them by giving Mama money
to buy one-day-old fish when the fish seller bicycled
down the street ringing his bell. But mostly Papa was
saving . . . saving . . . for what, Hanako wasn't sure.

Coming home from Kobe—bringing back rice—
was another happy time. And yet. The very next night,
after they returned from Kobe, Hanako lay in bed and
thought of Kiyoshi, and she wasn't able to fall asleep.
She suddenly almost wanted to kill him. She had given
him her cakes in the train station, and her shoes, and he
had repaid her by stealing rice! The anger rose up in her
mouth and tasted like rotted meat. She tried to get the
thought of him out of her head, but she couldn't. It was
wrong to be bitter, Papa always said so, but what could
you do to get such feelings out of your heart?

Then she realized light was still glowing in the living room. She got up to see why and was surprised to
see that Papa was using an electric lamp.

"We have electricity?" she cried out.

"It's expensive," he said. "I shouldn't be using it, but I couldn't find the oil for the lamp."

In front of him was an electric fan, or what was left of it. Papa took things apart when he needed to relax. Hanako didn't know why he found that relaxing, but he did. To her, it seemed it would be stressful, because what if you couldn't put it back together? But usually he didn't do it unless he was deeply disturbed or concerned about something. For instance, when he took out a loan to expand their restaurant, he managed to turn their only bicycle into a pile of gears and chains and random pieces of metal that he never put back together. One time he'd shown Hanako how an electric iron worked. It had a thermostat made of bimetal, which was two different metals attached to each other. When it got hot enough, one metal curved more than the other, which turned the heat off. At least, that was the way she remembered it.

The fan's front grate and blades were lying on the floor, and he was busily unscrewing another piece. The cord was cut through, and the metal wires inside the cord were split apart at the cut section.

"Papa, are you all right?" Hanako asked after watching for a minute.

"Mmm," he said, only glancing up. "What are you doing awake?"

"I don't know. I couldn't sleep. I was just wondering what you were doing."

He looked up again, studying her, then lay down his screwdriver. "I have a lot on my mind. But tell me, how are you fitting in at school?"

"So-so. Not so much yet."

He nodded seriously. "Do you miss America?"

She thought about that. "I'm not sure," she answered honestly. She thought about how she fit in this house, but she didn't fit in Japan. "I was wondering, when do you think we could start a restaurant in Japan?"

His eyes glazed over, then he said wistfully, "It was a good restaurant, wasn't it?"

"Yes. Can we open a new one?" she persisted.

"It's complicated. . . . I guess I never told you that for three years out of the decades my parents worked this farm, they turned a good profit. All three of those years, they sent me the money. That money helped me start my restaurant. Since then they've gotten deeper and deeper into debt."

"How come they can't make money?"

"The cost of fertilizer, the cost of renting the

farmland, the rent on this house, bad crops for a few years."

"So they've had bad luck?" Hanako asked.

"Oh, no, the same luck as most tenant farmers. That's what happens when you're a tenant farmer." He sighed. "And . . . your mother got four hundred dollars from her parents when they died. And I took out a loan from a Nisei man I knew. All these things, that's how we were able to start the restaurant. Those things will never happen again." He looked at the fan, seemed to be speaking to the metal parts. "I had just finished paying the man back when we were sent to camp. And a loan from the bank to expand, I paid that back too."

*And??* "But did you ever send Jiichan and Baachan money?"

He closed his eyes and rolled his head in a circle twice, then stopped with his head bent backward for a moment before raising it again. "Only once. I prioritized paying back the man, paying back the bank, buying whatever you and Akira needed. So we were out of debt, and maybe I should have gone into debt to send something to my parents. But I wanted to buy a house someday, and they wrote me not to send them anything. They wanted you to have a house. It was a dream they had."

"But, Papa . . ."

He looked directly at her and spoke fiercely. "And that's what I want you to do to me someday, if you have to. Buy your children a house."

"But, Papa . . ." She noticed the fan was rusty and dirty, like it hadn't been used in a very long time.

"I never cared about my future. I cared about *your* future before you were even born and before I even met your mother. What is the future for you and Akira? That's what's on my mind."

Hanako considered that, then said, "I care about your future, Papa."

"I know, Hana-chan. But you mustn't. You just study hard. Do everything you can to help your grandparents. Do everything you can. But go on to bed now; you need to get up for school."

He gave her a hug, and she went back to their bedroom. Akira was whimpering in his sleep, like he did sometimes. He sounded like a little animal. Sometimes he even cried out, but not like a human. He had done this his whole life. When he was a baby, she had looked at his wine stain and listened to him whimper in his sleep, and she'd thought he was the strangest and most beautiful baby in the world. Now she lay next to him, wrapping an arm around his side and listening to the odd sounds coming out of him. For some reason, it made Hanako think about how someday Akira would grow up, grow old, and die. She could not see his future, no matter how hard she concentrated. She remembered the last thing Papa had said when the military police took him away. "Do everything you can, Hanako!" And then, right as he was passing through the doorway, "Always take care of your brother!"

At the time she'd interpreted his words as "Take care of your brother." But now she realized the "always" meant that, in the future, she would *always* have to watch out for Akira. Maybe she was just feeling this because she had her arms around him now, and he was so small. But she thought she would have to make sure to live longer than him, in case he ever needed her for anything. When Mama and Papa grew old, it would be her and not Akira who would be responsible for them, just because. He was the oldest son, but she was certain it was not his fate but hers to take care of them. Maybe she would own a restaurant too, like a little noodle café here in town, with eight or even ten tables. And maybe she would see farther than this town, she would under-stand the emperor and even beyond. In America she'd felt she could judge President Roosevelt; she had felt she knew him. So. What she wanted was to take care of her home like Baachan but to see beyond it too. But listening to the whimpering near her ear, and feeling her brother's warm breath on her cheek, mostly, mostly, she just wanted to outlive Akira, so he would never be alone. And . . . just like that, she forgave the boy for stealing the rice. Kiyoshi was feeding his little one— nothing more, nothing less. That was the way it should be. From now on, Hanako would protect the rice from Kiyoshi if she ever encountered him again. But she was not angry. She could sleep now.

# THIRTY-TWO

At school Hanako had a day when she was a celebrity. Her father had brought home three American pencils, and he gave them to her to take to class. Her classmates wrote with pencils, but there were no erasers—they used dried squid bone to white out their mistakes. So when Hanako showed everyone her pencils with erasers, they caused quite a stir. That day she seemed almost popular. Then she gave away her pencils so everyone would like her, but that didn't work. It was as if she had never given anything to anyone.

Another day the *sensei* gave Hanako a second-grade reading book to work on. This made the other kids quite surprised. "I thought she was smarter than that!" one of them said.

When the teacher turned away, Hanako closed her book in defiance, slipped off the straw sandals that Baachan had made her, and looked under her desk and wiggled her toes. She loved being barefoot in school; it made her feet feel free. So that was the best thing she could think of about going to school in Japan. Then she returned to her reading. She was happy to discover that she could get through most of the first story, a fairy tale about a girl who wore a big hat that wouldn't come off, ever. The illustrations were gorgeous, even though the pages were faded and torn.

When recess arrived, the other girls began talking softly about a book they were all reading. All Hanako could make out was that it was a "bad" book, something they weren't supposed to be reading. They giggled and screeched as they discussed it. Hanako hung on the outskirts of the conversation, hoping someone would include her. But they all ignored her. So for once she decided to speak up.

"Do you know if there's a Japanese translation of *Little Women*? I love that book," she said. She added, "I'm a very good reader."

They all looked at her, then turned away and continued their conversation.

Hanako's face got hot. She was so tired of standing by herself. Suddenly, she asked, "Would you like me better if I cut my hair?"

One of the girls evaluated her. "Maybe," she finally said, and turned away.

But Hanako didn't think she could ever cut her hair, especially not for a "maybe." So *maybe* she would never have a friend here in Japan. But she thought about it: What was more important to her—*maybe* finding a friend, or her hair?

Then, during history, Sensei decided to suddenly ask Hanako what she knew of the war. Hanako, surprised, said, "Well, I know Japan lost and the United States won."

How can you be more silent than silent? But that's exactly what happened at that moment: everybody was even more silent than they had been a minute earlier. Hanako looked around uncomfortably, expecting everybody to be staring at her. But mostly they weren't. Some had downcast eyes, but they sat very still. Then the teacher went on with the lesson.

That day after school, Mama was changing Akira's

clothes when Hanako got home—he'd soiled them for some reason, something he hadn't done in several years.

"Mama, your face is dirty!" Hanako suddenly noticed.

"I took Akira out to the fields and left him alone while I was working," Mama said. "He didn't think to just pee in the grass."

"You were working in the fields?" Hanako asked incredulously. She knew Mama had helped Baachan once, but she hadn't realized she was still working in the fields. And she felt bad, because she could suddenly see that Mama was very tired—*very* tired!

"Pulling weeds," Mama said wearily. "I want to help as much as I can. They've done so much for us." She paused. "Remember, I had that vegetable garden in our backyard one year. So I can work in the fields."

"Your garden died, Mama!" Hanako paused. "I can help too. After school."

Mama replied sadly, "I think we will all need to help eventually. But you wouldn't have to help until you have vacation from school."

Even though Hanako had just offered to work—and had been sincere—she realized she hadn't expected Mama to say yes. But she immediately said, "Yes, Mama!" It made sense to help in the fields, just as she'd had to help in the restaurant. You had to do part of your family's work.

Mama put a fake cheerful look on her face and said, "Hana-chan, how was your day? Let's talk about that! I don't want to talk about *my* day."

Hanako's mind jolted back to her day, then back to Mama. Then to both at once. Mama was doing something completely new. So Hanako exclaimed impulsively, "Mama, I want to try something new. I'm ready to have my hair cut!" She shook her head once and thought about what she'd just said. Cutting her hair? The words had simply popped into her head.

Mama looked surprised. "Are you sure, Hanako? You love your braid! And you really don't know with hair. One day all the girls will be wearing it one way, and then two months later they want to wear it another way."

Hanako reached back and fingered her braid. She squeezed it as hard as she could. She did want to keep it. She remembered how when she was young like Akira, she didn't care much if she had friends. Her family was her world. But now, if she could have just one friend, it would be worth it to cut her hair. Wouldn't it? Suddenly, a "maybe" was enough. She wanted to try. She had to do what she could do—right? "I want to fit in more," Hanako said. "I do." She squeezed as hard as she could. "Please! I want to have a friend! Do it before I change my mind!"

So while Akira stared, fascinated, Mama cut off Hanako's braid with sewing scissors. She didn't cut it to the ears, just to Hanako's shoulders. "I can't do shorter," Mama said. "I can't bring myself to do it. It looks cute like this!" Then she cut Hanako's bangs. Then she spent about an hour making little snips here and there. She kept going "Hmmm." Hanako didn't know if that was good or bad. Mama was concentrating so hard, Hanako thought her mother's head might explode. Mama even started to sweat on her forehead, though it wasn't warm.

Akira lay on his stomach, chin in his hands. Sometimes he made a face like Hanako's hair looked great, and sometimes he made a face like it looked awful.

When Mama was finished, she picked up the braid and said, "I will give this to Baachan—she'll like it." She wiped her sweaty forehead. "Thank goodness I'm not a hairdresser, the stress is unbearable! But it looks very *kawaii*," she said. That meant it looked cute.

"Does it look better or worse than before?" Hanako

asked. "Can we get a mirror someday? Are there any . . . I don't know . . . *shops* somewhere?"

"I don't know much about that. But I can promise you that your hair looks darling."

"It looks worse than before," Akira said bluntly. "But it's *kawaii* too."

"Aki!" Mama scolded.

Akira was frowning; Hanako was surprised that she didn't even feel like crying. She felt a little sad that Akira didn't like it, but she also felt a little happy and hopeful and even excited. What was the harm in trying a new thing? If she didn't make a friend, her hair would grow back. At least she had a chance now. She whipped her head around, feeling her hair swing. That felt good. Mama lovingly laid the braid on the table. She gave Hanako a look that was honestly a little silly. Goofy, even. Like the way she had looked the first time Akira took a few steps as a baby. It was a my-little-baby-is-growing-up look.

Then Mama said she wanted to return to the field to work for another hour.

"But, Mama, you look so tired!" Hanako told her.

"Remember how tired you used to look some eve-nings when you got home from working at the restaurant?" Mama said. "Of course I'm tired. But I'm not more tired than your father or your grandparents."

"But, Mama . . ." Then Hanako couldn't think of anything to say.

So they all walked out together. Hanako felt the air on the back of her neck. That was something new. Still, she was starting to feel some regret, and now she was glad her grandparents didn't have a mirror. She tried to enjoy the way the days had been turning warmer, the grass wilder and greener. Everything was overgrown; the plants scratching at her calves. Hanako paused in the path. She felt older. She felt like a young woman. Well, not really a young woman. But older.

When they arrived at the fields, Mama headed immediately into the yellow field of wheat. There was already a blanket laid out on the ground. Akira began picking blades of grass and carefully arranging them into a . . . mess. He would pick a piece of grass, think for a couple of seconds, and then set it down any old place on the blanket. Pretty soon most of the blanket was covered. Hanako was a little jealous at the way he could get so engrossed in stuff. She herself would not be entertained by placing grass randomly on a blanket.

"Do you want to play tag?" she asked, but he shook

his head sharply. So she asked, "Do you want to play hide-and-seek?" This time he just ignored her.

She leaned over to touch her toes, letting her legs hang over the blanket so as not to disturb any of her brother's grass. Her hair fell into her face as she stretched. This was something new, and she liked the feeling of her hair bouncing on her cheeks. She stayed bent over and swung her hair.

"If you froze into place like that, you would be unhappy," Akira mused. "That's how Baachan feels."

Hanako sat up. "But Baachan isn't unhappy," she said.

"That's true." He pondered the blanket and carefully set down a blade of grass. "I made her smile five times today so far. I try to make her smile ten times every day." He drew a piece of paper and a broken pencil out of his pocket. It had hash marks all over it. He pointed at a group of five marks. "This is today."

Movement in the field caught Hanako's attention. It was her grandparents and her mother starting to come out of the field, though it was still light out. They were dragging big bags—Mama clutched two. What were they doing? When they reached the blanket, Jiichan stared at Hanako for a moment—her hair—but then hissed with wide eyes, "Every day we will take some wheat to sell on black market."

"*Nani?!*" Hanako spoke softly, stretching out the last syllable. "Is that all right to do? I thought the black market was against the law."

"Yes, is against law. Government tell you what to do with your crop. But I will not listen! We will make more money this way! Sell on black market instead of to government." Then he snapped at her, "Hurry!"

Mama handed Hanako a bag and repeated, "Hurry!"

Hanako suddenly felt like throwing up. She remembered how she had felt a little sick to her stomach when Mama had sewn the twenty dollars into her pajama seam. She had thought, *What if a soldier finds the money somehow?* And yet, if the government was trying to stop you from having what was yours, then that was wrong, wasn't it? But wrong or right, the problem with governments is that they were very big and you were very small.

"Hanako, look alive!" Mama barked.

Hanako's heart was pounding. She didn't really understand any of this. She knew people sold wheat and rice on the black market, because she had seen it on the tables. But she hadn't thought that the sellers might get it from people like her grandparents. She hadn't known where it came from, really.

"Hanako, you must move!" Baachan said urgently.

Akira suddenly hopped up and pushed her away. "I'll do it!" He grabbed the bag, but Hanako snatched it away from him.

"We take chance by steal from government," Jiichan said. "I am too old to be arrest, but I feel we must do this."

There was sweat all over his forehead, dripping down into his eyebrows.

"But why can't you just sell it the regular way?" Hanako asked.

"More money this way to feed you." His eyes were shining brightly.

"But . . ."

"Why don't you buy the land?" Akira asked.

"We have no chance. There is no money. My parent farm here, and we take over, but we have no chance to buy."

Hanako gazed at the brown burlap bag she was holding. She looked up: the sky was blue, beautiful, cloudless. She looked at the bag. *Her* bag. She thought about Kiyoshi. Did he feel fear when he stole things?

"I'm not scared," she lied to Akira. "I'm never scared." She clamped a hand around the bag and pulled, walking off without waiting for anyone. "Come on, Akira. I'm not scared!"

She heard the others following behind her and felt so frightened, she wanted to run all the way home.

"Tomorrow I bring wheelbarrow to make easier to carry," Jiichan said. "But I just think of this plan right now. I was not prepare with wheelbarrow. Tomorrow I be prepare." He had tears falling down his face.

No one said a word the rest of the way, just doggedly dragged their bags. As the house grew closer, Hanako felt more and more brave. They were doing the right thing! They would sell this wheat on the black market—yes, that was a good idea. Everybody did it—that's why the black markets had wheat and rice for sale. They would have more money. Akira would grow absolutely chubby. When they emerged from the woods, however, her bravery dried up into dust. Literally anybody could see them now.

And, in fact, as soon as they were in the open, Hanako saw a woman walking by, seemingly studying them. Hanako concentrated on looking like a normal person, just out for a stroll while dragging a big bag. Her head held high, she didn't even glance at the woman as they passed on the path.

"Hanako, I'm talking to you!" she suddenly heard Akira shout.

She turned quickly, alarmed. "What's wrong?"

"I was talking to you. I was right behind you, and you ignored me."

"I'm sorry, I didn't hear you."

"How could you not hear me?"

The woman was glancing back at them, then kept walking. But Hanako got a good feeling from her, like, "We're all in this together."

"What did you want, Akira?"

"I asked if your bag was heavy."

"It's not so bad," she replied, pulling it up the steps now.

Once inside the house, she waited impatiently for the others. Mama came in looking a little dazed and lost. "Well. Here we are," Mama said.

Jiichan came in then, heading directly into the big bedroom. Hanako and Mama followed him. He went to the closet and moved a little rug, uncovering a trap-door. "We made it!" he said triumphantly. "Hana, put your bag in."

She heaved her bag over and looked into the dark hole below. "Should I just drop it in?" she asked.

"You must climb down," Jiichan said. "There is ladder."

She looked down doubtfully. What if there was a rat down there? She had a friend who got bit by a rat once. But she made her way down a few steps of the rickety ladder. Then she held out her arms for her bag. Jiichan handed it to her, and though she almost lost her balance, she held tight with one hand, using the other hand to clutch the ladder. She set the bag near the ladder. It was very dark. Why hadn't someone given her a lamp?

In a few minutes all four bags were on the floor. They were already knotted on top, and the material was very thick. But couldn't a rat get at the wheat anyway? But probably the bags would not be down there long.

She scrambled back up, eager to get out of this hole. When Jiichan had lowered the door and moved the rug back over it, she took a big breath. "That lady won't snitch on you, will she?" she asked.

"Lady?" Jiichan asked.

"The woman we passed on the path."

"She would not tell!" Baachan exclaimed. "It her son we save that night. He spent long time in locker. We sleep right here whole time, like nothing different. He sneak out in middle of night."

Jiichan pursed his lower lip, his eyes going far away. "I remember that night. I lie in bed and think, 'I know him when he baby, then little boy. Now he hiding in my closet.' Seventeen year old. This was 1944. Before that, must be twenty to fight in Army. Sometime they even pressure fifteen-year-old boy to join."

"Imagine how scared he was in your closet!" Mama exclaimed.

Hanako thought of those boys with ducktails on the barge, what it would be like for one of them to hide in a closet for such a reason. Then she wondered with alarm if there would still be wars when Akira was grown up, and whether he would have to fight in one. The thought of it made her whole chest hurt. She would make sure to build a locker under her house too, in case he needed to hide in it. She looked at her brother's burgundy Australia, the way it moved when he blinked.

"Stop staring at me," he said. "It makes me scared."

"How can I make you scared? I'm your sister!"

"You're looking at me funny." He frowned, annoyed.

She turned away so as not to scare him with her staring. She thought about how he did not give a twit about the future, how he thought about the here and now. He did not think about being hungry tomorrow; he thought about being hungry or full *now*. He was scared or he was happy or he was sad *now*. He did not know how he would feel tomorrow. He did not think about future wars; he did not think about the next day or the next or the next. It was for everybody else to think of these things for him. She had a feeling that even when he grew up, it would be this way. He was just . . . Akira.

"Sometime life good," Jiichan was saying. "Sometime life bad. This is the world, *neh?*" Then he beamed at Hanako. "But don't worry. I know you scared today. But it good day. If you knew Japan one year ago, you would see this is true. Today is very good day, this I can promise. *So darō.*"

# THIRTY-THREE

ater, while Hanako cooked dinner, she could hear Akira and Baachan laughing in the living room. It made her happy, but for some reason that feeling of loneliness engulfed her. It was a funny loneliness, though. It was a Japanese loneliness, something she'd learned about from studying poems in school—just a sense that everything at that exact moment was kind of perfect, and yet also really sad. With the excitement of stealing their own wheat, nobody had even seemed that interested in her hair yet! She did not know if she was sad or happy right now—she was free but lonely, surrounded by love but hungry. She couldn't figure out how she felt. And then she did not feel like thinking anymore. She just

suddenly ran into the living room and jealously pushed
Akira away from where he lay against Baachan's chest.

"Hanako, that's not fair!" Akira said accusingly, tugging at her arm.

But she just closed her eyes and leaned against
Baachan and smelled her musty smell, a kind of old
smell, the smell of your grandmother. And then she
wasn't lonely anymore; she was only happy. Baachan
stroked Hanako's hair a couple of times. Then and only
then, Baachan said approvingly, "Ahhh, haircut very
cute." She petted Hanako's hair.

Akira started to push at Hanako to get her to move,
and then she pushed him away, not hard but firmly.

He placed his hands on his hips, furious. He looked
kind of adorable, so she relented and pulled herself
away from her grandmother. He said "HAH!" triumphantly and snuggled into their grandmother.

Hanako finished cooking the rice, listening to
the sounds of everybody talking especially excitedly
tonight. She guessed it was good they'd gotten some
extra wheat to sell. But later, during dinner, she started
to worry that someone would come to take away the
wheat they'd hidden. She wished Papa would come
home; it would make her feel safer. After she'd eaten

and cleaned up, she sat outside until finally she saw her father's dark form appear down the road. He was walking swiftly yet somehow seemed tired. So, as much as she wanted to talk to him about the wheat, she didn't want to trouble him. He left the house at five each morning and returned at eight each night, every day except Sunday. When he arrived, she could see how exhausted he was. "Hi, Papa."

"Hanako! Waiting in the cold again?" Then he cried, "What?!" He turned her face in one direction, then the other. She'd been so worried about the wheat, she'd forgotten about her hair!

"I asked Mama to cut it. I was tired of my braid."

He closed his eyes and reopened them, as if unsure what he was seeing. "But . . . That is, it's very cute."

She could see he didn't mean it, and for a moment she wanted to cry. Instead, she said, "Thank you, Papa." She could see the fatigue in his face. He looked like he was fifty. "I just wanted to wait out here for you."

He reached out to touch her hair, and then he lifted a lock before dropping it. "It's very cute," he said more convincingly. "Did you save your braid?"

"Yes. Mama is going to give it to Baachan."

"Well, then, it's a good thing, I guess . . ."

When they went inside together, Papa handed his rucksack to Akira, saying, "There's something for you in here." Many nights, he handed his rucksack to somebody and spoke the same words. Aki excitedly opened it up, reaching and reaching and finally pulling out three tiny, green, wooden houses. "Houses!"

"They're from a game called Monopoly," Papa said. "It's a board game. One of the soldiers gave them to me to give you."

"Thank you, Papa!" He looked joyously at his little houses and set them on the table to admire. Then he picked them up and sat in a corner to play with them.

Baachan left and returned in a few minutes with a big bowl of hot soup. Papa always ate very quickly as if starving, with everybody watching him and waiting for him to finish. Then he always stopped when there were a few bites left and said what he said now: "I'm full. Does anybody want what's left?" That was Akira's cue to jump up. Today, though, Aki wanted to keep playing.

"Aki, you're getting too skinny," Mama said firmly. "Come."

He got up obediently, pocketing his houses. He didn't use the spoon, just picked up the bowl and poured the remaining soup into his mouth, some of it dribbling down his chin. "The houses are lucky," he declared after putting down the bowl. "It means we're going to get a lot of rice." He spoke shyly at Hanako. "I'll share with you more. I'm sorry I don't share more."

"You don't have to share."

Mama scooted next to Papa. "You look tired," she said.

"I do?" Papa said, pretend-jovial. "I don't feel tired!" He smiled at Akira. "How could I feel tired when I have such a wonderful son as you?"

"This is true," Akira said with pleasure, the way Jiichan would.

Papa smiled so hard, his face got all crinkly.

"Papa, in school today I learned that you should be careful what you say when you talk about war," Hanako said.

Papa nodded thoughtfully. "What did you say about war?"

"I said Japan lost."

"Nobody can argue about that. But be careful what you say. We're guests here in Japan. All right? If you want to talk about the war, you can talk to me about it. Is that a deal?"

"Yes. I didn't want to talk about it, but I was asked."

"Just be careful," he said, more firmly this time.

"Yes, Papa."

Everyone fell silent. Hanako lowered her head but looked up at the grown-ups. Who would tell Papa that they had hidden some of the wheat? She thought Mama should do it. But then Akira blurted out, "We had so much fun today! We stole some wheat and hid it in the hole in the closet!"

Another silence. "What do you mean?" Papa said, looking displeased.

"We did not steal!" Jiichan explained. "It was our own wheat. We took some to sell on black market. I cannot steal my own wheat!"

"Hanako dragged a big bag of wheat all by herself! She was scared—I saw her face!"

"I was not scared! I'm never scared!"

"I saw your face!"

"Children!" Mama said loudly.

"Everyone STOP!" Papa shouted. Then he sat down to stare sullenly at nothing at all on the table.

When Baachan rose to take Papa's bowl to the kitchen, he said, "Ah, Okaasan. Wait a moment." Then he said, "I've been thinking about something, and now I've just made a decision."

Papa looked so serious. "What, Papa?" Hanako said nervously.

Papa cleared his throat, then cleared it again. "There's an American lawyer who wants to help all of us who renounced. His name is Mr. Wayne Collins. If you would like to get your American citizenship returned, he will help you. President Roosevelt tried to get rid of us, but Mr. Collins thinks we should be able to come back if we still believe we're Americans. He feels—and I feel—we made our decision under severe duress. All of us did."

Hanako immediately turned to her grandmother, who looked like someone had just slashed her in the stomach. But in a flash her face filled with incredible passion. "There is no future for my grandchildren in Japan! There is no food, the school is old, we have no clothes, you can never have another restaurant, you will never own land. If we are arrest for stealing food, what then?"

"But, Baachan! But, Papa!" That was all Hanako could think of to say.

"Hear me out. Your mother and I talked about this last night. We made our decision to renounce while our lives were in a state of turmoil, and we should make a new decision now that things are calm. Mr. Collins says Tule Lake was an insane asylum, and President Roosevelt never should have signed the law just to get rid of us. I've heard that in America the Nikkei are building new lives. It's not easy. . . ." He took a deep breath, then fell silent, nodding his head a couple of times. "I heard about Mr. Collins from another man who gave up his citizenship. I've already contacted him, just to hear what he had to say. I did it two days ago. But I've decided tonight that . . ."

"But, Papa. Papa?" Akira said.

"Yes."

"They will cry if we leave." Meaning Baachan and Jiichan.

"I know, Aki-chan."

"I will cry too," Hanako said.

"I know, I know."

Mama was holding the back of her hand to her mouth, her eyes on Baachan.

Hanako turned to her grandmother, whose eyes were blazing. But to Hanako she didn't look *sad*. She took Hanako's face in her hands. "I want future for you. I will cry, yes. But look at my back. If you stay, you may end up like me. In Japan it is not easy to change your fate." She swept her arm upward, toward the ceiling. "There is so much for you to do. You will not do it here. I say this before: especially for granddaughter of tenant farmer, it very hard for tenant farmer to escape her fate in Japan."

Jiichan cleared his throat twice like Papa had. Then three times, as if they were in a throat-clearing competition. He sounded as if he were trying to clear something really big out of his gullet. When they all looked, he stood tall and spoke like he was making an announcement. "Yes, it must be so. I am strong. You will not accept your fate because you know it is not really yours. You are American." He spoke like he was the president making a speech, except in his funny little voice.

It was very hard, because . . . Hanako knew that she did not want a back like Baachan's. She did not want to be a tenant farmer one day. If she were going to be a farmer, she would at least want the chance to buy her farm. She had not even known Baachan's fate was a possibility for herself; she had not really thought that she would end up that way. Baachan was perfect, but . . . it was not what Hanako wanted. Visions of her noodle restaurant withered away to nothing in her brain. She felt that old anger rise up in her, the anger that made her squeeze her fists, which she did now. But then Baachan ran a hand gently over Hanako's, and now it was the anger that withered away until it was gone. Gone, because Baachan's hands were somehow more powerful than her own.

# THIRTY-FOUR

So Papa was working on getting them back to America, but they hadn't heard more for a couple of weeks. Hanako even wondered if it would really happen. She began to think of her noodle restaurant again. One warmish Sunday, Jiichan and Hanako set off to climb a nearby mountain together. He said she had gotten too tense. And he said it was something just for him and her, since sometimes he liked to focus on her and Akira separately. Usually he paid attention equally to both of them, but he seemed to think that sometimes it was good to concentrate on just one at a time.

In the distance the mountain was green with foliage. Hanako felt a little shy to be with her grandfather alone. Farmhouses were scattered on the sides of the road they took. She took off her straw sandals and felt the cool grass on her feet.

They walked silently until Jiichan suddenly pointed to the grass. "*Zubona!* Usually it grow by river. You suck on leave." He leaned over with a grunt, tore off a leaf, and handed it to Hanako.

She put the plant in her mouth, sucked on it, and grinned. "Sour!"

Jiichan plucked off a leaf. "I like *zubona* when I boy." But after he sucked on his leaf, he spit it out. "Ah, why I ever like that?"

The mountain was towering over them now. Farmhouses were clustered along the base. The road led right up to a path, which in turn led right up the mountain.

"People live here by mountain in Kofun period. You know Kofun?"

She searched her brain. "Well, Akira says we're in the Shōwa period. . . . That's all I know."

"Kofun, ah, maybe fifteen hundred year ago. That would be about when giant tree there was just a baby." He pointed at a massive tree along the road. "That oldest tree in Hiroshima-*ken*."

Along the base of the mountain were many trees

Hanako didn't recognize. On the mountain itself were mostly majestic pines. Jiichan began the climb upward and did not seem to be growing tired. In fact, Hanako grew more winded than him as they ascended the path. She checked the base of each tree for mushrooms. Jiichan had mentioned a special, expensive mush-room called a "matsutake." Maybe there would be a rogue matsutake growing early. She didn't know what it looked like, but if she saw any mushroom at all, she would point it out to her grandfather.

"Maybe I'll find a matsutake!" she said.

"Matsutake!" He shouted it like a battle cry. "If you find, your *baachan* cook and you have first bite. Worth many money. Nothing else taste same. Ah, I should not say, since I never eat. But I have many imagination." There was a bush with flowers and another with hard red berries. "Many more flower in spring will come," Jiichan said.

They grew quiet again as they made their way up a steeper section. Suddenly, Jiichan sat down.

"Are you all right?" Hanako asked, concerned.

"I walk very much, but I don't climb high so much." Then he smiled and said, "Very good now." He got up and kept climbing. Hanako kept looking to see if her grandfather was all right, but he didn't seem tired at all now.

It took two hours to reach the summit. The whole way up they moved in the shade of pine trees. But still they were sweating. When they reached the top, Hanako ran to an outcropping of tan rock and put out her arms as if she were hugging it. She didn't know what kind of rock it was, but she saw a small stone on the ground and kissed it before putting it in her rucksack. She would save it as her special spending-the-day-with-Jiichan rock. Then they sat down to a lunch of rice and *tsukemono*—pickled vegetables.

Jiichan gazed out at the farmhouses in the distance. "First time I climb mountain in twenty year. Mountain special place to Japanese. Our whole country mountain everywhere." Hanako didn't say what she thought: *I know.* He was nodding away, then started humming before he stopped to speak again. "Twenty year ago I climb here with your father." His eyes went out of focus. "That day he tell me he go back to America when he eighteen. So that sad memory, but it also good he tell me because then I know to enjoy next two year most I can enjoy." He pressed his lips together and looked down at the remains of his lunch. "That night my wife cry very hard but very quiet so he not hear." He smiled at Hanako. "And now you here, and every night she happy." He nodded. "You special girl."

Hanako looked down bashfully. She said, "Thank you for coming here with me. Now I have a Japanese mountain rock."

"Girl who like rock. I wish I know this all my life. I see many rock in my life. I could have save for you. Then you have too many rock."

They laughed and finished eating. As they climbed back down, Jiichan said over and over as if it amazed him, "Girl who like rock! I wish I know. I wish I know!"

# THIRTY-FIVE

When Hanako had first gone back to school after cutting her hair, everyone had noticed— she could tell by the way they stared—but nobody said a word. It was like she was this kind of strange America-*gaeri* who occasionally did kind of strange America-*gaeri* things that they all took note of, and then they went about their normal lives and forgot about her.

But she starting thinking about how at camp, random kids were often joining in with other groups of kids without being invited. She just needed to put herself forward.

So one day at recess, a group of girls gathered

around Ayako, who apparently had received a note from a boy. Which boy, Hanako didn't know. But she walked straight over to the group and lurked briefly at the edges. She cleared her throat the way Jiichan sometimes did, and a couple of girls glanced at her, but that was it.

"Was it Nori? He's the cutest boy!" Hanako exclaimed in Japanese.

The girls all turned to her as one, and then Ayako said in a friendly voice, "Yes, he is!" As soon as she said it, they all looked around and giggled, as if Nori might have heard. Nobody seemed to mind that Hanako stood near them the whole time, listening and laughing when someone said something funny.

When the bell rang, one of the girls even looked back at her and said, "Come on!"

That just made her so happy that she half skipped all the way inside! If Wayne Collins got them back their citizenship, even if it took a year or two, she would have time to make some friends, she decided. She had no idea how long something like getting back your citizenship might take. In general, as she understood it, lawyers took a long time to do . . . whatever it was precisely that they did.

In class she felt pleased that she'd made so much

progress today. Her mind wandered, thinking of her friends at Tule Lake and how some of them had abandoned her after they learned her parents were renouncing their citizenship. Others befriended her for the same reason. She had lost her best friend, Reiko, even before Papa renounced.

In 1943 the American government had given the Nikkei in camps questionnaires attempting to separate "loyal" from "disloyal" inmates. The government—Papa often just called them "they"—wanted to induct the "loyal" men into the army, so they needed to figure out who was a loyal American and who could be discarded as disloyal. Papa had said "they" were midlevel government workers: "Any old idiot can decide your entire fate. That's the way government works." Papa had spoken his mind on this questionnaire. Where it asked whether he would be willing to serve in combat duty, he said he would do it *gladly*, if his family's civil rights were returned. There was another "loyalty question," but he had answered "yes" to that. So that single answer, where he mentioned their civil rights, was why he was brought in for questioning and eventually branded "disloyal" and the family was sent from Jerome to Tule Lake.

He was a "no-no boy." That's what the "disloyal" people were called. Hanako remembered feeling shame at first. Yes, shame even of her own father, for being a "no-no." All the way on the train to Tule Lake, she had felt ashamed. A lot of people from Jerome had been "no-nos," though, more than at any other camp. So that helped a little. It was just that her best friend and her family were *not* "no-nos."

Reiko. With her funny, loud laugh—and her speedy feet. When they were running away from mischief, Reiko always got way ahead and then waited for Hanako. They had been friends for a long time, because they'd gone to school together before the war and had both ended up in Jerome. Reiko's father had answered "yes-yes" to the loyalty questions. Then he had been drafted and fought for the 442nd, the combat unit made up of Japanese American men. It became one of the most decorated combat units in American history. Its motto was "Go for broke," and it had suffered massive casualties. Reiko's father had been killed helping to liberate an Italian town. Reiko's letter to Hanako about her father's death had been filled with fury, as if his death were Hanako's fault. But for no reason: Why was it *Hanako's* fault? Reiko called Papa a coward.

No matter how much that had hurt Hanako, in Tule Lake she had become incredibly proud of her father for standing his ground and asking for their civil rights back before he would serve. And she was incredibly proud of Reiko's father and so sad that he had died. But she understood why they could no longer be friends. It was because both of their fathers had done what they knew was right, and those were two opposite things.

"Tachibana-*SAN*!" The teacher was rapping her stick on Hanako's desk! That was all the *sensei* said, though. She started lecturing on poetry, no doubt what she'd been doing while Hanako wasn't paying attention.

Sensei wrote a poem on the board, and they all recited it together:

> From the white dewdrops,
> Learn the way
> To the pure land.

The bell rang, and after cleaning the floor, a couple of the girls said good-bye to her! She bowed her head respectfully as she said good-bye back.

She walked home down the quiet path, surrounded

by trees and grass and blue sky. It had not been a bad day, not at all. Now everything was so peaceful. She could not imagine what it would be like to have bombs falling on her city. It just went to show that there was always something worse than your situation, and probably always something better as well. All she could do in life was what Papa said: "Do everything you can." But it was also possible, she knew, that things could be so bad that there was nothing worse. She knew this because she had seen Hiroshima.

When she arrived home, Mama was outside rocking Akira, who was crying. Hanako dropped her backpack and ran up. "What is it?"

"He's sorry he broke open his geode."

Hanako saw the broken rock on the ground, and it was sparkly inside. Very pretty! Hanako knelt before him. "But it's beautiful inside! Aki, it's the most beautiful thing I've ever seen!"

Aki shook his head no. "I'm having a bad day. I want to go back to camp." He grabbed Hanako's arm and looked at her pleadingly. "I'm hungry. I haven't had peanut butter since we got here! Let's go back to camp."

"Aki!" Mama said in a moment of anger. "Don't talk like that!"

"But I *am!*"

Hanako picked up his hands, noticed his sharpies were getting dull. "I tell you what. I'm going to cut your nails extra-pointy tonight. And I promise you that someday you can have everything you want to eat. I'll cook . . . spaghetti and ice cream for you!"

He stopped crying. "How do you cook ice cream?"

Well . . . she hadn't exactly meant to say that. "It's a surprise."

Akira seemed to be weighing her words, then carefully gathered up the pieces of the geode and cupped them in his hands. He was half smiling, his face satisfied. "Can I put these in your special bowl later?"

"Of course. You can have my bowl," she said, and immediately regretted it, even though it made him happy.

They went inside, where he set the pieces of the geode on the *kotatsu* table so he could show everyone later. Next, they played what seemed like a hundred and twenty rounds of Go Fish. Akira was deeply involved, concentrating for several minutes sometimes before deciding what card to ask her for. Then someone knocked at the door. Hanako slid it open, and there was a little boy who looked about four. Down the walkway was a woman who must have been his mother. She was holding an unlit lantern, as it was still light out.

The boy held up a pair of small shoes. "I have nice shoes for rice," he said.

His mother called out, "Look cute!"

"We don't have rice, I'm sorry," Hanako said. She thought about the wheat Jiichan had stuffed into the locker. The boy was quite adorable. But she said firmly, "We have nothing." Tomorrow Jiichan was planning to sell the wheat in the locker on the black market while she was at school. They had "stolen" much more, and Jiichan separated the grain from the straw. They had quite a bit. Hanako tried not to think about it, in case the boy could read her mind. The boy ran to confer with his mother, and then they walked off. Hanako noticed that he was barefoot. Akira was leaning around Hanako.

"*Konbanwa,*" he called out to the boy. "Good evening," though it wasn't evening yet.

"*Konbanwa,*" the boy said back.

"He's hungry," Akira said. "I feel bad."

"You're hungry too," Hanako said coldly. "That is more important." To her. It was more important to her.

"Why is it more important if I'm hungry?" he asked curiously.

Mama interjected, "Nobody is more important than anybody else, Hanako." That was a scold.

But Hanako raised her chin and refused to concede. To her, Akira was more important. But sometimes at night, when she felt hungry, she had an awful thought: that she was more important than anybody in the whole world. When you're very hungry, that's unfortunately the way you feel. Sometimes it took everything she had to be able to share a single carrot with her brother. It took such a big effort that she would feel worn out afterward, like she had just walked ten miles. Sometimes she would give him half her last carrot, and later in bed she would cry about it. Did that make her a terrible person? She just didn't know.

## THIRTY-SIX

Hanako woke up in the middle of the night. She heard muffled yelling. For a moment she froze in fear, but then she pushed herself up and moved quietly to the bedroom door. She wondered if she should wake up Papa. But he was always so tired. She slid open the door, then closed it behind herself. The sounds were coming from the other bedroom. It had to be Baachan's voice she was hearing, but it was so frantic and intense, it was unrecognizable to Hanako. Were her grandparents fighting? That seemed impossible to believe.

She crept toward their room, until she could hear more clearly. Baachan was sobbing. "You must tell them to stay! You must tell them!"

Hanako felt like . . . like something truly awful had just happened, like someone she loved had just died. She put her hands over her ears as Baachan yelled, but then she *had* to hear and took them off again.

"It is good for the children to go," Jiichan was saying in Japanese. "They are hungry for better food than we can give them. They need a good education. There is no future for a tenant farm girl in Japan except to get married and work on a farm she will never own. She will never make money, and then she will die. They must leave."

"Please, *please* tell them to stay! You are his father—he will listen to you!"

Then there was no more talking or shouting, just sobbing.

Hanako stood in the dark living room undecided. Should she go to their room or back to hers? She closed her eyes and thought hard. Then she opened her eyes and moved forward.

She waited outside their door for a few more minutes, then said softly, "Baachan?"

The crying immediately stopped. Jiichan opened the door. "We have awoke you?"

"I get up in the middle of the night all the time,

almost every evening," she said, though she hardly ever got up in the middle of the night. She was almost as tall as Baachan, but she suddenly felt very small and very young. "We can stay, Baachan," she declared.

"I am sorry," Baachan said. She leaned over, trying to bow, but she couldn't because of her back. Then she knelt down. "I am sorry. I should not have said. You must leave; I know this."

"We can stay, though," Hanako insisted. "We don't even have anywhere to go in America."

"You will find your place," Jiichan said urgently, like it was extremely important for her to leave Japan.

"Anyway, we have more time, maybe two year with you," Baachan said. "It will be happy time of my life. I will not cry when you leave. I promise I will not cry again."

"Oh, I cry all the time!" Hanako said. "There's nothing wrong with crying. Look at Akira—he cries almost every day!"

"The child may cry to the parent," Baachan said, swatting at the air. "I must not cry to you. You are try to grow up. It does not help if I cry."

Jiichan placed his hand fondly on Baachan's back.

"You old woman! You cry your whole life! You will not stop now!"

Baachan smiled then, and he smiled too. They seemed to have forgotten Hanako was standing there as they smiled at each other. He wrapped his arms around her, and Hanako knew it was time for her to slip out. She moved through the living room slowly, so as not to walk into anything, and when she lay down, she felt wide awake. But she did not feel like crying, not at all. She just felt . . . like she wanted to lie here forever, in this house, surrounded by her family. She concentrated on her family being all around her. Akira was whimpering, though, very sadly. Nobody had said so, but she knew that if she did not have much future in Japan, neither did he. He would end up working on the farm as well. Not owning it or anything. Not making money. Just working to survive. Six days a week if he was lucky, seven if he was not. If they stayed, that was surely his fate.

## THIRTY-SEVEN

The next day was Saturday. The Japanese had a half day of school on Saturdays. But nobody had woken Hanako up, and when she got out of bed, she saw that it was too late to leave now. The house seemed silent, and in the living room she found a note saying that Mama had taken Akira next door, where they'd been invited for tea. Everyone else would be at work, even though Hanako could hear that it was raining. There was a knock on the door—Hanako was in her underwear—so she put on her coat and ran to answer.

It was Kiyoshi! And very suddenly her anger returned! It just exploded inside of her! What did he want from her now? At least he'd bothered to knock this time.

Kiyoshi held out something wrapped in news-paper. His face was proud as he bowed deeply, still holding out the package. "This is for the rice," he said in Japanese.

She froze while the anger began to fade away. His hair was wet from the rain. And where was Mimi? Kiyoshi stood up straight and pressed the package into her hands. So she reached out and slowly unwrapped it. It was a kimono—a *purple* one. It made her heart flutter like butterfly wings. She could not say it was beautiful, exactly—that is, not beautiful in the way a wedding kimono was. But it felt like nice silk, and the flower decorations were pretty.

Upon pulling out the kimono to inspect it further, Hanako saw that it was prettier than she had thought. The bottom six inches were a darker purple, and then the very bottom was trimmed in lilac. There were scat-tered white flowers in the dark purple section. It was actually quite dramatic. She put it on over her coat; she had never worn a kimono before. It was too big, so it would be even bigger on Baachan.

She felt different, like she was in a different world, in a different time, like this kimono had the power to transport her. She imagined being older, standing

next to a man she loved. Baachan and Jiichan would have been happy the day they married. Baachan would not have thought that someday her back would be bent. Probably she would have hoped for more than one child. Hanako felt as if, in this kimono, she could understand how Baachan felt on her wedding day.

Then she remembered that Kiyoshi was standing there. He was looking at her with genuine curiosity. She took off the kimono and carefully folded it up. She wasn't even sure when Baachan's birthday was, but she would save it for then. She inhaled deeply; the air smelled of rain. So she had done a bad thing by hinting to Kiyoshi about the rice, but now a good thing had come out of it. Maybe she would never be in the right on this subject, but at least she would not be so terribly in the wrong now. Maybe.

Kiyoshi bowed. "You might not think it, but I try to be honorable. That's how my parents raised me. Is it good enough for the rice?"

"Yes, there's something very special about it." Actually, she used the word *irei*, which meant "unprecedented" or "exceptional." She wasn't sure that was the way *irei* was supposed to be used—was it too formal? But she was concerned with something more important.

"I was wondering, where did you get it?" Hanako asked. "Did you steal it?"

"I worked for it."

She wasn't sure if he was lying—she just couldn't tell. "What did you do for it?" she asked suspiciously.

"I put Mimi on my back and knocked on every door asking if they had a purple kimono. I said I would work for it. Not in this village, in a different one. Mimi and I have walked a lot." He held up one of his shoeless feet, and Hanako saw it was raw.

"Oh! Does it hurt?"

He laughed—*at* her, like she wasn't very bright. "I was in a bomb—I don't care about the bottom of my feet!"

She glanced toward the door. "Maybe we have a bandage."

He shrugged, as if uninterested.

"Well. Thank you very much for the beautiful kimono. It's a gift for my grandmother. And thank you for being honorable." She bowed to him, and he bowed again. "But where is Mimi now?"

"She's in the orphanage in the city. Sometimes we stay there. I left her there because it's raining so hard. Usually she's with me every second. I walked here in the rain."

"So you live in the orphanage now?"

Kiyoshi frowned. "No. I don't like it. Too many rules. It's not like the way my family treated me. I always got my way at home." He stuck out his lower lip petulantly, just like Akira might, then idly scratched at where his ear had once been. "My scars still itch . . ." He began to scratch quite hard—furiously, even.

"Don't hurt it!" Hanako called out, as if he were ten feet away.

He looked at her like he was certain now that she was very stupid. "It doesn't hurt! It itches!" Then he tried scratching his back. "I don't know why, sometimes I itch all over at the same time! Scratch my back for me!" He sounded frantic over how itchy he was as he turned his back to her.

Hanako reached out, her hands lingering doubtfully near his back. Her hands dropped, then lifted again to twist her braid nervously . . . but it was gone. Kiyoshi wasn't wearing a jacket today; finally, she lifted his wet shirt with her left hand and tried not to gasp. His back was covered with scars. They were raised up from the surface of his skin at random, some like splashes and some bigger and attached to other big ones. She felt almost panicked, just at the pain and what must have been the terror in the moment when he got those scars. The noise . . . the horror. Then, as strange as it was to scratch the back of someone she didn't really even know, she began to anyway, as gently as she could.

"Harder!"

But she couldn't. "I don't want to hurt you."

"Mimi scratches harder than *you*!"

So she scratched harder. His scars were so bumpy! And he was so skinny! His waist was smaller than hers.

"Harder, I say!"

She felt like she might swoon, like one time when she cut her knees and they bled profusely. She had been running wild with some other kids and had slipped and scratched both knees. How she had cried! It had hurt! But her scratches hadn't even left marks—nobody could even tell where she'd been hurt. Now she pressed into Kiyoshi's scars, moving her nails up and down and across his skin. His scars turned red as she scratched, and it made her feel seasick.

"Ahh, thank you, that's enough," he said. "Thank you. My back hasn't felt so good in a long time! You did a better job than Mimi."

She let his shirt drop down. She didn't know what

he saw in her face when he turned back around, but he snapped, "Don't feel sorry for me—I don't like it."

"I don't! I mean, I'm sorry. I mean . . ."

He touched the front door. "I had a door once," he mused. "We had a pretty good house." He patted a wall. "A very solid house. My father and uncles built it themselves." He looked at her like Mama did sometimes, when she was trying to see into Hanako's brain. "Can I tell you something I've never told anyone?"

"Yes," she said eagerly. She didn't want to think about his old house, his scars, the bomb.

"This is something I will never tell Mimi. But I've wanted to tell someone since it happened. I was reaching up into our apple tree when the bomb went off. I loved apples. I was knocked unconscious, and when I woke up, my back felt like it was on fire. . . . Maybe it *was* on fire. I looked around for my parents to help me. I was supposed to be at the factory like all the kids from my class, but I felt so tired that day that my parents let me stay home. That's why we were at the apple tree, because my mother always said apples were one of the healthiest foods. She was hoping one was ready to pick, though it was only August." He was talking swiftly, like now that he had started telling his story, he had to get it out all at once. "Anyway, I woke up after the bomb, and I saw a—I guess you could call it a person . . . wandering nearby. I didn't know if I was looking at the front of their body or the back. They had no face and no hair. Then I realized it was my mother. I don't know how I knew." He looked at Hanako as if she could *help* him somehow.

Hanako couldn't move, her arms raised slightly, her mouth slightly open. All she could think of to say was "Oh . . ." Her mind went blank. She started to say she could scratch his back again, but . . . the pleading look on his face—what did it mean? She picked up one of his hands and held it in hers. "I—I can picture it. . . . You're doing a good job telling the story." Was that a stupid thing to say?

But he looked relieved. "Can you picture it? Can you? I want someone to understand! So I picked up a board. I was going to kill her so she wouldn't suffer, but then I couldn't." His face got all contorted, his eyes squeezed shut. He opened his eyes again, now filled with tears. "I was a coward. I'm disappointed in myself. *I hate myself.* We just stood there looking at each other. She tried to reach out, but she couldn't really lift her arm. I think she was trying to talk, but she couldn't—

she didn't have a mouth. Maybe a minute passed while she suffered. Then she lay down, just like she was lying down to sleep. She didn't collapse—she lay down gracefully. She always did everything gracefully. My mother was the most graceful person I ever knew." He was crying now but managed to say proudly, "Mimi is going to be just like her."

And so. And yet! Hanako's mind went back and forth. She wanted to give him rice, and yet . . . she loved her brother so much. She loved her whole hungry family. So much! But then she thought of how her father had said, "Do everything you can." Maybe . . . maybe? So she asked, "Can you work in the fields for my grandparents? Your hand . . ." She glanced at his claw hand that she was still holding.

Fury—maybe even hate—flashed across his face. "I can do anything with my right hand that I can do with my left!"

"Maybe I can ask my family if you can work for them? They will need help. They raise wheat and rice and vegetables. They could pay you with food . . . maybe."

His eyes suddenly got that evaluating look, the one that scared her. Like he was trying to make sure whatever she was saying was a good deal for him, or whether in fact he could manipulate her into a better deal.

"That might be a good idea," he finally decided. "But for rice. I'll only work for rice," he added, bargaining.

Hanako nodded, bobbing her head up and down over and over. "I'll ask them. How will I find you?"

"I'll come back when I can. I might have to go to school if I stay longer in the orphanage."

"All right. Well . . . Thank you for the kimono. I've never seen one like it."

He bowed his head stiffly and held up his hand in a casual wave, but before walking off he asked, "What's your name again?"

"Hanako."

"I've never met a Hanako," was all he said.

She paused before asking, "Kiyoshi? And then? What did you do next? After your mother died?"

He cocked his head and looked at her with genuine curiosity, as if he had asked *her* a question. Then he said, "I looked for my father and saw him in a heap. I rushed away—it was too awful to see my parents like that. So I wandered around in a daze, and I saw many other people wandering. People with blackened skin, bleeding people, people who looked like they must be dead, and yet they were walking. I headed toward the countryside; even through the pain, I kept walking. Then I had to stop. I just lay down and decided to die. It was time to die, for certain. The pain in my whole body was everything in the world as I lay there. I guess I passed out, and when I opened my eyes, it was night. It was while lying and looking up that I really noticed, for the first time in my life, how beautiful and full of stars the night sky was. I had been working so hard, and there was so much going on during the war. I never had a chance to look at the night sky like that before. That was when I decided to live after all."

He turned around and walked off into the rain. She wanted to ask him to come in and wait out the downpour, but at the same time she found herself actually a little scared of being alone inside with him. He was a boy who might try to be honorable, but he was also a boy who would do what he had to do for his sister. She knew this like she knew her name.

It was raining furiously by now. She couldn't even see where Kiyoshi had gone. "Kiyoshi!" she shouted. She should invite him in after all! She ran down the steps and called again. "Kiyoshi!" For a full minute she stood shouting. Then, standing there alone in her coat and underwear, the rain falling as hard as she'd ever seen it fall, falling almost in sheets, she burst into tears. She cried for . . . everything . . . for the girls and boys with perfect hair locked up in camp, for the way her father's face had aged, for her sweet, sweet grandparents. But mostly, right at this moment, she cried for the horrible pain Kiyoshi must have felt the day the bomb fell. The pain outside that she hoped was gone for him now, and the pain inside, which she knew would never leave.

# THIRTY-EIGHT

Hanako hid the purple kimono in the closet, in her mother's empty suitcase. She was afraid of wrinkling it, but she did not know where else to hide it. Though she kept a lookout, she did not see Kiyoshi anywhere. Days passed, then weeks. Thinking of him, she also looked for an opportune time to ask her grandparents if they needed help in the field. But when she finally did, they said not now.

Spring vacation from school started in March. Jiichan was extra busy preparing the paddy for the rice planting while Baachan made a special bed to plant the rice seeds. Later, once the seeds sprouted, they would be transplanted into the paddy. At that point Mama,

Hanako, and Akira would help with the transplanting. The reason they weren't helping now was that Jiichan and Baachan needed everything perfect so that they would get a good crop. "I cannot concentrate enough if I know you watch," Jiichan explained. "And you cannot help, because it must to be perfect."

The transplanting would also need to be done perfectly, but Jiichan was most worried about the "foundation." He kept saying, "Foundation must be best you ever do, every year."

When it was time to transplant, the five of them stood looking upon the field. Jiichan, wearing a bright blue shirt that had been hidden away in a closet, was holding an old *taiko* drum. Baachan wore a bright blue cotton kimono and her big straw hat. Jiichan said he didn't know the ancient rice-planting rituals, nor had he ever been to a modern rice-planting festival such as some villages held. But he and Baachan performed their own small ceremony every spring before the transplanting. "If last year crop good, we do same ceremony again. Otherwise, we make small change to next year," he told them, then added, "In spring spirit come down from mountain to watch over all the rice field."

He used his fingers to play a simple but hypnotizing

rhythm on the drum. He and Baachan swayed their bodies with the drumbeat, so Hanako, Akira, and Mama joined in. "I pray for many good rain to help rice grow," Jiichan called out.

Baachan said loudly, "I pray for many rice to feed my grandchildren."

"Hanako!" Jiichan shouted.

She reared back in surprise—she didn't know she was expected to speak! What should she say? Arghh! "Uh, springtime is . . . uh, the time for planting rice!" she cried loudly into the wind.

Akira was ready:

> Cool melons–
> turn to frogs!
> If people should come near!

Mama seemed a little self-conscious, but then shouted fiercely, "Please, fields, feed my children!"

Then Baachan and Jiichan took off their special clothes, revealing their regular outfits underneath.

Everybody got to work. The seedlings were several inches high. A pleasant breeze blew ripples across the long stretch of muddy water in front of them.

"Perfect planting weather," Jiichan proclaimed.
Then he turned to his grandchildren. "I make this long
time ago for when I have helper," and out of a bag he
drew two long pieces of heavy twine secured at both
ends by pegs. There were beads tied into the twine.
Jiichan gave an end to Hanako and pulled her over
to one side of the paddy. Then he stuck in a peg and
instructed, "You hold this in. Do not let it move. I beg
you for not let it move."

He walked across the paddy as Hanako rested a
foot on her peg. When Jiichan reached the other side,
he began to push his own peg into the mud, pulling

the twine taut. Hanako was so busy watching him that she lost focus, so when he pulled on the twine, her peg slipped loose. She quickly put it back, pushing her hands deep into the mud. When she stood back up, her grandfather was watching her with his hands on his hips. Then he stuck his peg in. Hanako hung on to the peg for dear life!

Baachan, cupping twenty or so seedlings in her hands, said, "Now I show you how to do. You take seedling"—she held one up—"and plant into ground like this. Put it right here at bead." She plucked the seedling neatly into the mud, and it stood straight up like it had been growing there all along! It actually looked happy! Then she quickly and efficiently set two more in at the next two beads. "Now you put one at bead."

Baachan handed one to Hanako and watched. Hanako carefully stuck hers into the ground. It tilted at an angle. It looked sad! She looked up doubtfully at Baachan, who was looking very, very disturbed.

Then Baachan cheered up. "I show again." She gently pulled out Hanako's seedling and placed it so that it stood straight up . . . and somehow looked happy.

Hanako tried again, and her seedling didn't stand

straight, but it did stand straighter than her previous attempt. She was rather pleased, but when she looked at Baachan, her grandmother's lips were pressed together.

It took twenty minutes for Hanako to get it right. She was shamed, because Akira was working with Jiichan, and her brother's seedlings were flawless. He was spending a long time on each one. He stared at the mud like a chess player thinking out a move. Then he moved in slow motion and plunked the seedling into the mud.

She'd noticed that in all the fields she'd seen in Japan, the plants were perfectly aligned.

The field used one of the nearby rivers for irrigation and was deliberately flooded, the water reaching half-way up Hanako's calf. On her own now, Hanako delicately placed a seedling into the mud and was surprised that it stood straight up. She did another, but she could see that the plant wasn't exactly straight. She wondered whether it really mattered whether it was straight up or not. She pulled it out three times to get it right, but then she worried that it was worse to keep pulling it out than for it to grow slightly crooked. What if she were hurting the seedling? It would never be happy!

Hanako did twenty feet, and it took her about an hour. Meanwhile, she couldn't even count how many rows her grandparents had done. Her mother was third fastest. Akira was the slowest, but to Hanako, his little row seemed like a work of art.

She stood up and arched backward. Her spine was already bothering her. She worked for another two hours, and finally Baachan came over and said, as if relieved, "That enough. You work hard enough. We all take break. Except your *jiichan*. He don't like break."

Hanako had never been so glad for a break in her life. But just as she stepped out of the paddy, Akira squealed, "Look at Hana's legs!"

Hanako looked down and screamed. Leeches!

Mama and Baachan hurried over. "What happen?" Baachan asked.

"Leeches!" Hanako cried, pointing. There were three of them attached to her shins. They were dark green and ridged and longer than her pinky. She had never seen a leech before except in books. They were so ugly, they were otherworldly. And they were attached to her leg! As if they thought it was theirs!

"Ah, yes, field has leech." Baachan reached into a pocket and pulled out a slender piece of plastic. "Guitar pick. Your *jiichan* use to play. You put pick under jaw of leech."

She flicked off each leech. Blood trickled down Hanako's ankles.

"Leech make blood not clot," Baachan explained. "Maybe you keep bleeding, but don't worry. You take break now."

Akira stared, fascinated, at Hanako's leg. He didn't seem sure if he should be worried or excited. Then he settled on worried. "Where will she get more blood?" he asked doubtfully.

"Oh, she don't lose too much. This I know. It look like many blood, but you have many, many, many blood inside you."

The blood looked like bright red watercolors running down Hanako's leg. But she couldn't feel a thing.

Baachan started to wipe it off with a *tenugui*, but Akira said, "Wait, can I look at the blood more?"

So Baachan let him watch, and then he wiped down Hanako's leg himself. "I'll take care of you," he told her confidently.

When Mama and Baachan returned to work, Akira ate his lunch of boiled cabbage. They'd run out of rice yesterday, even though Papa had sold the "stolen" wheat.

He sold it for paper money. At work Papa was getting paid in salt, because he felt it was worth more than paper money, but he had not been able to find rice the last time he was at the black market.

Watching her brother devour his food, Hanako thought about America, where he would be able to eat all he wanted someday—in a year or two or three, she wasn't sure. Papa said he had called Auntie Jean and Uncle Kent, to see if they would help Papa, Mama, Hanako, and Akira when they got to America. Auntie worked as a maid and Uncle as a janitor—same as before the war. They lived in a one-room apartment, so they were able to save money. They had two children who never got anything special except a little rice candy, even before camp. And they had not lost money before the war because they had not owned much that they had needed to sell. All they'd had was in savings from a life of hard work. They were saving money so that they could be sure to have enough to send their kids to college. Hanako did not know them well, just saw them once a year at Christmas. She used to think about how they seemed so cold, and yet all they did was work for her two cousins. Anyway, even though their apartment was small, they had agreed to take

Hanako's family in until Papa found good work.

She lay on her stomach, then pushed her chest off the ground, arching her back. That felt so good! Then she lay on her back and gazed at the beautiful sky, a few white clouds passing through the blue. Somehow the sky seemed more beautiful here than the sky over Tule Lake, but she knew that must be all in her mind. "I'm in Japan," she said out loud. "I'm planting rice." Day after day in Japanese school at Tule Lake, she'd thought about whether she would really ever go to Japan and when. And now here she was, eventually to be gone again, leaving behind her brokenhearted *jiichan* and *baachan* . . . both of whom were now moving swiftly down the rows, planting, planting, planting.

Hanako trudged back into the field and began placing more seedlings into the mud. She was surprised to find that she was better at it than she had been before. She still moved slowly compared to her grandparents, but there were fewer "leaners" that she needed to replant. She tried to forget that there were probably leeches on her legs at that very moment. She remembered reading once about how they injected anesthetic into your skin so you couldn't feel them biting into you.

And then something took her breath away. She

heard an unfamiliar noise, and she looked up to see a flock of white birds flying low over the field, their wings making a noise like sheets flapping in a hard breeze. Baachan and Mama stood up to watch, but Jiichan doggedly worked. The birds swooped up then and higher into the air until they vanished.

Akira tugged at Hanako's arm. "I know what that was."

"Cranes?" she guessed. "Ducks?" But they hadn't looked like cranes or ducks.

"That was the spirits from the mountains," he said knowingly. "We'll have a lot of rice this year." He pointed at his head. "Brains, *neh*?"

# THIRTY-NINE

The next morning, Hanako and Akira slept very late, as they liked to do. When Hanako finally woke up, Akira was still snoring softly. Her back ached. She thought the rumbling in her stomach had woken her up. But then she realized that Mama was calling to her, not urgently.

She hopped out of bed and hurried to the living room in her underpants and undershirt—she still did not have new pajamas. Kiyoshi and Mimi were standing there! Mimi pointed at her and laughed. *"Shitagi!"* That meant "underwear." Mimi started laughing so hard, she couldn't stop.

"Oh!" Hanako ran back into the bedroom and

grabbed Mama's pajamas—the purple coat was in the living room. The pajamas were big, but she hurried back into the living room anyway.

Hanako wasn't sure who she should address first. Her entire family was staring at her as if waiting for her to speak. She decided on Papa. "This is Kiyoshi and his little sister, Mimi."

Kiyoshi bowed deeply and stayed down while Hanako continued, "And . . . and, Papa, he's a friend of mine, and, and, Papa"—okay, it was now or never, so she blurted out, "Can he work for Jiichan and Baachan in the rice fields? Please?"

Kiyoshi turned his focus on Papa. The boy got that evaluating look in his face. Then he said, "I'm a very hard worker. I work so hard, I'll do the work of three men."

Papa evaluated him in return. Then he said, "Hana, I'm sorry to ask, but can he work?" His eyes rested on Kiyoshi's injured hand.

For a moment Kiyoshi seemed to be frozen. Then he demanded, "Watch!" He picked an empty teacup off the table with his claw, tossed the cup high into the air, and caught it easily as Baachan gasped. "My hand is even better now than it was before. It's better now because I work on it every day."

Papa and Jiichan glanced at each other without speaking.

And finally Jiichan nodded. "We hire young people many year. But we cannot pay much. Not much at all." To Kiyoshi, he explained in Japanese, "You come back in the early morning one week from now. You must work hard, though."

"He'll work hard!" Hanako exploded. "I promise! Jiichan, he's the one we saw in the train station!"

"He mustn't steal, though," Mama chimed in.

"He won't, I promise!" Hanako assured them, and hoped it was true. She reminded herself to tell her grandparents to hide the rice in the locker at all times.

Mimi had wandered over to where the purple coat lay draped over a basket. "Can I have your coat?" she asked plaintively, stroking it like it was a cat.

Hanako rushed over and took the coat from her. "No, I'm sorry. That's my special thing!"

But she had scared Mimi, sending her running over to her brother to bury her head in his legs.

"I'm sorry," Kiyoshi said to Hanako. "She has nothing, and she's little. She doesn't understand. We don't want your special thing."

He bowed deeply to all of them one at a time, even to

Akira, who had just appeared in his own underwear. Then, seemingly on a whim, he even bowed to Mimi. "Next week, then." He picked up his little sister and departed.

Hanako heard sniffling and saw it was her grandmother. "Baachan! Don't worry, he'll work hard!"

Nobody spoke, just kind of squinted at her. All five of them!

"What is it?" Hanako asked with alarm.

Papa half groaned, half moaned before saying, "I. Have. Made. So. Many. Big. Decisions. Over and over the last few years." He paused. "I should say 'we.' *We've* all made a decision." He studied the floor, as if he saw something extremely interesting there. He even kicked at this imaginary thing with a foot. Then he continued, his forehead wrinkling as he looked at Hanako. "A judge has decided that Wayne Collins won't be allowed to get our citizenship back with a class-action lawsuit. A class action would mean he only has to prepare one court case, and all the thousands of us could get our citizenship back at once. Instead, he must do each of us one by one. That means . . ." He held out his hands as if it were obvious, but it wasn't, not to Hanako. "It could take many years. Many, many years. It will take sooner for some and longer for others."

Hanako tried to understand what he was saying. She did *not* have her brother's brain! "So we'll be staying here for a long time, then?" she asked at last. Every time Papa and Mama made a decision, it shook her up deeply, no matter what the decision was. They were leaving in maybe a couple of years? Shook her up deeply! Staying for a long time instead? Shook her up deeply! So she would be a tenant farmer after all? She jerked her head a couple of times, trying to comprehend.

"That's what we need to tell you. Your mother and I will need to stay here until we get our citizenship back. It could take as long as five years." He looked down again. "It could take twenty." He turned his head to the side, holding his eyes closed for half a minute. "We are . . . your mother and I have decided . . ."

Hanako stood very still. "What, Papa?"

"We are going to need to send you and Akira back to live with your auntie Jean."

Hanako's whole body felt white-hot. "But . . . you mean we wouldn't live with you?"

Papa sat on the table. Hanako had never seen anyone do that before. It seemed such an odd thing for a Japanese person to do. He looked at his palms, touched two of his fingertips together. For no reason. "Hanako, we must send you back. There is no future for you and Akira here." He stood up like that was the end of the conversation. "It's hard to get ahead in America, but at least it's possible."

"My parent were tenant farmer," Jiichan reminded her. "My grandparent, too. My great-grandparent were less even than that."

Baachan was crying, a string of drool falling to the *tatami*. "You will never own anything; you will always worry for food. I like very much you own something. Eat, ah, peanut butter." She pronounced it "but-er-roo." "We do not even own this house. We live here many year. We do what we want with house, but we do not own." There was a silence, and then she added, "Even if only table." She gestured at theirs. "This table come with house when we rent. There are many table in America you can own. Many peanut butter. Akira will get sick of it, there is so much!"

Hanako felt so many things at that moment. She felt things that were total opposites! She felt that she never wanted to leave her parents and grandparents, and she felt that she did not want to be a tenant farmer her whole life. She did not want to spend her life with leeches covering her legs, she did not want her back to bend out of shape, and yet she never wanted to leave this house. Hanako reached for her braid . . . but of course it was still gone.

Papa closed his eyes tightly, a couple of tears squeezing out anyway. "A table . . ." was all he said. "Hana, it's not the table." He paused, turned to his mother. "Okaasan, what I mean is that I understand what you're saying. You know, maybe it's me being selfish. But I don't want to think that all I'm doing is working to survive so that my children have to work only to survive. All right then, a table, if you will! Why shouldn't you own your own table?" Then he slumped over as if in agony. He lifted his head, opened his arms to Akira. Akira ran hard into him, bumping into Papa's stomach as they hugged each other.

"Ow, you're hurting me!" Akira screamed.

Papa loosened his grip. He stared into Akira's eyes like he saw something very sad there.

"You're scaring me!"

So Papa let him go, and Akira ran to Mama.

"But, Papa," Hanako said. She was trying to get everything straight in her head. She wasn't sure she understood! "Papa?" She felt almost delirious—and then she thought of Kiyoshi—all alone taking care of his sister all by himself. Doing anything he could for her. And she cried, "Do you mean I'm going to be responsible for Akira all by myself?"

"Of course not! You're just a child!"

"But why won't you come with us?" Akira shouted. "Mama, come with us!"

"We can't—we can't go anywhere in the world," Mama said sadly. "We can only go here, because we aren't citizens anywhere."

Akira put his palms over his ears. "I'm not going! I'm not listening, either!"

But Mama held him and rocked him and sang songs that Hanako had not heard since Akira was a baby, songs about falling asleep and moonbeams and angels.

Akira was staring into space with his special dead-eyed look. "But they like their own kids better!" Akira said. "You like me better. You like me better than Hanako."

Hanako didn't think that was true, but for now Mama didn't deny it. She winked at Hanako.

"Of course I do. I love you best in the world," Mama said soothingly.

"You love me more than anyone."

"Of course I do. Everybody loves you best."

Hanako started to say she loved him best also, just to make him feel better, but then a thought occurred to her.

"They do—they love their own kids best!" Hanako suddenly exclaimed, as if accusing Mama and Papa of something. "Akira will have me to love him best, but . . . who will I have?" She burst into tears.

Akira pushed free of Mama and ran to Hanako now, falling into her arms. "I'll love you best, Hana!"

They held on to each other for dear life. Hanako felt if she let go of her brother, they would both drown right in the middle of the living room.

"Hana, Aki . . . ," Mama was saying. "Did you know, Hanako, that my sister was there when I delivered you in the bathtub at our little house? I saw her clean you off. She didn't have children yet, and I had to remind her to give you to me. She didn't want to let go. She will take good care of you. If I didn't trust her, I would never send you back to America."

Hanako was suddenly five years old! She stomped her foot and crossed her arms. "I don't remember that!"

"You were just a newborn," Mama said.

Hanako's chest felt so hot that she slipped a hand

under the pajamas to feel it: it felt normal.

Papa cleared his throat. "As long as we're talking about all of this, there's one more thing you must hear. If we are lucky enough that your *baachan* and *jiichan* are still alive when your mother and I get our citizenship back, *if* we get it back, I will stay here to take care of them. I will not leave them alone. But your mother will return at that point."

Hanako gaped. "That could be twenty years!"

"We don't know," Papa said, holding out his palms as if to prove they were empty, as if to prove he was not trying to trick her. "We don't know."

"We will not live long," Jiichan said soothingly. "Do not worry that we will take your father away from you."

"I want you to live long!" Hanako said, still shouting. Then she added, "I want him to stay with you!" She did not want them to be alone, ever! Ever!

And so . . . what was happening was in fact what had to happen. Given their choices. And something dawned on her: Kiyoshi had no such choices. He would probably never own so much as a table.

But then, very suddenly, Hanako had a thought—an important thought. "But Papa said America destroyed our lives! He said that once."

Baachan grunted loudly and sat down on the floor. She often grunted when she lowered herself. Sometimes her grunts were almost groans. She leaned back and tried to look up at Hanako. "Hana-chan. I don't know many other country, but I think every country can destroy your life if thing go wrong. Every one. But you need go to place where you have best chance at good future. You have only two choice: Japan and United State."

Hanako stared stonily at the *tatami*, right at a hole. All the things in her grandparents' house—all the things they didn't even own—were old. They had worked in the fields their whole lives, and now *they* were old. But she thought of the few things they did own, like the small stuffed animals with hers and Papa's names on them. There was probably one for Akira as well. If her grandparents owned a million things, maybe they wouldn't even have thought to save those stuffed animals.

Baachan got up and began stroking her hair. "It very nice to have you here. I appreciate so much. Best time of my life, and I never forget." She nodded her head a few times. "I never forget." Her eyes got a faraway look. Then her face grew bright. "Yes, I already remembering when I first see you. I never forget that."

ater that evening, when Hanako and Baachan were in the kitchen cleaning up after dinner, Hanako asked, "Will you please come to America when my parents get their citizenship back?"

Baachan smiled at her patiently. "Oh, I may be dead by then."

"No!"

Baachan nodded. "Even if only five year, I hope I be alive, but maybe I be dead. Don't look so worry; when you old, you understand will die someday. Anyway, I stay here now. I too old to move. I don't even like walk so much anymore." She smiled again. She had been looking at Akira and Hanako all night and smiling.

Baachan left for her bath, and Hanako washed and dried the dishes and put them away. It would not be an easy trip, going back to America. She thought of the journey to Japan on the ship and how awful it would be making that same trip back, this time *without* her parents. But she knew that sometimes merciful people could just appear suddenly. It happened. There was a time in Jerome when she got lost in the barracks in a storm. Her dress was covered in mud. All the barracks looked exactly alike. And out of nowhere a middle-aged couple had found her. The man had picked her up. She hadn't even remembered her barrack number, but somehow they had figured out where she belonged. Maybe sometimes you just had to go out into the world and trust what would happen. You had to trust that there were good people in the world. Like Mr. Collins. Like that couple. Like her family. This was life. This, she knew, was also *kintsukuroi*. Putting broken things back together with gold. That was what Mr. Collins was doing, it seemed to her, but it would take a long time.

# FORTY-ONE

apa talked to Mr. Collins several more times. He said he did not think the man could possibly sleep more than a few hours a night. Otherwise, how would he have time to talk to all the renunciants? Mr. Collins had found a young woman who'd come over to Japan with her family, though she herself had not renounced. And now she was returning. Papa would be paying her to watch over Hanako and Akira on the ship. The only problem was that she was leaving soon. Very soon.

In a week.

Akira threw up when he found out. Then he ran and got his green Monopoly houses and threw them across the room. After that, he went to the corner and stood there and refused to move. If anyone came near him, he would scream. Usually, Hanako was used to him and took him in stride. But watching him in the corner that way, she started to feel very fearful of the responsibility. She did not understand how Kiyoshi could stand the responsibility of taking care of a young sibling. Didn't he like it better when someone took care of *him*? But . . . choices. He had no choices.

Every night after dinner, Baachan wrapped her arms around Hanako, and Jiichan wrapped his around Akira, and they sat by the table just like that, sometimes not even talking.

"This is fair," Baachan said. "Your parent have you your whole life, but we have for only short time. So we need hold you now."

"You will see your parent again," Jiichan agreed. "But we are old."

Then one night Papa said loudly, "I have an idea! Is there a photographer in the village? Let's take a picture!"

It turned out there was a man about a mile away who owned a camera, so the next day Papa stayed

home from work, and they went to see him. He wasn't
surprised at all when they knocked on his door, just
nodded and told them to come in. He said, in Japanese,
"I have heard there were America-*gaeri* here in the
village."

He had them sit on stools of different heights, each
holding a prop: Mama an umbrella, Papa a hammer,
Jiichan an oil lamp, Baachan a ceramic cat, and Hanako
and Akira fake flowers. The photograper took two
shots, and Papa paid him while Hanako and Akira
were putting the stools back in a corner.

Their ship would sail in two days, so Hanako and
Akira would not see the photograph when it was devel-
oped. On the night before they were to leave, they left
the dirty dishes on the table all night!! Then suddenly
Mama hopped to her feet and started cleaning obses-
sively. She cleaned things they hadn't even messed up
that day.

Finally, she said, "It's getting late." She sank to her
knees, closing her eyes, and Hanako could see she was
praying, like she had at the Christian revival meetings
in the Jerome camp. Sometimes Mama had brought
her and Akira to them.

"Mama, are you praying to God?"

"I don't know. Shhh." She leaned her forehead into her clasped hands while her lips moved.

Papa joined her, in the exact same position. Nobody talked for the longest time. Then Papa and Mama stood up, and Mama got busy again, packing for Hanako and Akira.

Papa knelt in front of Hanako and held her face in his hands. "When you get on the ship, remember that you traveled across the ocean once, and you can do it again. The trip won't last forever. Maybe you will even make new friends."

"You will know who you can trust," Jiichan said. "I never have time to teach you how, but you my granddaughter. You have my feet! You will feel it in your body. Like I tell you about on mountain. Remember? Heh, I have good memory for old man! But I cannot teach you now, Hana-chan—it would take two year at least."

Papa continued, "Your mother and I are very proud of both of you. We will think of you every moment. Every single moment. So when you have time, just stop what you're doing sometimes and think of us. All right? And I promise we'll also be thinking of you."

Hanako nodded. Then waited. Were those his only instructions?

Mama stuck her head out of the bedroom and asked, "Hanako, did you want your abacus?"

"No, Mama, I never want to see that again, actually." She had never gotten very good with it. At planting rice, either. Apparently, she didn't have very talented fingers.

Papa held her gently, then said, "Your grandparents want all your attention. All right? Just remember to stop and think of us sometimes. All right?"

"I promise. I'll make Akira do it too." She did not think she would have to "make" her brother do this at all, because he would never stop thinking of their parents even for a minute. Neither would she!

Papa nodded and released her.

"We like having child. We forget after so many year how much we like," Baachan said. She pressed her hand against the center of her chest. "Inside here, I feel how much I like. But more I like it, more I want for you to go and have good life."

"They will have good life, no need to worry now!" Jiichan exclaimed. "I am sure of it! They will work hard, but have good life."

Hanako and Akira glanced at each other, then Akira half screamed, "We have something for Baachan and Jiichan! In case . . ." *In case we never see them again.*

Hanako and her brother ran into the bedroom to get packages they'd prepared. They'd wrapped their gifts in something Mama had bought for very cheap in the village: it was "cloth" that seemed to also be paper. The shopkeeper had said that during the war, and even now, some people made their clothes out of this inexpensive material. But they had to keep their clothes dry, because if they got wet, they would disintegrate.

So the wrapping was cloth, but it was also paper. Just like Mama and Papa were Americans, but they also were not. Because in war, nothing made sense.

First Akira handed his gift to Jiichan. It was tied with string that Papa had gotten at work.

"Ohhh," Jiichan said. "Present for me! I don't get present in many long time." He admired the package for a few seconds. "I know, I know," he said modestly. "I pretty good grandpa." He nodded. "I pretty good, if I say so myself. Maybe you could say I am outstanding good. *Neh?*"

Imitating him, Akira said, "Maybe you could say I

am outstanding good. *Neh?*" Everyone laughed. Akira looked very pleased. So did Jiichan.

Now Jiichan untied the string and the cloth fell open, revealing half of the geode, all sparkling inside.

"I'll keep the other half forever," Akira said. "I also gave you the crumbs." And indeed, there were bits of sparkle inside the wrapping.

Jiichan nodded. "Yes, I pretty good," he murmured. "Thank you, Aki-chan. I will miss you. You pretty good too. As good as me. Huh?"

They seemed so much alike that suddenly Hanako had a thought. "Jiichan, what is your name?" she asked.

He looked very bashful, yet very satisfied, and he said, "Ah, yes, I am Akira also." He smiled through tears at Hanako's brother. "So you see, we are both Akira."

Baachan added to Hanako, "In Japan, we do not name our children same name as parent. But we very satisfy that your brother has his *jiichan*'s name." Then her eyes flashed excitedly, like a child's, as she looked at the package Hanako was holding.

Hanako gave her present to her grandmother. Baachan opened it with shaking hands. Her expression didn't change as she pulled out the purple silk.

"It's your wedding kimono!" Hanako and Akira cried out.

Baachan gazed at it, her eyes going so far away that she did not even seem to really be in this room any longer. For a second she didn't seem happy, and Hanako worried that she had somehow offended her grandmother.

Baachan sat for a very long time without saying anything, just staring into space. Everyone waited. *"Kou in ya no gotoshi,"* she finally said. "Light and darkness fly like an arrow," meaning time passes quickly. An old Japanese proverb grown-ups liked to say. Baachan didn't say "thank you," though, just gazed sadly at the kimono. She stroked it, murmuring, "I have not touched silk in many year."

"Is it as pretty as your wedding kimono?" Hanako asked eagerly.

"It is not, but it mean more to me, Hanako. It mean much more to me. I will not sell even if I starve." Then she very neatly folded up the wrapping, though it was just cheap, ordinary material.

Baachan moved slowly to a shelf and pulled down a box. "We have spoken of this. I will not be at your wedding, but you must wear this. I make with my own hand," she said to Hanako.

Hanako took the box and pulled off the lid. Inside was a headpiece of purple flowers.

"I take this to America, bring it back here, and now it will follow you wherever you go in life," Baachan said. Then she paused and thought. "If you want to wear white like they do in America, never mind purple headpiece. I forget you wear white. Never mind, I be sad if you wear just for me. But take it with you to America." Her eyes welled up. "Stupid I forget you will wear white."

Hanako touched her arm, but Baachan batted it away and wept.

Hanako placed the box in her suitcase. On that night she and Akira got in the tub together, before anyone else. They had to get to sleep. In the hot, hot bath Akira mostly stood up because the water was so deep for him. Then he would lean over sometimes to get his hair wet. He had a whole routine that involved rinsing himself over and over. He was quite active, even though people were supposed to relax in the bath.

Watching him, she thought of all the things they had lost:

Their home.

Their restaurant.

Her cat.

Several years of their lives, in camp.

Many friends.

And soon: their parents, for a few years, and their grandparents, probably forever.

When they got out of the water, Hanako did not want to be with anyone at the moment, not even her family. She announced firmly, "I'm going outside." Nobody told her not to, so she went out in her purple coat and took a full two hundred and fifty steps away from the house, then sat in a cool patch of grass. She looked into the darkness, saw lights glowing in the windows of some houses. She held her coat close . . . and decided right then that she would leave it for Mimi. Then the girl could own one thing in her life.

And so.

Hanako had lost things, but she had also gained things, and she was ready to chase her future. She was scared, but she felt braver than she ever had before. She had met a boy who had seen his mother without a face, and she had scratched his horrible scars. That, somehow, was one of the things that made her brave. And she had met her grandparents, whose love had rinsed the anger from her hands. She had seen many mountains that even a world war had not destroyed.

And so we move forward in life.

*Neh?*

AFTERWORD

In 1941, about 127,000 Nikkei lived in the continental United States. More than 110,000 were forced into detention camps. More than 60 percent of camp inmates were American citizens. It is thought that as many as six thousand Tule Lake inmates eventually renounced their citizenship—a significant majority of American-born adults living there.

When Wayne Collins filed his class-action lawsuit for them, a judge ruled in their favor, saying, "It is shocking to the conscience that an American citizen be confined *without authority* and then, while so under duress and restraint, for his Government to accept from him a surrender of his constitutional heritage." But that decision ended up being voided by a different judge. So Mr. Collins had to file about ten thousand affidavits for both renunciants and witnesses, working tirelessly to restore citizenship one by one for those who wished to return to America. He often worked without pay. The first restoration of citizenship came in 1951, and the last in 1968.

(In real life a judge did not actually decide until 1951 that Wayne Collins could not try the renunciants' case as a class-action lawsuit. In the book this decision happens in 1946. Otherwise, I tried to remain true to the facts, though I'm sure that despite my best efforts, mistakes were made.)

Mr. Collins died in 1974, having changed the lives of thousands of innocent men, women, and children. That's why this book is dedicated to him.

In 1946, land reform began in Japan. The government passed a law to force big landowners to sell land for prices that were fair to the owners, and then the government let former tenant farmers "buy" the land, meaning they gave the tenants a loan to purchase the land, and the loan needed to be paid off within thirty years. This spread ownership throughout the farming community, especially among peasants. Japan experienced major inflation in the years that the reform was ongoing; the land the peasants now owned soon became worth much more than it had been worth when they signed the contracts to buy it. It's complicated, but it meant that instead of having to pay off the loans on their land within the normal thirty years, many were able to pay off their loans in two or three years. So, as it turns out, Jiichan and Baachan could have soon owned their farm after all!

# ACKNOWLEDGMENTS

I am so very grateful to those whose real-life stories are treasures beyond belief. Yasuko Margie Sakimura changed my whole concept of this novel when I met her, and she patiently allowed me to interview her numerous times. And *mahalo* to longtime Hawaii resident and atomic bomb survivor Larry Miwa and his son Stephen Miwa, for contributing their exquisitely detailed family stories. Tom Miyamoto, from a family of "no-no boys," was deported on the same ship to Japan as Margie's family. He allowed me to read his writings on his experiences and answered many, many questions over the years. Thank you as well to Tom's brother, the late Ichiro Miyamoto, as well as to Kyoko-Lillian Furumoto, Grace Hata (who bought the fake sweet cakes when she got to Japan), Taeko Helen Shinmachi, and the late Tad Yamakido.

Atheneum is a magical house to be published by. The care they take with each book and the support they offer their authors is surely unparalleled. My editor, Caitlyn Dlouhy, is fortunately younger than I am, so I am hoping that someday I will retire before her, because I honestly doubt I would survive in the wilds of publishing without her immeasurable talents and kindness. Publisher Justin Chanda is quite a bit younger, so I think I am safe on that front! I assume he must have a stern side, because, well, he's a publisher, but he's been so kind to and supportive of me, it has occasionally brought tears to my eyes. Russell Gordon has designed all my Atheneum books—when I heard he was leaving the company, my first thought was "My life is ruined!" (But I wish him the best anyway!) And thank you as well to Jeannie Ng, an extremely exacting copy editor and a very patient person when I spam her with copyediting queries. (Jeannie quote: "When you spam, you SPAM.") Elizabeth Blake-Linn always makes sure the covers look perfect, and I love all of the covers so much! So thank you! Alex Borbolla is also *wonderful*, as is the entire Atheneum crew.

My appreciation for Reiko Nakaigawa Lee knows no bounds—there is nobody in the world like her, and I could not have written this book (and others) without her help, discernment, and generosity. And endless thanks to Brian Niiya, editor of the indispensable website Densho Encyclopedia. Both of them read the manuscript and offered much-needed advice and criticism. Margie and Tom also read the manuscript—their patience has been such a blessing.

I am grateful as well to Martha Nakagawa, Junko Sekine, Hiroshi Shimizu, Sachiko Takita-Ishii, Mary Wong, and Samuel Yamashita.

I first started writing this book more than a decade ago, putting it aside now and again and turning to other books until I met Margie. I believe I went on the Tule Lake pilgrimage around 2006 to start my research. For anyone considering it, the pilgrimage is an amazing experience. There is no other way, for instance, to appreciate the size and squalor of the stockade the government held the protestors in, no other way to sit on the bus and talk for hours with people who lived in Tule Lake so many years ago. I apologize profusely to anyone I interviewed in those early years and may not have mentioned here because I have moved and lost some of my notes.

I'm pretty sure some people secretly got a little sick of me over the years—as in, "Is this annoying woman ever going to actually write this book, or is she going to keep asking me questions until the end of time?" So thanks to all for their patience!!

# A Place to Belong

`` `` `` `` `` `` `` `` `` `` `` `` ``

## By Cynthia Kadohata

### Discussion Questions

1. The story opens with Hanako's family preparing to travel to Japan by sea after a four-year internment at Tule Lake. Hanako is happy to be out of the camp, but is conflicted about moving to Japan. She tells her brother, Akira, "'We don't belong in America anymore.'" What do you think it means to belong? Think about belonging in the context of a family, a country, and a culture? Why do you think many Japanese Americans lost their sense of belonging? What is evidence of belonging? How do you treat people and how do they treat you when there's a collective feeling of belonging?

**2.** One of the story's prominent themes is life's dual nature. What does duality mean to you? Can you locate other examples of this in the text? Consider the passage where Hanako remembers something Papa said to her about Mr. Taylor, Camp Jerome's cruel director: "'Mr. Taylor has a life. He was a baby once. Maybe he has children; maybe not; maybe he will someday. He has hard days and easy days. He has emotions. These are the things that keep me from killing him.'" What meaning does Hanako take from her father's words?

**3.** Discuss the meaning of "What rises, falls. What falls, rises," and how this adage is illustrated in the story. In difficult situations, Hanako often thinks, "and yet." How do these two words reflect Hanako's ability to consider things from multiple perspectives? How does this ability help in her situation? Have you ever had to think about things from someone else's point of view? How did that impact the outcome of your situation?

**4.** After the family realizes Hanako's and Akira's duffel bags are missing, Hanako understands, "That was the way war was—things just became gone." Papa realizes her sadness and says, "'Let me tell you, when I was in

Bismarck, when I had nothing, not even a family, it taught me who I am.... You're still Hanako. That twenty dollars in your seam doesn't make you Hanako.'" What does Papa want Hanako to understand from his words? How can having nothing teach you important things about life and yourself?

5. The purple coat Hanako got at Tule Lake is one of the items she brings to Japan. Why is Hanako's purple coat so precious to her? Beyond the ability to keep her warm, what does it represent to Hanako? After she trips and falls in the mud, Hanako hears a "hysteria in her voice" as she yells at Akira not to muddy her coat. Why does the thought of dirtying her coat make her so upset? How does the importance of the coat change over the course of the story, and why? Why does Hanako decide to give the coat to Mimi? Do you have an item like Hanako's coat that you feel strongly about? If so, why does it mean so much to you?

6. Hanako is deeply thoughtful, sensitive, and prone to worry. Why did touching the 2.5 million-year-old volcanic rocks in Tule Lake help her to feel "that eventually all would be right with the world"? How does

Hanako gradually learn how to live "in the moment"? Why do you think this is an important lesson for Hanako to learn?

7. Hanako is confused about who she is, saying, "'But . . . I don't know if you want me to be American or Japanese.'" Why does Hanako feel pulled in two directions? Can you name other situations that illustrate how she feels? What advice would you have for Hanako?

8. Discuss Hanako's relationship with Akira. Cite actions throughout the story that reveal her deep connection to her brother. How does Akira serve as a metaphor for living in the present?

9. The theme of survival runs throughout the story. Discuss actions and decisions Hanako's family and other characters in the book make in order to survive. How do they justify their actions? How do they feel about having to make these decisions? Discuss Baachan's statement, "'Akira is sick. To feed him is more important than not to steal.'" Describe why Hanako feels like throwing up when she realizes

her family expects her to steal the wheat. Reread the section where Hanako talks about feelings that come to her when she is hungry. Why does hunger give her the "awful thought" that she is "more important that anyone in the whole world"? Why is the thought so awful to her?

10. While on the train to Hiroshima, Hanako notices the poverty in the Japanese countryside; she thinks back to her former life in California and how relatively better off they were there compared to what she sees out the train window. This is an early example of Hanako's understanding of how her life circumstances are relative to the life circumstances of others. Discuss other examples from the text where Hanako ultimately sees her life in the context of the world at large, and can weigh her problems against others who are suffering.

11. How does Hanako demonstrate that she's highly observant and attuned to the world around her? Reread chapter 14. How does this chapter illustrate Hanako's powers of observation and her questioning mind? Do you think these traits were impacted by her experiences in the camp?

**12.** Hanako is empathetic beyond her years. Discuss the scene where she offers a *katapan* (cracker) to the man with no pants. How does this small act reveal Hanako's enormous ability to feel for her fellow man? How can you channel Hanako's example in your own life?

**13.** One of Papa's mottos is "Do everything you can." How does Hanako's experience seeing the destruction in Hiroshima make her feel that these words are meaningless? How does she put these words into action in the train station, at the farm, and with Kiyoshi? How does Kiyoshi become an important figure in Hanako's life? After Hanako gives him the butterscotch candy, why does he say, "'It's not food. It's . . . it's like it's making fun of me'"? How does hunger become like a character in the story? Give other evidence of this.

**14.** Throughout the story Hanako is reminded of the temporal nature of life: time is fleeting, and the world and everything in it is constantly changing. In addition to wanting to fit in, how is Hanako's decision to cut off her braid an example of the changing nature of life? How would you have reacted to these changes if you were in Hanako's shoes?

**15.** Hanako displays enormous bravery in the face of her family's situation. How does Hanako show courage on her first day of school? How does she become more independent during her time in Japan? Why does she equate growing up with "being by yourself more"? How does being hungry force her to grow up?

**16.** When the family gets off the train and begins their journey on foot to Jiichan and Baachan's house, Hanako is worried that Papa doesn't know the way. Papa reassures Hanako that he does, saying, "'I just had to find it in my memory.'" Discuss the importance of memory and the nature of memory as themes in this story. How does memory sustain Hanako as she struggles to begin her life in Japan? Can memories be both helpful and hurtful?

**17.** After the horrors of witnessing the destruction of Hiroshima and its effects on the Japanese people, Hanako experienced the healing pleasures of a warm bath and a cup of tea, and "felt such a surge of optimism that she wondered for a second whether she'd been hallucinating when she saw Hiroshima." Why does Hanako feel this way from the seemingly simple experiences of bathing and drinking tea? How does this illustrate both the power of a kind act and the difficulties in comprehending tragic events?

**18.** Jiichan tells Hanako, "'There is many bad, but there is also many good. So we move forward in life, neh? When we can, we move forward.'" Discuss examples of how Hanako and her family live by this idea. Why is this idea so powerful?

**19.** Discuss the concept of *kintsukuroi* or "the thing you break you must fix with gold." What "gold" does Hanako use to help herself and her family move forward? How can Hanako feel happy when she is still hungry, knowing that food will be scarce for some time to come? Do you think there can be both an emotional and a physical hunger?

**20.** Hanako is faced with many dilemmas over the course of the story. What do you think about her decision to give a potato to the old woman? Explain your reasoning. What does it mean to "harden your heart"? Do you think Hanako was right not to trade the family's rice for a kimono? Why does she feel "rather mixed up" after she gives her shoes to Kiyoshi and bargains with him for a purple kimono for Baachan?

**21.** What is unconditional love? How do Jiichan and Baachan display unconditional love for Hanako and Akira? How does Baachan's love and self-sacrifice dissolve Hanako's anger? Can you name a time when you've shown unconditional love for someone in your life, or they've acted out of unconditional love for you?

**22.** Hanako realized that "sometimes you just had to go out into the world and trust it would happen. You had to trust that there were good people in the world." How does Hanako learn the meaning of trust? Do you think trust is an easy thing to earn?

*Guide written by Colleen Carroll, literacy specialist, education consultant, and author of the twelve-volume series, How Artists See and four-volume How Artists See, Jr. (Abbeville Press).*

*This guide has been provided by Simon & Schuster for classroom, library, and reading group use. It may be reproduced in its entirety or excerpted for these purposes.*

Turn the page for a look at another of
Cynthia Kadohata's books,

# Weedflower

THIS IS WHAT IT FELT LIKE TO BE LONELY:

1. Like everyone was looking at you. Sumiko felt this once in a while.
2. Like nobody was looking at you. Sumiko felt this a lot.
3. Like you didn't care about anything at all. She felt this maybe once a week.
4. Like you were just about to cry over every little thing. She felt this about once daily.

But not today! Sumiko jumped off the school bus and ran behind her house. Her family was working; she saw their small forms surrounded by bursts of color in the flower fields. "Jiichan!" she shouted to her grandfather. She waved an envelope at him. "I'm invited to a party!"

"Can't hear!"

"I'm invited to a party!"

Everybody was looking at her, but nobody seemed to understand what she was saying. Oh, forget it! She ran into the stable to look for her little brother, Tak-Tak, but he wasn't there. Baba just looked at her expectantly. She patted the old nag's yellow nose and said, "I'm invited to a party." Baba didn't change expressions.

She hurried inside the house to change into her work clothes. That morning Sumiko and some other kids in her sixth-grade class had received invitations to a birthday party this Saturday. One of the popular girls was holding a party and had decided at the last minute to invite everyone in the class. The invitation was embossed, and the lettering inside was gold. Sumiko had read the inside about a dozen times:

*We are pleased to invite you*
*to a birthday party for*
*Marsha Melrose*
*12372 La Mirada Terrace*
*Saturday, December 6, 1941*
*1–3 p.m.*

The invitation reminded Sumiko of the expensive

valentines her cousin Ichiro gave to girls he especially liked.

She changed clothes behind the blankets her aunt and uncle had strung across the bedroom. She shared the room with Takao, a.k.a. Tak-Tak. Auntie and Uncle had strung the blankets up three weeks earlier when Sumiko turned twelve. She felt guilty because she actually liked the blankets, even though Tak-Tak had cried over them. He was almost six and he followed her around day and night. She loved him like crazy. But she still liked the blankets.

Sumiko stuck the invitation into her shirt pocket so that she could look at it now and then while she worked. This was the first class party she'd ever been invited to.

Through a fluke, Sumiko lived in a school district with few Japanese. She was the only Japanese girl in her class, whereas if she'd lived a few miles away, several Japanese girls would have been in the same class. The white girls were nice enough to her during recess, but she had never been invited to play on weekends or sleep over at anyone's house or anything like that.

She didn't used to worry about it as much as she did lately. The way Jiichan told the story, Sumiko had been born cheerful, had become sad when her parents died when Tak-Tak was a baby, had begun to get cheerful again, and now was just "starting to act like a female." He'd said that because she had asked for a mirror for her bureau so she could decide when it was time to start curling her long hair. Instead of a mirror, she'd gotten the blankets.

"Hurry!" Tak-Tak called out. "Or we won't have time to brush Baba."

She stepped around the blanket divider and saw that her brother had come in. "I'm invited to a party." She waved the invitation at him.

He looked at her blankly. He wore black-framed glasses that stayed attached to his head with an elastic band Auntie had made. The lenses were so thick, his eyes always looked big.

Tak-Tak clearly didn't understand the significance of her invitation. Finally he said, "We have to brush Baba. You promised me before you went to school."

He looked a little forlorn over the thought that she might have forgotten what she promised him. "Did you clean Baba's brush?" she asked.

He held up a clean horse brush. "I'll race you!"

She let Tak-Tak stay one step ahead of her as they ran outside to the stable. "You beat me!" she cried as they fell into some hay.

Sumiko smiled as Tak-Tak jumped up from the hay to brush the horse. Tak-Tak really adored Baba. Her nose dripped all the time, but that worked out fine because Tak-Tak liked gooey things. Sumiko sat up and looked out the stable door. Her cousins Bull and Ichiro were still tending the flowers, nineteen-year-old Bull wide and strong and twenty-three-year-old Ichiro slender and lean, graceful even in his farm clothes. Uncle was working at the far end of the fields among the carnations, which he always liked to take care of himself. The carnations grew in a makeshift, open-field greenhouse, where they were protected from extremes of sun or wind. Uncle was cutting some for tomorrow's wholesale flower market. Ichiro and Bull were pulling weeds among the stock. Local flower farmers called flowers grown in the field kusabana—"weedflowers." Stock were weedflowers that emanated an amazing clovelike fragrance. Of all the flowers her family had ever grown, Sumiko loved them most.

Ragged white cheesecloth rippled above parts of the fields. Last spring Sumiko and Auntie had sewn cheesecloth tarps for the men to hang over the fields to protect the flowers—except the stock, which didn't need protection.

Uncle dreamed of setting up a glass greenhouse someday and growing perfect carnations, but so far that was just talk. Only the wealthier Japanese farmers owned glass greenhouses. Uncle said you could control the elements better with a greenhouse. Perfection was the Holy Grail to Uncle. Sumiko thought that a lot of the flowers were perfect, but Uncle often looked critically at his carnations and said things like, "They would be perfect if we had a glass greenhouse." He never even considered whether the stock could reach perfection—after all, they were just weedflowers.

Most of the greenhouse growers came from families who'd moved to America before laws were passed preventing those born in Asia from becoming citizens. Uncle and Jiichan had both been born in Japan. People born in Asia were not allowed to become American citizens, and those who weren't citizens were not allowed to own or lease land. Because her cousin Ichiro was born in the United States, the farm's lease was in his name instead of his father's.

Sumiko turned her attention back to the stable to check on her brother. Tak-Tak had climbed a stool and was brushing Baba's mane. Tak-Tak loved Sumiko best of anything in the world. But Sumiko thought maybe he loved the horse second best.

Now she saw her grandfather walk into the outhouse. That was always the first thing he did when he finished working. "I have to start the bathwater," she told Tak-Tak, who barely noticed as she hurried away. In the bathhouse she got kindling from a pile and placed it under the big tub. She lugged a few logs off the woodpile and placed them atop the kindling and started a fire. As soon as the bathwater started steaming, she would place a wooden platform in the tub so the bottom wouldn't be too hot to step in.

"Sumiko-chan!" her grandfather called from the outhouse. There was a crack in the wood that he always peered out of. Sometimes he liked to talk to the family right through the outhouse wall! He had no dignity because he was so old. Still, he made Sumiko smile a lot. She ran to the outhouse.

"Yes, Jiichan."

"When is party?" he said.

"I thought you didn't hear me."

"Whole neighborhood hear you," he said.

"It's Saturday."

He didn't speak. Sometimes he just stopped talking, and you didn't know whether you were supposed to wait at the outhouse or not. If you asked him if he wanted you to wait outside, he would snap that you had interrupted his train of thought. If you waited without asking, he would look surprised when he came out.

"I thinking, maybe it better I drive you to party instead of your uncle," he suddenly said. "I wait in car nearby in case you get hurt." Though Jiichan had lived in the United States for several decades, he didn't sound like it. Sometimes he spoke chanpon, which was a mix of Japanese and English; sometimes he spoke Japanese; and when he talked to Sumiko and Tak-Tak, he spoke mangled English.

Jiichan already seemed as obsessed with this party as Sumiko was.

"Jiichan! I'm not going to get hurt at a birthday party!" she said to the outhouse.

"I just thinking. But if you got no respect for old man opinion, never mind, never mind."

Sumiko laughed. "I'm going to be fine. Maybe they'll

ask me to sing a song!" Was that what they did at birth-day parties? She liked to sing. Once she'd even been chosen to sing a song alone during a school assembly. She'd gotten a little flustered and sung the same verse twice, but otherwise, she'd done great. She imagined a crowd of classmates surrounding her at the party.

"Sumiko!" Jiichan said. "Are you listening?"

"Sorry, Jiichan. What did you say?"

"I say go get your uncle!"

She shouted out, "Uncle! Jiichan wants you!" Uncle looked up from the fields and headed in.

"You break my eardrum," Jiichan said.

Sumiko returned to the bathhouse to check the water (not hot enough yet), went into the stable to check Tak-Tak (still brushing Baba), and hurried to the shed to grade the cut carnations Ichiro had just brought in from the field. He smiled as she passed.

The shed was yet another drafty building on the farm. Empty taru—barrels—that soy sauce came in were piled on top of one another along the walls, wait-ing to be filled with carnations for tomorrow morning's market. Sumiko was supposed to grade the flowers and put them into the taru. That was one of her main jobs.

Flower farmers charged more for their most beauti-ful, biggest, nearly flawless flowers. Sumiko graded the best carnations #1 and the next best #2. Only carnations were graded inside the shed. The stock were graded right out in the field.